"Jace, I don't know if we should complicate the issue with a fleeting romance that can't go anywhere."

"You mean can't go anywhere if I don't accept Nathan into my life?"

"No. That's not what I mean at all. I mean, I live in Washington. You live in Holly River. I'm going home in twelve days, one way or another."

Jace curled a finger under Kayla's chin and lifted her face. Her beautiful eyes glowed with a turquoise blush in the shade of the barn rafters. He took off her baseball cap, letting her hair fall to her shoulders. Shiny honey-and-wheat hair. He couldn't describe the special color with one word. He wanted nothing more than to taste her full lips, to hear if he could make her sigh a sweet murmur of desire.

Dear Reader,

Dad in Training was such fun to write. Maybe that's because my hero, Jace Cahill, is the kind of guy we've all known, maybe even the kind of person we've all wished we could be. Laid-back, fun, the don't-take-life-too-seriously sort who seems to skid into adulthood with perfect balance and standing on two feet. And maybe some of us have even gotten to know the deeper, perhaps darker side to this guy, the part that delves beneath the strumming and picking of his guitar to the one who actually writes the songs.

I hope you enjoy getting to know Jace. I hope you appreciate his struggle to accept responsibility without losing his joy of life, his appreciation of nature and the fulfillment that comes from his own inner peace. This book might have been called *Jace Grows Up*. And by the end, maybe you'll come to accept that, with a bit of effort, a bit of luck and, the best of all things, a strong, abiding love, we can all be better.

I love to hear from readers. Contact me at cynthoma@aol.com.

Cynthia

Cynthia Thomason inherited her love of writing from her ancestors. Her father and grandmother both loved to write, and she aspired to continue the legacy. Cynthia studied English and journalism in college, and after a career as a high school English teacher, she began writing novels. She discovered ideas for stories while searching through antiques stores and flea markets and as an auctioneer and estate buyer. Cynthia says every cast-off item from someone's life can ignite the idea for a plot. She writes about small towns, big hearts and happy endings that are earned and not taken for granted. And as far as the legacy is concerned, just ask her son, the magazine journalist, if he believes.

Books by Cynthia Thomason

Harlequin Heartwarming

The Cahills of North Carolina
High Country Cop

The Daughters of Dancing Falls
Rescued by Mr. Wrong
The Bridesmaid Wore Sneakers
A Boy to Remember

Firefly Nights
This Hero for Hire
A Soldier's Promise
Blue Ridge Autumn
Marriage for Keeps
Dilemma at Bayberry Cove

Visit the Author Profile page
at Harlequin.com for more titles.

This book is dedicated to all the free spirits who adapt and learn and love and are better for their efforts. My brother, Doug Brackett, a Bob Dylan–loving, guitar-playing old hippie, is one of them.

CHAPTER ONE

FAMILY. THE WORD could be as irritating as a burr between a guy's toes or as comforting as a soft pillow. Unfortunately, for Jace Cahill, the burr metaphor was the one he most thought of. Sure, he loved his brother Carter, his sister, Ava, and his mother, Cora. They were good people. But he'd practically thrown a party when his father, Raymond, died almost two years ago.

Animosity hardly described the relationship between Jace and his father. In fact, an accurate word probably didn't exist in current vocabulary. Raymond had taught Jace two important things. Avoiding family drama was a good thing. And living alone was a blessing.

But today Jace was working on the schedule of raft trips down the Wyoga River, and his brother was seated across the counter from him, and that was all good. Now that

August had come to the High Country of North Carolina, Jace knew his potential for getting money from the pockets of tourists was running dry. They would head back to wherever they came from, and the Wyoga would run cold and swift now that summer was almost over.

"So, how was your season?" Carter asked Jace. "Did you make a killing here at High Mountain Rafting at forty-five dollars a clip?"

Jace motioned for one of the younger guys who conducted the rafting trips to come to the counter. Jace didn't lead the river trips unless he absolutely had to, if someone didn't show up for work or asked for a day off. Jace knew every inch of the Wyoga River, but he was just plain tired of navigating from the back of a raft filled with anxious adults, screaming kids and overly zealous adventurists.

"A killing? Not hardly," he said. "But I made enough to keep Copper in kibble."

A picture of Jace's eight-year-old ultra-calm Labrador retriever sat on the counter for all the tourists to admire and to keep Jace from flipping out at the repetitious questions from the folks who tried to convince themselves to take the plunge. Ha! An accurate description, because on at least half of the river trips, usually one person actually did plunge into the rapids.

"How fast is the river's current?"

"Will we be issued life jackets?"

"Does anyone ever fall off the raft?"

And Jace's prepared answers: "Slow. Yes, often, if they don't listen to instructions. Why do you think we have that wall of slickers and goggles and life vests?"

"You know," Carter began, "maybe it's time for you to consider selling this business and taking over the Christmas tree farm. Nothing would make Mama happier, and you might be getting too old for rescuing folks every other day."

"I don't rescue people that often," Jace said. "I only guide about once a week these days." He raked his hand through his wavy light brown hair, stopping when he reached the spot where twine had held his short ponytail until two days ago when he'd had it cut off during a spontaneous moment that he still wasn't sure if he regretted or not. "And you know how I feel about Snowy Mountain Tree Farm. I've never had an interest in it. And may I mention, neither have you."

"Yeah, I know," Carter admitted. "But Mama's always held out the hope that you would take over her inheritance. Grandpa left that acreage to his daughter, thinking she would hand it down to her sons."

Jace frowned. "One of whom is a cop, not a tree planter, I might point out."

"Yeah, and one of whom is a disgruntled adventure guide," Carter said. "Speaking of being a cop, I'd better get to the station. This town won't protect itself."

He stood from the stool he'd been occupying as Jace gave instructions to the young man who would guide the tourists waiting outside by the reclaimed school bus the business used. Every day during tourist season the bus transported eager rafters across the Tennessee line to the input area of the river. "Have you got your jokes memorized?" he asked the kid. "Keep 'em entertained, Billy. You need the tips. I don't pay you nearly enough."

The young man laughed, grabbed his paddle and safety gear, and headed into the parking lot.

"You going to Mama's for dinner?" Carter said as he walked to the door.

"Nope. You and your bride enjoy her barbecue pork. I've got a gig at the River Café. Gary and I are making a fat hundred bucks for playing the patio."

Carter stopped at the door. "Looks like you've got a late arrival." He stared across the parking lot at a woman and a young kid who'd just gotten out of a small but sleek crossover vehicle.

"They won't make it now," Jace said. "Billy's full up and he's already pulling out." He leaned over the counter and stared at the woman. "Whoa, she's a looker. With customers like that coming in the door, you can't think I'd actually give up this business to grow Christmas trees." He grinned at his brother. "Maybe I'll arrange a personal tour with me at the helm."

Carter chuckled. "Behave yourself, Jason Edward Cahill. Your big brother's a cop, remember?"

Carter was in his patrol car before the woman reached the entrance to High Mountain Rafting. She came up the three steps and in the door of the outfitter shop, gently prodding a boy ahead of her. The fact that she had a kid was something of a downer to Jace. He enjoyed being an uncle to his brother's stepdaughter, but he had no interest in being a father himself. He had no interest in being anything other than what he was—a part-time rafting guide and an underpaid folk guitarist.

And besides, if this woman had a kid, she was probably married. Oh, well, it didn't hurt to enjoy the view of long legs in dark denim jeans and a curve-hugging T-shirt. "Well, good morning," he said, purposefully exaggerating the North Carolina drawl women seemed to like. "You just missed the bus pulling out for the morning rafting trip. Can you come back this afternoon?"

"Maybe," the woman said. "But I'm mostly hoping to get some information."

Here we go again. Same old questions. *Does anyone ever fall out? How fast is the river?* But heck, he could put on the charm for this lady. Average height, maybe five-six, she had shoulder-length hair the color of rich Carolina honey, a mix of golden blond and auburn. Her eyebrows were perfectly arched above long lashes and cool blue eyes. Prominent cheekbones drew attention to creamy coral lips. Yep. This woman was special.

She raked her hand through the hair streaming from a center part and let it fall in a tangled mass of waves. Slipping her over-size dark sunglasses on her head to hold the hair, she gave him an intense stare. "Are you Jace Cahill, the owner of this business?"

"Guilty as charged," he said. "Hope you're not from the North Carolina state tax assessor. I've paid my dues to be here, and my licenses are current."

His admittedly corny remark was met with a firm press of those gorgeous lips. Maybe she didn't have a sense of humor.

She stuck her hand across the counter. "Hi. I'm Kayla McAllister." Nodding toward the boy, she said, "This is Nathan."

Jace shook her hand, nodded at the kid, who looked to be about nine, same age as Carter's stepdaughter. "Hello, Nathan. You wanting to hit the rapids?"

His eyes widened. "No, not really."

"Well, if you just came in for souvenirs, I've got a bunch of them." He indicated a display case along one wall filled with black bear statues and Native American memorabilia.

Give a kid a prize and a jar of Carolina-made jam, and he was usually on cloud nine. "Go ahead and pick something out," he added.

"That's okay," Nathan said, slipping his hand inside Kayla's.

A kid turning down a toy? Some things just didn't compute.

"It's fine," Jace said to Kayla. "Tell your son to pick one. I give them out all the time. Sort of a loss leader for this business."

"He would if he were interested," she said. "I guess he's not. And besides, he's not my son. He's a family friend, and I usually let him make his own decisions."

"Okay then. Understood. But it's okay to change your mind, kid." Jace settled back on his stool behind the counter. "Now, what information do you need? That, too, happens to be free today."

"I'm just curious about these adventure places I've seen in the High Country. Wondering what kind of training you need to operate something like this. And you mentioned licenses…"

He pointed to a wall beside him. "Take a look. Sales tax forms, North Carolina small business license, federal withholding papers and more." Thank goodness his certificates were all up to date and clearly posted. The state officials were sticklers about proper display. "We have to provide instructions and water gear to everyone who comes aboard a raft," he said. "And our guides have to be trained in water safety and lifesaving procedures."

"How long have you owned this business?" she asked.

He smiled at her. "You writing a book?"

Her cheeks colored. "No. I dabble in travel writing. Hope to sell this story to a Charlotte magazine. You want to be in it, don't you? Free advertising."

"Haven't got a problem with free advertising, as long as you make me sound good. I've owned this place for ten years."

"Do you lead most of the rafting trips yourself?"

"Nope. Not anymore. I leave that mostly to the younger guys who don't mind jumping into the cool waters of the Wyoga."

She angled her head slightly to the side. "Why do they jump in the river?"

"Because some stu—misguided tourist decided to take an unauthorized dip. But don't worry. If Nate here changes his mind about rafting, I'll strap him to the mast and make him wear a seat belt."

She smiled, perhaps finally appreciating his sense of humor. She had full lips around perfect white teeth. Was she naturally this beautiful or did she pay for exorbitant upkeep? Botox and dental whitening or just lucky? He figured she was about his age, maybe thirty-two, so he was betting the years had so far been kind to her.

"Why did you decide to open this business?" she asked.

He noticed that so far she hadn't written anything down. A reporter? Jace didn't think so. But he answered. "I saw a need. All the adventure places were in Boone, and I figured we could use one in Holly River. We're a small town, but we attract tourists."

"And you've been successful?"

What did this lady want? His profit-and-loss statement? "I've done okay," he said. And then, since he wanted to change the conversation to something about Kayla, he decided to ask a question of his own.

"We allow almost all ages on our rafts," he said. "But mostly we appeal to the guys.

Maybe your husband would like to take Nate on the adventure of a lifetime." His standard line to describe his service. He figured she'd like it.

"I'm not married," she said. "But maybe we'll come back this afternoon. I think I could appreciate a real adventure."

Suddenly he felt a bit guilty for exaggerating the thrills of the Wyoga. At its roughest point, the river rapids were only a class two on a scale of five. Not exactly on a par with the latest amusement park rides.

Satisfied that he had learned just enough about Miss McAllister, he said, "Haven't seen you around, and I've seen most everybody. Are you new in town? Just visiting?"

"Just visiting."

"How long you staying? We have a number of businesses in town that are worth a curious reporter's investigation."

"I can stay as long as two weeks," she said. "Then I have to be back at work."

"Which is where?"

"DC. I work in the Capitol building, assistant to a congressman."

A political junkie? If so, Jace sensed that any common ground they might have enjoyed had just suffered a seismic shift. His only interest in politics was an occasional fishing trip with the mayor. No problem. There was enough about this woman to hold his attention.

"I'd be happy to show you around while you're here," he said. "The nice thing about owning my own business is that I sort of have built-in references. Ask anybody in town about me. And I can plan my afternoons off. This is beautiful country, and who better to guide you than a man who makes his living doing just that?"

She thought a moment, tapped her finger on the counter. "Yes, that would be nice."

"Shall we start with dinner tonight?" He remembered his gig at the café and frowned. "Make it tomorrow night instead?"

She nodded. "I'll look forward to it. But I hope we can go somewhere that caters to children. Nathan will be with us. Maybe a restaurant with a video game room?"

Okay. His vision of the perfect first date just plummeted. But they could go to the Louisiana Barbecue joint. Video games inside and corn hole and volleyball outside. Should keep the kid occupied while Jace's attention was right where he wanted it—on Miss Kayla McAllister.

"We're staying at the Mountain Laurel Inn, cabin C," she said. "Is seven o'clock okay? Nathan usually goes to bed around nine thirty."

"See you then." Maybe he could tire the kid out so he'd turn in a bit earlier. Worth a try.

NATHAN WALKED QUIETLY beside Kayla and sighed deeply. "What's wrong, Nathan?" she asked. "Is something bothering you?"

"No."

Nathan had been so sullen in the office of High Mountain Rafting, Kayla hoped he was feeling okay. She sensed he was withdrawing more and more into his own world these days. And why not? According to the psychologist who was working with him, this behavior was not unusual for a nine-year-old boy who'd recently lost his mother.

Kayla opened the passenger door of the crossover vehicle that had just brought them the seven hours from DC to Holly River. Nathan looked up at her with doe-like brown eyes just like his mother's. His sandy-blond hair was the same color as Susan's, too, but a recent haircut had made him look more like a little man than the raggedy-haired kid who'd been Susan's pride and joy. Kayla thought a new look would help Nathan adapt to the other, more serious changes in his life.

"Something is kind of bothering me, Auntie Kay."

She leaned against the passenger door. "What is it, sweetie?"

"We're not going on a raft, are we?"

"No, Nathan, not if you don't want to. I was just curious about the man who runs the place. I probably would try it, but we're not going to do anything unless you agree to it."

Relieved, Nathan crawled into the vehicle.

"We'll find oodles of other fun things to do while we're here. There's an old-timey railroad nearby and I understand we can search for beautiful gems from local mines. And if, in a few days, you decide you'd like to try rafting, then we will."

Kayla walked around to the driver's side, took one last look at the entrance to High Mountain Rafting and slipped behind the wheel. "We'll have dinner with Jace tomorrow, and maybe after you get to know him, you'll trust him enough to want to raft down the river." She prayed that this dream of the future would become a reality. "I'll bet it's fun."

Nathan shrugged one slight shoulder. "Maybe."

"He seemed like a nice man, didn't he?"

"I guess."

Truthfully Kayla hadn't been all that impressed with Jace Cahill. Like many of the men she ran into in Washington, Jace seemed more interested in her looks than anything else. Kayla had been blessed with good genes, great hair, a rosy complexion— all the qualities women seemed to want. And she had lived her life trying to downplay those superficial advantages. She wanted people to appreciate her for her mind, her drive, her skills at making a name for herself in Washington. She did not want to be re- membered for physical traits bestowed upon her by some capricious act of fate.

Still, she couldn't ignore the fact that Jace Cahill had been blessed with a few pleas- ing qualities himself. Soft, touchable light brown hair that appeared kissed by the sun. A strong, athletic build, broad shoulders and a slightly crooked smile that must endear him to many people.

Unfortunately he seemed to know that he approached that elusive ten out of ten category that good-looking men seemed to chase. He was a bit too sure of himself, too cocky. His answers to her questions were quick, mock-serious responses that left her wondering what, if anything, was really important to him.

Jace might be the perfect huckster to talk tourists into paying a small fortune to brave the Wyoga River, but she didn't see anything in his character today that would make him a good father for Nathan. Poor man. She imagined those deep butternut eyes widening in surprise, that sculpted jaw dropping in shock when she told him he was Nathan's biological father. She hoped he would recognize and accept his responsibility and be more to his son than just a contributor to his existence.

CHAPTER TWO

THAT NIGHT AT the Mountain Laurel Inn in cabin C, when sleep did not come easily, Kayla lay in the twin-size bed with its floral comforter and mound of soft pillows and thought about Susan. In the bed next to her, Nathan slept soundly, but he likely would wake up from a recurrent nightmare. Kayla would soothe him, assure him everything was all right and he would go back to sleep. And tomorrow night Kayla would take the second step in ensuring Nathan's future. She would tell Jace Cahill he had a son.

"Oh, Susan," she said into the dark room. "I'm trying. I really am. I don't want to break the promise I made to guarantee that Nathan has a loving future, and you know I care deeply for him, but a child? At this crucial point in my career?"

I wish we'd had more time to talk about this, to plan. This is all happening so fast.

Kayla's thoug... h... sp... ago, a beautiful ... before the brain tu... doctors had said the... could do, and Susan w... hood be oom, where ... round-t-clock nurses.

"I be to tell you some... said ... vo/ weak, her dry s impytant."

Ka... her best friend ever... whatever you

"Yeah an's guardian. Kayl red hard at Su... ing to a the pain and etched es. "No, honey... "Your re Nathan's guar... know little guy, but yo... and fath family."

"Gene, but they can't rai... She had a Kayla s hand wit... little stre ad left. They can't... don't kno g about my son. Th... co ld peopl want Nat... han growing up lik... I did... ense of a venture, wi h... out fun!" S wed, the effort costing

CHAPTER TWO

THAT NIGHT AT the Mountain Laurel Inn in cabin C, when sleep did not come easily, Kayla lay in the twin-size bed with its floral comforter and mound of soft pillows and thought about Susan. In the bed next to her, Nathan slept soundly, but he likely would wake up from a recurrent nightmare. Kayla would soothe him, assure him everything was all right and he would go back to sleep. And tomorrow night Kayla would take the second step in ensuring Nathan's future. She would tell Jace Cahill he had a son.

"Oh, Susan," she said into the dark room. "I'm trying. I really am. I don't want to break the promise I made to guarantee that Nathan has a loving future, and you know I care deeply for him, but a child? At this crucial point in my career?"

I wish we'd had more time to talk about this, to plan. This is all happening so fast.

Kayla's thoughts went back to a few months ago, a beautiful spring day twenty-four hours before the brain tumor took Susan's life. The doctors had said there was nothing else they could do, and Susan was brought to her child-hood bedroom, where she was cared for by round-the-clock nurses.

"I have to tell you something," Susan had said, her voice weak, her lips unnaturally dry. "It's important."

Kayla held her best friend's hand. "Whatever you want, whatever you need."

"You're Nathan's guardian."

Kayla had stared hard at Susan's face, try-ing to read past the pain and hopelessness etched in her eyes. "No, honey," she said. "Your parents are Nathan's guardians. You know I love the little guy, but your mother and father are his family."

"Genetically yes, but they can't raise him." She had squeezed Kayla's hand with what little strength she had left. "They can't! They don't know anything about my son. They're cold people. I don't want Nathan growing up like I did without a sense of adventure, with-out fun!" She swallowed, the effort costing her precious words. "I want him raised with loving care and happiness. My parents…no."

A feeling of panic had crept into Kayla's heart. She couldn't raise Nathan. She worked many hours a day. She had plans. "Susan, have you made this legal? Is it written down somewhere?" Part of Kayla wished that this decision had not been finalized and was only a parting wish from a dying woman. Sherry and Paul Wagoner had the resources to give Nathan a good life. They would see him educated. They would provide what he needed. Maybe not the tenderness Susan wanted for her son, but it would be enough.

But would it? In the two months since Susan's death, Nathan had been with his grandparents. He had become increasingly withdrawn, timid, almost as if he were afraid of shadows and his own thoughts. Even his physical characteristics had changed. He'd become thinner and pale as if he were afraid of the sunlight. And Kayla never thought she would see signs of stress on such a young face.

"It's legal," Susan had said. "You are his official guardian. My attorney has the paperwork."

"But Susan…" Kayla hadn't known how to tell her friend, how to explain that she had remained unmarried for the ten years since college for important reasons. She'd been focused on her career, her goals. She didn't have room in her one-bedroom apartment in DC or in her life for a nine-year-old, especially one who needed so much at this time of his life. Sherry and Paul would continue with his counseling, something Kayla couldn't afford. Eventually Nathan would become more like the happy, energetic boy he'd once been.

"I don't know what to say," Kayla had mumbled.

"I know. It's a shock."

It's more than a shock, Kayla had decided. It was an impossibility.

"I'm his pretend Auntie Kay," she'd said. "I care about Nathan, but I don't know if I can accept the responsibility of raising him. There would have to be so many changes, changes that wouldn't be fair to Nathan. I can't be the full-time mom you were." Was it right to be so brutally honest to a dying woman? Kayla had pushed aside the mounting feelings of guilt and convinced herself that it was.

Susan had closed her eyes, tried to draw a deep breath. When she next looked at Kayla, her eyes were bright and fierce. "There is one other option," she'd said, and then paused for another breath. "His father."

That horrible day, Kayla had listened carefully to the details about Jace Cahill, the man Susan had met her senior year of college—a charming, affable, basically goalless individual who skated through college pursuing a physical education degree. Kayla remembered Susan telling her about the man she'd fallen hard for, but Kayla had never met him. Now, on this day when every word was difficult for Susan, Kayla heard the story of Jace.

By the time Susan discovered she was pregnant, she'd learned that family life was not in Jace's future. Nice to almost everyone, a great kidder, Jace was serious when he said he didn't want children, didn't want to be tied down. Susan had never mentioned him to her friend again.

They both graduated and Susan broke up with Jace and turned to her parents for support during the most difficult nine months of her life. Susan explained to Kayla that she'd always hoped Jace would reach out to her again, decide he couldn't live without her. But that never happened. And so she'd never told him about the pregnancy.

In her dreams, her wildest dreams, Susan had imagined Jace meeting the remarkable boy they'd created together and falling in love with the delightful, sweet little person who was Nathan Joseph Wagoner. But that hadn't happened, either, and Susan started a successful graphic design business and devoted her life to her son and her job.

"I think Jace would be a good father," she'd said to Kayla that day in her bedroom when her strength had nearly deserted her. "At least the Jace I remember. He's single, lives in a small town in the High Country of North Carolina. He has a business." She'd cleared her throat, found the energy to continue speaking. "His information is in my safe-deposit box."

She'd pointed to her nightstand drawer. "Open it."

Inside Kayla found an envelope with a small key.

"That's the key to my box. Go to Jace,

Kayla. Introduce him to the son he never knew existed. See if he will take him and love him." Her voice started to quake. Tears fell down her cheeks. "If you can't raise him, take him to his father."

Kayla had promised to do that.

Susan had closed her eyes, drawn strength from somewhere deep inside. "He never wanted children," she said. "I pray to God that he will change his mind now. Whatever happens, Nathan's future is in your hands."

So now, as the clock between the two twin beds in cabin C ticked into the wee hours of the morning, Kayla felt the awesome ache of responsibility on her chest. Or was it the profound weight of guilt? With his grandparents the past two months, Nathan had certainly not thrived. But Kayla didn't want to admit to feeling guilty.

She couldn't accept the role of mother to this hurting child. She'd worked too hard to get where she was today. She couldn't change everything about her life to accept the conditions thrust upon her by a dying woman. But today she had brought Nathan to Holly River, North Carolina, so she had kept her promise.

A vision of Jace's face crept into Kayla's consciousness. A strong, slightly weathered face that hopefully reflected a kind man. "It's up to you, Jace," she said into the darkness. "Don't disappoint us."

SATURDAY MORNING STARTED out like most days for Jace. He got up early, made a cup of coffee and sat on the front porch of his hundred-year-old cabin on Sycamore Lake. Copper, undoubtedly the finest yellow Lab ever to walk the earth on four paws, ran around the yard sniffing and marking and generally having a fine time. Then he came onto the porch and sat beside the log chair Jace had chosen as his personal throne. After all, a man's home is his castle, and this rustic bit of North Carolina hominess was all the castle Jace wanted.

"Got big plans tonight, Copper," Jace said to the dog, whose ears perked up as if he were understanding every word. "Got a date with a fine woman." He scratched the dog on the top of his silky head. "I know how particular you are about women, and I believe even you would be blown away by this one."

Kayla McAllister had been the first

thought entering Jace's brain when he'd woken up with the sun. A woman had never caused Jace to lose sleep, but when he pictured Kayla, he decided she might be worth a couple of restless tosses in the middle of the night.

He'd stop at the bank this morning and pick up a roll of quarters so the quiet kid—Nathan, was it?—would have enough ammunition to maintain his video game fever. Maybe he'd find a kid his age to toss the beanbags in the corn hole game. Jace knew most of the locals, so he could introduce the boy to Holly River Elementary's finest, which would leave Jace free to explore the intimate details of Miss Kayla's life.

Jace wondered who would be playing at the Louisiana Barbecue tonight. Probably Edgar Manville and the Blue Ridge Mountain Boys. Always a good sound, but would Miss Washington DC appreciate the strumming and picking? And if she didn't, could Jace make an exception for a female who didn't love country music? In this case, yes.

He started up his old truck and headed into town. First stop was for a second cup of coffee at the River Café, where he ran in to Sam McCall, his brother's best friend and Holly River's newest rookie cop, and the closest thing to another brother the Cahill boys had—not counting Robert.

"What are you grinning about?" Sam asked from the barstool where he'd parked himself at the counter.

For some reason, the ladies seemed to like Sam, and the clerk from the all-night convenience store was seated next to him now. Jace figured Sam was being polite and charming even if he had no interest in dating her. Sam was Irish through and through. Complexion fair as the sun and red hair shiny as gold at the end of a rainbow. Sam naturally charmed everyone he met, but he was a good cop and could command respect when he needed to. And he had a heart that could be broken, which was proven a few weeks ago when a lady he'd been dating, a waitress at the café, had gone afoul of the law and skipped town before Sam could lock her up. Jace knew Sam wasn't over it yet.

Jace took the stool next to Sam and ordered a coffee to go. "Met an out-of-towner yesterday," he said. "I asked her out for tonight."

"Oh? What excuse did she use for turning you down?"

Jace pretended to punch Sam's shoulder. "This one actually said yes. Of course she hadn't met you yet."

Sam grinned. "I'll try to stay off her radar and give you a fighting chance. Is she a tourist?"

"She said she's here researching some of the local color for a magazine. Doesn't ring exactly true to me, but I couldn't accuse her of coming into High Mountain just to meet me." He added cream to the coffee brought to him in a paper cup. "She's got a kid with her."

"Really? That doesn't bother you?"

"Not so much. She said the boy isn't hers. He's a family friend."

"That's good. At least you won't be signing up for daddy duty."

"Me? Never." Jace chuckled, picked up his cup and headed for the door. "Have a good day, Sam. Be careful out there."

"Dude…it's Holly River. We've had our one serious crime for this year." Sam's expression mellowed. "And I got stung pretty badly from it."

Poor Sam. Not all women were heart-breakers, Jace thought, but right now Sam McCall probably didn't believe that.

Jace wasn't pleased to discover that one of his regular guides wasn't going to show up today. That meant he had to take tourists down the Wyoga for the first trip. Plus, that afternoon, the last rafting excursion was late returning, leaving Jace less than an hour to get to his cabin, shower, dress, feed Copper and be at the Mountain Laurel Inn by seven. Wearing better-than-normal jeans and a T-shirt with an actual collar, and cleanly shaved, Jace headed back to town, hoping the rest of his night went more smoothly.

BEING WITH KAYLA was a bit of heaven on earth. She was funny and interesting, liked country music—a truly big plus in her favor—and seemed fascinated by everything he said. Still, Jace wondered if she expected him to buy that dubious story she'd told about writing the article. Either way, he was happy to oblige her with detailed answers to her questions.

Yes, he'd lived here his whole life. He loved the High Country. There wasn't a better place for family and friends to get together and enjoy nature and the most beautiful weather east of the Mississippi. He learned to snow ski when he was six years old and returned to the slopes every winter.

Sure, family was a big part of his life. He was proud to say that his brother was chief of police; his sister would soon move back to Holly River to become chief administrator at the Sawtooth Mountain Children's Home. His mother lived in a big old farmhouse outside of town with one of Copper's relatives whose lineage went back almost as far at the Cahills'.

Thank goodness Kayla didn't ask about his father. That was one subject Jace didn't care to discuss, or even remember. The old man was gone now, and there were no glowing sentiments on his tombstone.

If Kayla was heaven on earth, the kid tagging along beside her was a touch of devilish glue. He stuck to Kayla as if without her, he'd fall through a crack in the earth never to be seen again. Jace got him to play a few video games, but just when Jace and Kayla were beginning to get cozy, the kind of cozy Jace had thought about all day, little Nathan would run out of the game room, plop down beside Kayla and say the game wasn't any fun.

At one point Jace led the kid over to a group of boys about his age. Jace asked if Nathan could join their game of corn hole. The boys, with the typical blasé behavior that seemed to identify most preteens, issued a noncommittal group nod. Jace took that to mean an engraved invitation, and he left Nathan with the boys.

For the entire time Jace watched Nathan, the kid never once held the beanbags. He just remained on the sidelines of the game, leading Jace to wonder if that was the way he lived his entire life—on the sidelines.

"So let's talk about you," Jace said to Kayla when Nathan was occupied with his sneaker toe and a clod of dirt.

"What would you like to know?"

"How did you get involved with politics?"

"I've always been interested. Even as a teenager I served as an intern at my congressman's office. Then I studied political science at the University of Maryland. Someday I hope to be an elected official myself and help people through the passing of fair laws."

Jace couldn't ignore the light in her eyes when she talked about her chosen career. Yeah, she was a political junkie all right, and apparently ambitious. She might find fault with Jace's laid-back way of life, but he was determined to interest her in some of his finer qualities, which had always worked for him.

"I can sum up my situation pretty quickly for you," she said, interrupting the pleasant thoughts that had filtered into his brain. "I'm an only child. My parents live in Maryland. Because of my schedule, I only see them a half-dozen times a year, but even so, we're close. Just like you and your family."

"That's good. So how'd you end up with the Energizer Bunny over there when you decided on this trip?"

She frowned, obviously not appreciating the reference. "Nathan's been having a hard time lately. His mother and I have been friends for years, and I thought this trip would do him some good."

"And has it?"

She gave him a serious stare. "Too soon to tell, but I hope it will."

Jace took a pull from his Bud Light. "Take him out to the Sawtooth Trout Farm. I guarantee he'll catch a fish."

"That's a wonderful idea," she said. "But I don't know a thing about fishing. Maybe you could go with us."

Oh, heck no. The trout farm was stocked with pudgy little trout that practically jumped into a kid's pocket, all to make Mom and Dad feel good about the twenty bucks they'd put down for pole rental. Jace was a fisherman, but he believed in giving the fish a chance. Besides, he was hoping for alone time with Kayla.

"You don't have to know anything," he said. "The owner of the farm will even bait the hook for you." He scratched at the label on his bottle. "I've got an even better idea. Let's drop the kid at the trout farm and you and I take the beginner's trail up Sawtooth Mountain. Nice and shady the whole way, and the views are spectacular."

She nibbled on a french fry. "I think Nathan would really enjoy that, as well. When would you have time?"

Jace obviously wasn't getting his point across. He leaned across the table and placed his hand on Kayla's arm. "Sweetheart," he said, "you're only going to be here for two weeks...make that thirteen days now. I'm hoping for some adult-only entertainment."

She took a sip of iced tea. "I wouldn't count on it. I'm responsible for Nathan. He pretty much has to go where I go."

"Look, my sister-in-law has a daughter Nathan's age. I'm sure she would look after Nathan if we wanted to get away for a few hours. Plus, there's a whole roster of college girls at Taylor-Crowe who are looking for childcare assignments. We could hire one of them."

She looked him square in the eye, almost making him uncomfortable. "You don't like kids much, do you?" she asked.

"They're okay." He rubbed her wrist with his thumb. "But I think I like you better."

And he did like her. Despite the obvious baggage she had with her, she was fun and pretty and seemed as at home in the mountains as she must in the nation's capital. Jace wanted to know everything about her. He called for the check. He would start his discovery process with a good-night kiss if he had to bribe the kid to get it.

Jace's confidence in getting to know Kayla rose when they returned to the Mountain Laurel Inn. Kayla unlocked the door to cabin C and placed her hand on Nathan's shoulder. "What do you want to say to Mr. Cahill, Nathan?" she said.

Nathan gave a little smile. "Thanks. It was fun."

"You're welcome," Jace said. "And you can call me Jace. Everybody does."

"Now go inside, honey," Kayla said. "You can turn on the TV. Just wait for me in the living room, okay?"

Now this was more like it. He'd hoped for some time alone with Kayla, and apparently her thoughts had been running in the same direction. He stared at her pink lips and allowed his mind to wander.

Kayla shut the door behind Nathan and walked a short distance from the cabin. When she stopped, Jace put his hands on her arms and started to draw her close.

Kayla's back straightened like a broomstick. "Don't do that," she said.

"Why not?" He left his hands where they

were but didn't coax her rigid body to get closer. "I thought this is why you sent the kid inside. So the adults could have a few minutes to end the night in the best possible way."

"You're wrong."

"You didn't have a good time?"

"Sure, it was fine. But I sent Nathan inside so we could talk."

He dropped his hands. "Okay. Seems to me we've just spent the last three hours talking, but if you want to talk some more, I'm game."

She gave him a forced smile. "This is important, Jace."

What could she have to say that remotely concerned him? "I'm listening."

She cleared her throat. "I'm not writing an article. That was just a way to get you to talk to me."

He frowned, not knowing what to expect next. "I figured as much."

"Do you remember a girl named Susan Wagoner from your time at the University of North Carolina?"

He really didn't, but he gave the name some thought. After a moment a pretty face surrounded by curly blond hair popped into his mind. Oh, yeah. Susan. She was cute, adventurous, a good sport… He nodded. "I remember Susan. We dated awhile."

"That's right. And then when you were about to graduate, you two broke up. Do you remember that?"

Again he needed a moment to bring up old memories. "Oh, yeah. She broke up with me. But until then, we had a pretty good thing going. How do you know Susan, and why are you bringing her up now?"

Her eyes clouded; her face grew serious. "I'm sorry to tell you, but Susan died two months ago. She was my best friend."

He shook his head in sympathy. "That's tough. I'm sorry for your loss." That was about all he could think to say. He hadn't seen Susan in ten years, so any real empathy he might have had was lost in a haze of time past.

"Nathan is her son," Kayla said.

"Oh, now I get it. You said the kid has been having a hard time lately. The death of his mother has to be weighing heavy on him. Why do you have him? Where is his father?"

"That's why we came to Holly River, Jace."

"That boy's father lives right here in Holly River?"

She didn't say anything else, so Jace tried to put the puzzle pieces together. He'd liked Susan back in the day. They'd had a healthy relationship, but it just hadn't worked out for them. She wanted a future, marriage, kids. And he'd clearly told her that…

"Wait a minute," he said. "You're not suggesting that…" His words stuck in his throat. His breath caught in his lungs. "No way are you saying…"

"Yes, I am, Jace. Nathan is your son."

CHAPTER THREE

JACE TRIED TO draw a deep breath, but it seemed that the air kept getting stuck on the way to his lungs. Finally he managed to speak. "What sort of game are you playing, *Miss Reporter*?" The last two words dripped with sarcasm and the panic he was experiencing. A son? This couldn't be happening.

"I know how you must feel," she said. "But…"

"Really? You know? When is the last time someone walked up to you, lied about who they are and handed off a nine-year-old kid like he was a rescue from a dog shelter?"

"That's not what's happening here," she said. "I'm not handing him off. You need to listen to me."

She paused while even more venomous words fought to find their way out of Jace's mouth.

"It's true that I'm not writing an article.

But I needed to get some information on you before I told you why I'd come. I had to know if you are solvent financially, single, as Susan told me, and if you are basically a decent man."

"Well, you've discovered that I own my own business. I'm not married. But as for the last part, you're about to find out that I can be considerably less than decent, especially if someone is running a scam."

Her eyes lit with an inner fire that almost made him regret his words. Almost.

"That's what you think? That I'm a scam artist? Do you believe this is easy for me?"

"I don't know, and frankly I don't care. How many guys have you tried it on? They say practice makes perfect."

Her lips thinned before she shot back, "That's just mean and totally uncalled for. That little boy in there is the sweetest, most gentle child. And his mother meant more to me than any other person on earth. She was like family to me. The last thing I ever thought I would do is come to this out-of-the-way town to find a man, a *stranger*, who might, if his heart is big enough, take Nathan."

Jace placed his fist on his chest. "This has nothing to do with the size of my heart! If I remember Susan correctly, and I'm beginning to, she was responsible, organized, a good student. I can't imagine her leaving her child to a man she hasn't seen in ten years."

"I guess you can't imagine her dying, either. And besides, you don't need to keep calling him *her child*. Nathan is as much yours as…"

"Fine. I got it."

"And what choice do you think she had? For heaven's sake, Jace, she didn't plan to die!"

He exhaled a deep breath and struggled to gain control of his emotions. That last line had gotten to him. Nobody planned to die. A sweet young woman who'd been part of his life was gone forever, and no matter what happened with the kid, that was a tragedy.

"Was she sure?" he said. "I mean how did she know that I…"

"Look, you can run any tests you want to, but if you remember anything about Susan, then you know she wasn't the type of girl to jump from bed to bed. She loved you, Jace, really loved you. And two months ago, in the darkest hours of her life, she decided to take a leap of faith and trust you.

"And another thing," Kayla said on a quick draw of air. "If you'd taken the time to look at Nathan, you'd see certain similarities between you and him. He has a slightly long forehead and full eyebrows for a kid his age. And he's tall. He'll probably grow to well over six feet." She dared him with a scathing look. "That description ring any bells?"

He was getting in too deep. The shock he'd felt earlier was turning into full-blown panic. "That description could fit any number of guys…"

"And it fits you, you jerk!" She bit her lip as if she wanted to take back the name calling. "I'm sorry. I know this is difficult for you, but we have a situation here that needs calm and logic so we can plan what we must do. Nathan is just a little boy. And he's all alone."

"I don't know if I buy that," Jace said, sensing a way out. "A mother doesn't leave her kid without provisions in case she dies. Susan wouldn't have done that. She had a warning that her life was ending. Nathan must have a guardian."

Kayla's back stiffened. She inhaled deeply. "There is a guardian."

"Well, fine, who is it?"

"That's not an issue right now," Kayla said.

"The heck it isn't."

"What I mean is, the guardian wasn't consulted before Susan made her decision. And because of that, the guardian is unable to fulfill the duties assigned. She simply isn't at a point in her life where she can take on the responsibilities of a child."

"Why not?" Jace paused long enough to see a glint of guilt in Kayla's eyes. She looked away quickly, but he'd seen it and he knew. "You're the guardian, aren't you?"

Kayla's eyes squeezed shut. When she opened them, she stared at Jace. Determination was evident in the set of her jaw. "Susan never talked about it with me. The day before she died is the first I knew that she'd named me as guardian."

"And you don't want the kid? He's the son of your best friend, someone who's like family to you, and you don't want the job of raising him."

Kayla looked as if his words had had a physical impact. She turned away from him and clutched her stomach. "It's not a matter of wanting him. I can't. You have to understand that. I have a job, an important job, and I have goals."

Jace walked around her, forcing her to look up at him. She seemed vulnerable, as if she knew her words sounded shallow. Maybe he was shallow, too, but this lady was wading in ankle-deep water.

"I get it," he said. "I'm just a flunky who books people on day trips down the river. My goals don't matter. My lifestyle can be altered at the drop of a hat, right?"

"I don't know you well enough to say that," she said. "But from what I've seen, yes, I think it would be easier for you to take Nathan. And you have a family that could help you. And all this doesn't even take into account that you're his father."

Suddenly he felt iron bars closing around him, tightening in his chest. This was happening too fast. There had to be a way out. "That's still to be determined," he said.

"I told you, arrange for any DNA test you want."

She was so sure of herself that little doubt was left in Jace's mind that Nathan was his. Kayla McAllister was credible. The timing was right. For the months he'd dated Susan, they had been monogamous. She'd been faithful to him as he'd been to her. But when she'd indicated she wanted a future with him that included marriage and children, he'd bolted, as he'd done countless times before. To Jace Cahill, who lived alone in a cabin surrounded by trees and critters, nothing was as important as freedom.

"Why didn't she tell me?" he asked, surprised at the calm tenor of his voice. In fact, he had to admit that it bothered him that Susan hadn't confided in him. Had he been that indifferent, that callous back then?

"What would you have done?" Kayla said. "Gone running to her home in Virginia with a marriage license in your hand?"

He shook his head. "No. But I would have offered to support the kid, if not emotionally, at least financially. I'm not a complete degenerate."

"Susan didn't need you for that. Maybe

you didn't know it, but Susan was raised in a life of privilege. Her parents took care of her." Kayla bit her lip again as if she regretted what she'd just said. "Don't get the wrong idea about Susan's mother and father. What I mean is…"

"What you mean," Jace said, a completely logical way out of this mess now evident, "is that Susan has parents, and Nathan has grandparents who are perfectly able to take care of him and no doubt willing to accept the job."

"Susan didn't want that. Her parents would be terrible guardians for Nathan. They are cold, unfeeling, even more so than when they raised Susan. They are completely incapable of relating to a sensitive child like Nathan, who doesn't need to live the rest of his life feeling as if he is a burden."

"Okay, maybe so, but she did the next best thing. She made you his guardian."

"Yes, she did. But then she did another next best thing. She told me about Nathan's father, his biological father. You, Jace, you are the logical one to raise this child. And you have exactly thirteen days to prove to me that you can form a bond with Nathan that will protect and support him until he's grown. Can you do that?"

Jace scoffed. "I've got to prove myself to you?"

"Of course. You can't think I would simply hand this child over as you said before."

The bars tightened. Jace felt as if he couldn't breathe. Now he had to show proof that he was father material. How could this woman walk into his life and tell him what he had to do, how he must live his life from now on?

"Thirteen days," he said. A period of time that he'd thought might be one of the best thirteen days of his life. Not anymore. His hopes of romancing through the next two weeks with Miss Kayla McAllister were reduced to dust in the wind. Now he either had to up his man-of-honor game or act like the jerk she already thought he was. "One thing, Kayla. How much does Nathan know about this? What have you told him?"

"Basically nothing. This is just a vacation for him. And I'm trusting you to keep this between us for now in case this doesn't work for some reason."

"No problem there," he said. "Tell you

what. I'll let you know where I am on this issue in thirteen days." He turned and walked away.

KAYLA WALKED INTO the cabin and found Nathan reading a book. "Nothing good on TV?" she said.

"I don't know. I brought this book from Grandma's."

"Reading is great. Do you want me to be quiet so you can go on with the story?"

He closed the cover and waited for her to sit beside him on the sofa. "I'm almost done with it. Why were you talking so long to Jace outside?"

Kayla had hoped to broach the subject of her long conversation with Jace after she'd had a chance to gather her thoughts, but that was not to be. Nathan had always been a curious child.

She picked up a soft pillow from the arm of the sofa and snuggled it against her chest. In truth, the meeting with Jace had gone about as well as could be expected. He'd been upset, shocked, understandably skeptical, but for the most part, he'd managed to keep his cool. By the time he left, Kayla was fairly sure that he was giving their predicament the consideration it deserved. Far from being ready to accept his role as Nathan's father, at least he'd admitted to being willing to give the situation serious thought. What more could be expected from a man who'd never been married, a man who'd never even considered the possibility, from what he'd said tonight.

"Actually we talked about you," she said. "And other things. We talked about the barbecue tonight and the fun music. This seems like a nice town, doesn't it?"

Nathan shrugged. "Why did you talk about me?"

Kayla didn't know when, if ever, she would tell Nathan that Jace was his father. She didn't know if Nathan would ever be ready to hear it. But until she made that crucial decision, she could begin to lay the groundwork for the two of them to form a relationship. This meant stretching the truth a bit at this stage.

"Jace wanted to know what things you like to do."

"He wouldn't want to do the stuff I like," Nathan said.

"Why would you say that, sweetheart? Didn't you like Jace?"

"He's okay. He didn't say much to me. He talked mostly to you."

"I'm sorry about that. Maybe Jace just found it easier to talk with someone nearer his own age. He doesn't have much experience with children."

"That's not it," Nathan said. "I think Jace wanted this to be a date with you, and he didn't like that I was there, too."

Kayla smiled and ruffled his hair. "Sometimes you are just scary smart, Nate."

"Did you like him?"

"Actually I did. He's interesting and funny."

"Are we going to see him again?"

"Would that be okay with you? I promise I will be with you all the time. And I'll tell Jace that's it's only fair that we do things you would like."

"I don't think I like that corn hole game."

"Then we won't play it. Now about seeing Jace again?"

"I guess it would be okay. Just tell him to talk to me once in a while."

Kayla held up her hand, prompting a high five. "You got it, kiddo."

One male willing to give this relationship a try. One male not so much. In Kayla's mind, it was a decent start.

CHAPTER FOUR

THE NEXT MORNING, the usual peace of the waking hour was spoiled for Jace. Likewise the calm he experienced while sipping coffee on his front porch was not as usual, thanks to the matters on his mind. It wasn't just the disappointment that his expectations with Kayla were crushed, though he had thought about the date for more than twenty-four hours.

Oddly, in the short time they'd talked in his office, he'd experienced more than a physical attraction with her, which was rare for Jace these days. Maybe it was her interest in him, though now he understood the reason behind it. Maybe it was the way she reacted with the kid—comforting and respectful. He took a sip of coffee and shook his head. The irony was too much to ignore. He'd felt a closeness to a woman who was a complete stranger. He'd felt nothing at all for the kid by her side. His son.

Sunday stretched before him. The rafting trips were covered since Jace had a plan for the morning and a gig at the winery in town. Until then, he would stay busy around the cabin and try to keep his thoughts about Nathan to a minimum. But right now, the coffee was strong, the breeze gentle. The sound of an automobile on his little-used mountain road told him his morning solitude was about to be interrupted.

His brother Carter drove into the gravel parking space in front of Jace's cabin. Sunday was Carter's day off, but since he'd gotten married, he hadn't wasted a Sunday visiting his brother. So why was he here today? Wearing jeans and a casual shirt, Carter got out of his personal vehicle and walked to the porch. Copper ran from the nearby woods and raced around Carter as if his pockets were filled with treats. "Down, you little beggar," Carter said, rubbing Copper's muzzle.

Jace checked his wristwatch. Not even eight thirty. "What are you doing here?"

"Thought I could get a cup of coffee,"

Carter said. "Besides, a man can't visit his brother?"

"Not one who's enjoying the benefits of wedded bliss," Jace said, jerking his thumb toward his front door. "Pot's inside. Go get a cup."

Carter pulled a straight-backed wooden chair close to his brother before going inside. He was back in under a minute, the cup of java steaming in his hand. He sat in the chair, breathed deeply and let his gaze wander over the property. Then his attention settled on his kid brother. "What's with the fancy clothes? I expected to find you in sweats and a raggedy T-shirt. You look like you could be going to church."

Jace glanced down at his neat jeans, collared shirt. "Going to Wilton Hollow to see our brother."

"Our half brother, you mean."

Carter hadn't yet gotten comfortable with discovering that their less-than-honorable father had had an affair with a former employee at the Cahill Paper Mill—an affair that culminated in the birth of another son for Raymond Cahill. Unfortunately Raymond had cared about as much for this son as he had Jace.

The boy, Robert, was now twelve years old, and he had issues even more serious than the ones that plagued Jace when he was born. The diagnosis of Robert's autism had to have been a crushing blow to their father, who hated weakness of any kind.

"Call Robert what you want," Jace said. "But he's our flesh and blood."

"You've been seeing a lot of Robert," Carter said.

"I've been trying to get out there at least once a week. Don't know why that should surprise you, Carter. You're the one who found out that Robert existed and took me out there to meet him."

"It doesn't surprise me exactly," Carter said. "It's just that Robert is so hard to communicate with."

Jace smiled. "I think you're a bit scared of Robert."

Carter scoffed at the ridiculous notion. "Of course not. I just don't get him. I understand that his problems aren't his fault..."

"No, they're not. Nature plays little tricks on us sometimes. To understand Robert takes patience, that's all," Jace said. "He and I have had a couple of meaningful encounters. At least he seems to remember me when I show up now."

The brothers sat in companionable silence until Jace asked, "So why aren't you with your wife? Is there trouble in paradise?"

"No. Actually Miranda kicked me out of the house this morning."

"Sounds like trouble to me."

"Well, there's no trouble. She and Emily are baking me a cake, and they want it to be a surprise. But being a cop, I put the clues together...flour, baking powder, sugar..."

"Yeah, you're an investigative genius," Jace said. "A cake? What's the occasion?"

"You forgot again, didn't you? My birthday is on the same day in August every year, Jace. You'd think you'd know it by now."

Jace slapped his palm against his forehead. "I'm sorry, bro. Mama even called me a few days ago to remind me about dinner tonight."

"Don't worry about it."

"No, no. I'll be there. I'm going to Wilton Hollow this morning. Then Gary and I have a gig at the winery this afternoon. We're playing from one to four. I'll come out to the house after that." He paused before adding, "Can't forget to put the present I got you in my truck."

Carter scowled at him. "You mean you can't forget to stop and buy something. Don't waste your money. Nothing I need."

"Oh, I know that. Since Miranda came back in your life, you're happy as a pig in... Well, you know what I mean."

Carter drained the last of his coffee. "I won't keep you now, Jace, but speaking of happy, you don't look so perky yourself this morning considering I heard you were at the Louisiana Barbecue with a nice-looking gal last night. Could it be the one who came into the shop the other day?"

Darned small town. The chief of police, aka Jace's older brother, would have heard about the date, probably from the minute Jace picked up Kayla at the inn. He nodded. "Yeah, her name is Kayla McAllister. She's from Washington, DC."

"A big-city girl, eh?"

"Yeah."

"And the kid with her?"

Even the best gossipers in town didn't

know about his connection to Nathan. "Not related to her. The boy, Nathan, is the son of one of her friends, somebody who recently died. Kayla brought the boy here to help him forget his grief for a while."

Carter sat forward in his chair. His eyes reflected the inner spark of curiosity that had always guided his actions in the police department. "Why'd she bring him here? I mean, I love Holly River, but it seems to me there are a lot more exciting places to take a kid."

Jace's heart began to race. Suddenly he wanted to tell his brother all about the revelations of the night before. He could trust Carter, and the two brothers knew a lifetime of taking on the other's burdens. And just maybe, Carter could shed some logic on this tough situation. Maybe he could suggest a way out of this mess.

"Can you keep a secret?" Jace asked. "I mean, keep it from *everyone*?"

"By 'everyone' I assume you mean Mama and Ava."

"Yes, and Miranda, too. This secret is big, explosive even."

Carter's brow furrowed. "I don't like to

keep secrets from Miranda, so if this secret concerns her in any way, then don't tell it to me."

"It doesn't. Just concerns me and that boy, Nathan."

"You and Nathan?"

"Yeah." Jace's mouth felt dry. He swallowed and began to relate his tale about his memorable date with an even more memorable lady—until the bombshell was dropped. "Back at the Laurel Mountain Inn, when I tried to kiss her, she stiffened up and said no."

Jace attempted a smile though he didn't feel like smiling. "She was emphatic. She just wanted to talk."

"Okay. And what did you talk about?" Carter's clasped hands twisted between his knees. He obviously was waiting for a bombshell himself.

"Get ready," Jace said. "That kid is my son."

Carter didn't speak for a long moment and when he finally did, his voice was raspy, his words low and mechanical. "Your son?"

"That's right. There was this girl, in college."

"No way. You're not stupid, Jace. You never would have risked a baby. You always used protection, didn't you?"

Jace looked down at the porch floor. "Most always."

Carter stood, went to the porch railing and wrapped his hands around the rough wood. "Well, this is a potboiler. Are you sure? Is there proof?"

"I'm having a test done. Got to get the kid's DNA sample. But I think I'm the daddy."

"And you knew nothing about this? I mean for ten years you've been blissfully unaware that this college girlfriend had a baby?"

"Her name's Susan." Jace nodded. "*Blissfully* is the right word. Believe me, there was no bliss in discovering the truth last night. I've been a mess just thinking about what this means."

"I can imagine," Carter agreed. "I'll tell you what it means, brother. If it turns out you're the kid's father, then you have responsibilities."

"I darned sure know that!"

"And Kayla wants you to take the boy and raise him?"

Jace shrugged. "That was her plan. She's the boy's legal guardian, but she claims she can't take on his upbringing. Maybe when she gets to know me she'll decide I'm not parent material, either."

"And maybe she won't. Nathan isn't her kid. She doesn't have to assume his upbringing."

Jace sat on the edge of his throne, his elbows on his knees, his eyes raised to his brother's face. "You know me, Carter. I can't raise a kid. What do I know about children? I love Miranda's kid…"

"Yeah, Emily treats you like you're some kind of superhero. Maybe you should think about…"

Jace's head began to shake. His palms raised in front of him, he signaled that the idea would never work. "I don't want a kid," he said. "Look where I live, miles from town. Look how I lead my life—handing off river trips to whoever will take them, making a few lousy bucks playing my guitar…" He stared at his brother. "Forgetting birthdays…"

Carter walked over and put his hand on Jace's shoulder. "That can all change. You're a good man, Jace. You might surprise your-self at how well you take to fatherhood."

Comforted by his brother's touch, Jace calmed, took a deep breath. "Get real, Carter. I'm a goof-off, and you know it. And this kid didn't cause any reaction in me. I couldn't tell you the color of his eyes if Kayla hadn't pointed them out." He rubbed his nape. "What should I do? Kayla and Na-than will only be here twelve more days. I didn't make any plans to see them again, but I'm sure I will. Kayla is nothing if not determined."

"See how you feel the next time you see them. And if you need more professional advice than I can give you, talk to Ava. Be-cause of her new role at the children's home, she's been reading every book ever written about raising children."

Panic coursed through Jace's veins. "Don't tell her, Carter. Not her or Mama. If Mama finds out about Nathan, her grandson, she won't let me hear the end of it. And Ava will just conclude that I'm a scumbag."

Carter smiled. "You're not a scumbag, Jace. You've been hit with a life changer. You need time to think it over. You're going to have to support this boy financially, but if after these twelve days have passed, you know for certain that you will never feel a kinship to him, well, maybe a solution will come to you."

"Yeah, maybe," he mumbled. Did a solution exist where the guy gets the girl for twelve fantastic days and the scenario about the son only existed in his imagination?

"In the meantime," Carter continued, "I'm here for you if you want to talk. Go see Robert today. Play at the winery. Come to Mama's for dinner. At least your current day is planned without added stress. Who knows what tomorrow will bring—maybe a clear path to please everybody."

Jace watched his brother walk down to his SUV. "If only," Jace muttered to himself. Then he went into the house, checked the lock on the doggy door to make sure Copper could get outside and filled a metal bowl with kibble.

"See you later, boy," he said to the dog. The drive to Wilton Hollow was forty-five minutes. Jace knew what he'd be thinking about the entire way.

CHAPTER FIVE

SINCE THE FIRST time Jace had visited his half brother, Robert, two months ago, Jace had paid special attention to the boy's mother, quiet, staid Gladys Kirshner. Jace regarded Gladys as another of Raymond Cahill's victims just like he was, like Robert was. They were an odd, damaged group, Jace, Robert and Gladys, and anything Jace could do to make Gladys's lot in life easier, he was willing.

He was the only one of the three legitimate Cahill children who hadn't tried to talk their mother, Cora, out of continuing the payments Raymond had started for Robert's care—a guilty man's salve for his wrongdoing. Cora wouldn't hear of it and continued sending fifteen hundred dollars a month from her paper mill profits. "Your father and I had a marriage. His debts are my debts."

That statement had marked the end of any discussion.

"It's so good to see you," Gladys said when she opened the door to Jace. She seemed almost nondescript in her brown pants and tan shirt. There was no sparkle to Gladys. "Robert's been talking about your visit today," she said. "It warms my heart to see him enthused about something."

"Is it Jace?" The shrill shout came from Robert's bedroom just before the boy appeared, walking steadily and excitedly on his sturdy legs.

Robert looked good today, bright and alert. His long dark hair had been combed. His plaid shirt matched his tan jeans. He wore shoes, something he rarely did. After all, he didn't leave the house these days unless it was to visit a doctor. Jace intended to change that very soon.

Robert looked like he might hug Jace, but at the last minute he pulled back. Spontaneity wasn't something he was comfortable with. Jace gave him his biggest smile. "You're looking dandy today, buddy," he said.

"Robert's therapist said he's showing improvement since you started visiting. He's more outgoing and seems more willing to try new things."

The county only paid for Robert to have caregivers two mornings a week. Robert's therapist, a kind woman named Harriet, was an expert in assisting children with autism. She did what she could, and the visits gave Gladys time to go to the grocery store and run errands.

"Did you make your own sandwich this week?" Jace asked him.

"You bet. I'll show you."

The chore of deciding which ingredients went where on the bread had always been a difficult activity for Robert, one that increased his anxiety. But Jace had worked for over an hour with him during the last visit, and when he left, Robert was building a sandwich like a deli pro. A small step, but one that made Robert proud.

Today Jace had brought a stack of yellow plastic cups. Yellow was a color that didn't upset the boy. They sat on the worn carpet in the living room with a small toy truck Jace had bought from a thrift store. Jace began hiding the truck under a cup and asking Robert to find it. He soon understood that even if he couldn't see the truck, it was still there.

As the minutes progressed, Jace added more cups, creating a play version of the old shell game. Robert's eyes were alert as he followed the movements of Jace's hand. Soon he was picking out the cup hiding the truck every time.

When Robert tired of the game, Jace talked quietly with him. Sometimes the boy responded, sometimes not. But this had been a good visit, and Jace was encouraged when it was time for him to leave.

"Come back whenever you can, Jace," Gladys said at the door. "Robert responds so well to you."

"I'll be back soon," Jace said. He was always a bit sad when he left Robert, and today was no different. There was so much he wanted to do for his half brother, but it was a slow and arduous task. He often wondered if Robert remembered the big, boisterous man who'd visited him until Robert turned six. After that, when Robert had become unpredictable, Raymond had stopped coming.

Jace got in his truck and drove toward Holly River. He chose a soft country station on his radio and listened to the music as he contemplated the difference Robert had brought to his life.

"So why can't you feel a connection to your own kid?" he said aloud. "You feel more for the half brother you just met than for a little boy who carries your genes."

Jace knew the answer. His responsibilities to Robert were voluntary. His time limited. When he left Wilton Hollow, he went back to his own life, the life he loved, the one without distractions. He looked forward to his visits with Robert. For an hour he could be a decent brother to a kid who craved attention. But so far he hadn't felt the beginnings of affection for Nathan.

He picked a drive-through restaurant and ordered a burger, fries and a milkshake. The food felt like cement in his stomach when he reached the Sawtooth Winery at twelve thirty.

"Terrific," he said as he took his guitar case from the back seat. "Now I've got to deal with indigestion." But at least he wouldn't see Kayla or Nathan today and have to face the truth about his past indiscretion. That's what he thought, but he was halfway through his second set when he saw them walk under the grape arbor and find seats on the patio.

JACE WAS A trained guitarist. He rarely needed sheet music. He knew which chords to play for which songs. His fingers were lithe and strong, perfectly calloused. Yet when he saw Kayla and Nathan, his finger pads slipped on the guitar neck and his music-making mind went blank. He missed a total of three chords before his brain caught up to his shock.

His best friend and keyboardist, Gary Mitchell, shot a quick glance at him and expertly covered the mistake. Luckily this was Gary's solo number, so Jace hadn't completely screwed up the song.

At the end of the number, during polite applause, Gary leaned over to Jace and said, "What happened to you in the middle of that song?"

"I got distracted," Jace said. "Someone came in that I didn't expect to see today."

"Is it that pretty lady with the little boy?" Gary asked.

Jace nodded.

"She looks like she knows you. You've been the focus of her attention since they sat down."

His attention fixed equally on Kayla, Jace said, "She does know me, not that she's all that happy about it."

"Wow, buddy, you didn't leave another one brokenhearted did you?"

"Not yet."

"Then you're keeping secrets from me," Gary said.

If Gary only knew how accurate that statement was. Jace was keeping a huge secret. "I just met her," he answered. "She came in the shop the other day."

"I hope you flirted with her," Gary kidded. "If I weren't a happily married man…"

Kayla looked fantastic in white shorts, a red-and-white-striped T-shirt, and a matching ball cap. Nathan also wore a ball cap, the necessary accessory to keep the bright North Carolina sun off his face. Nathan's cap was blue and didn't match anything he was wearing, at least not the baggy cargo shorts and World Wrestling T-shirt.

As Jace's gaze remained transfixed, Kayla

nudged Nathan, and they both waved at him. Both were smiling as if seeing him were their number one priority for the day. Jace nodded.

"Let's take our break early," Gary suggested. "We're almost at the end anyway. Then you can go talk to the one you shouldn't let get away."

"That's not necessary," Jace said.

But Gary had already made the decision. "Folks, we'll sing one more number and then take a little break." He hit a few notes on the keyboard and added, "Come on with us now as we take a lazy journey down those country roads."

Thank goodness. Jace could play the all-time favorite John Denver song with his eyes closed. And not that he was vain, or that it mattered, but his voice sounded good on this number, too.

They finished the set on a high note. Everyone in the Blue Ridge Mountains seemed to like that song. Jace set his guitar in the steel rack by the playing area, took a deep breath and stepped off the makeshift stage.

Kayla was still smiling as he approached her table. Nathan, on the other hand, was spinning his cork coaster and not paying any attention.

"What brings you guys out here?" he asked. "Nathan has a desire to visit a winery?"

"Sure, Jace," Kayla said. "I always bring nine-year-olds in my care to a winery."

He knew she was being sarcastic, but a quick glance at the kids playing on the expansive lawn next to the vineyard assured him that kids did enjoy an afternoon in the sun at one of Holly River's prettiest spots. The vineyard had become a family gathering place on Sunday afternoons. The two large vineyard dogs were chasing the children and barking excitedly. Jace took the third chair at the table.

One of the girls from the winery sales department came up to them. "You sound good today, Jace," she said.

"Thanks."

"Can I get you something? On the house of course."

"Nothing but water for me," he said. "But the lady might appreciate your signature rosé." He looked at Kayla.

"That sounds lovely. And a root beer if

you have it for my partner in crime here." She smiled down at Nathan, a truly genuine smile, not the rehearsed one he figured she was giving him.

"Seriously," he began, "how did you know I'd be here today?"

"Any one of the dozen signs I've seen plastered around town clued me in that 'Gary and Jace' were performing today."

Oh, right. Gary was a good promoter.

"I didn't know you could sing," she said.

"I mostly play. Can harmonize a bit, I guess. Gary is the real musician." He leaned back in the chair, trying to effect a comfortable, casual attitude. Figured it probably wasn't working.

"Well, the sound is good. I enjoyed it. Do you have another set to play?"

"Yep. One more."

Kayla glanced at Nathan. "We'll stay, won't we, sweetie?" The kid nodded with almost complete disinterest. "How about after?" Kayla asked. "Want to grab a pizza? My treat this time."

"Thanks, but I can't," Jace said, wondering why he suddenly wished it weren't his brother's birthday. Being with Kayla and enjoying a pizza had all the advantages he'd imagined when he first met her. Being with the kid, however... "Big family gathering at my mother's house this evening," he continued. "It's my brother's birthday."

Kayla thought a moment while the wine was brought to the table. "A lot of people will be there?"

"Oh, yeah. Probably twenty or more."

"Then do you think your mother would mind a couple of party crashers?"

Jace bolted upright in the chair. "You want to come to the birthday party?"

"Would it be a problem?"

No, it wouldn't, at least not for Cora, who welcomed everybody to the farmhouse. Not to mention her love for any humans under four feet tall. Plus Emily would be there. If anyone could find an enthusiastic bone in Nathan's body, it would be Em.

But bottom line, Kayla's showing up at the house would be a tremendous problem for him. He still wasn't over his indigestion from the hasty lunch, and he'd only told his brother this morning about his latest situation. It might be too soon to introduce Carter to Kayla. Might be too soon to introduce them ever!

"It would be fine," he heard himself say. "The more the merrier." He stood. "Follow me after the set ends."

"Will do."

Now what had he done? Invited his biggest problem into his family circle. He must be crazy. And she had to have been a bit crazy to have suggested it. What would this woman do to get to know everything about Jace Cahill? But one thing was for sure. This day would be embedded in his mind forever, so he probably wouldn't forget his brother's birthday again.

JACE AND GARY were finished a few minutes before four o'clock. This gave Jace plenty of time to get out to Sweet Valley Road by five, when his mother had told everyone to show up. He pulled out of the vineyard parking lot, checking his rearview mirror. Kayla was right behind him. He could easily lose her on these country roads. He knew every curve and every pass in these mountains, and all the good places to hide. But heck, no way would he sink that low. Besides, those white shorts showing off long legs… He slowed his truck so she could keep up.

At four thirty he drove onto the lane that led to his family home. Already a few cars had taken prime spots in front of the house, so Jace pulled close to the apple orchard and parked. Kayla took the spot right beside him.

"Beautiful home," she said, getting out of her car. "How old is this house?"

"Better than a hundred years," Jace said. "Belonged to my great-grandfather first and sort of got handed down. It's not the fanciest house on this road, far from it, but it does have a lot of history behind it."

For a moment Jace wished his mother had kept the house up better since Raymond died. The porch floor needed staining. The railings were dull and peeling. Some of the Victorian trim could use a spruce up. But Cora wasn't putting her money into the house these days—not since she decided to send Gladys Kirshner fifteen hundred dollars a month to continue the care Raymond had started for Robert when the boy was diagnosed. No amount of persuasion by Carter and Ava could change her mind.

Jace had basically stayed away from this

family drama, like he did most always when uncomfortable topics came up. Besides, he liked Robert. He wanted to see him have every advantage he could. From experience, Jace knew it wasn't easy being the weak child of Raymond Cahill.

Kayla didn't seem to notice the flaws in the house. She stood on the front lawn staring up at the hanging flower baskets Cora always kept pruned and watered. A look of contentment settled over her features. Wow. This city lady liked country music and apparently an old country home. If it weren't for the nine-year-old issue that stood between them, Jace could imagine a few days of uninterrupted bliss with her.

"Jace, you're here!" Cora hardly ever missed the sound of a car pulling up to her house. And if she did, Buster, the family's old Labrador, took up the slack and barked a warning. Buster was hot on Cora's heels when she came out onto the porch.

Wearing an apron and a cotton dress, and glowing with a slight sheen of perspiration, she hurried down the steps and wrapped her third born in a tight hug. She smelled wonderful, a mix of nutmeg, cinnamon and sweet barbecue. Jace had always loved her hugs. They were fierce and protective. In fact, he'd always thought he was her favorite, or at least he noticed that she gave him extra attention when his father berated him.

"Well, who do we have here?" Cora said, beaming at Kayla and Nathan. "Who's this handsome young man?"

Jace cleared his throat, motioned for Kayla and Nathan to come closer. "Friends of mine," he said. "They came into High Mountain the other day and then showed up at the winery this afternoon. Thought they might enjoy a taste of real Carolina hospitality."

"We'll do our best not to disappoint," Cora said. Buster trotted up beside her, and Nathan backed up a couple of steps.

"This nosy dog won't hurt you, honey," Cora said. "He's big and kinda scary-looking, but he's just a goofy ol' puppy deep inside."

Nathan approached the dog and gently rubbed Buster's head. Buster responded by resting his snout against Nathan's leg and administering a long, sloppy kiss. "He likes me," Nathan said, his eyes wide.

"Sure he does," Cora said.

"And I like big goofy dogs best," Nathan added.

Jace filled in names for everyone, and Cora suggested they go out back where Carter's family and a few early arrivals had gathered. "Miranda, Ava and I will be handling kitchen duty, so you go on back and have fun."

"I would be glad to help out," Kayla said.

"Nonsense. This is your first time here. Go on now."

"Did you ever have a dog?" Jace asked Nathan as they walked around the house.

"No. But my mother said I might get one when I'm ten and we move out of our apartment. But now I guess I won't."

Jace frowned. He'd grown up with all sorts of animals. A kid who'd never had a big goofy dog just didn't seem right.

They'd barely rounded the corner of the house when Carter, dressed in jeans, a T-shirt and an obviously homemade birthday hat on his dark hair, rushed to meet them. "You made it, brother," he said, slapping Jace on his back. Then he leaned in close and whispered, "Is this the lady? And that's the kid?"

"Good guess. They showed up today at the

winery, and Kayla sort of invited herself to this party. I couldn't say no."

Giving Kayla a quick once-over, Carter grinned. "Why would you want to?"

"Don't forget the real issue here," Jace said. "It's not the girl. It's the kid."

"Oh, right." Carter studied Nathan for a few seconds. "He must look like his mother because he's a heck of a lot better looking than you are."

Jace made introductions, which put an end to his brother's teasing. As much as Jace enjoyed kidding around, he simply couldn't see anything to make light of in this moment.

"My wife, Miranda, is in the kitchen," Carter said to Kayla. "She'll be anxious to meet you."

"I'll look forward to it," Kayla said.

"Uncle Jace, you're here!" A spinning cyclone of blond curls and churning legs charged toward them. Emily slammed into her uncle and wrapped her arms around him. "Nobody knew if you'd come or not," she said.

"When I heard you would be here, there was no keeping me away," he said. "Emily, this is Nathan, a friend of mine. He's your age, and I thought you could show him around the farm."

"Sure. Hi, Nathan."

Poor kid. His lopsided grin proved he was already smitten by Carter's beautiful stepdaughter. "You want to go see the animals?"

Nathan nodded, but never made it out of the yard. Miranda, looking pretty as ever in a flower-printed dress, came out the back door of the house. "Emily," she called. "Grandma Cora has a beater covered in chocolate frosting. She thought you might like to lick it."

Emily's gaze darted from the source of the treat to Nathan. A new friend or a chocolate-covered beater. Tough decision. "I don't know, Mom. I'm with Nathan right now."

"It's okay," Miranda said. "Grandma's got two beaters. Bring him along."

Emily grabbed Nathan's hand and they trotted to the back porch. Satisfied for the moment to have Kayla to himself, Jace walked her around the yard and introduced her to some Cahill family friends.

"Your family seems wonderful," she said as they walked toward the barn.

Jace thought of the time his father was alive, the time when his family didn't seem so wonderful, at least where he was concerned. "We're just big on birthdays," he said. "And holidays, and Sundays, and occasionally a Wednesday night."

"I think you're big on each other."

He couldn't deny it. As much as he tried to stay uninvolved in his family's dramas and problems, he knew he wouldn't want to be on this earth without them. He was lucky to have three solid people who cared about him, who would support him no matter what. He imagined Nathan in the kitchen licking the beater and wondered if that support would extend to a kid he never knew he had until yesterday. No doubt. It would.

There was also no doubt that Jace was enjoying this private time with Kayla. He had to be honest. When she walked into the winery today, more than his playing hand had reacted. His heart stumbled as clumsily as his fingers had.

As if reading his mind, she said, "I really enjoyed the music today. You play well. And you have a nice voice."

Usually playing and singing came so naturally to him, he didn't have to think about what notes or words came next. Today, after seeing Kayla listening attentively to his performance, he'd tried extra hard. He took her arm as they entered the barn. "Are you sure that isn't the wine talking?" he said.

"One glass? I don't think so."

The barn smelled of leather and sweet hay along with the rich, musty smell of a stall that needed to be cleaned. He'd get to that before he left this evening. Mostly what he noticed was the flowery scent coming from the woman by his side. Was it her shampoo? Did she wear cologne? Whatever it was, he liked it and wanted to get closer.

They stopped in front of the stall that held a contented Clementine. Jace stroked the cow's nose. "We've had her ten years," he said. "She gives a good amount of milk. We refrigerate it, and once a week Carter takes it to the dairy plant in Boone. I'm pretty sure that what we make on her milk doesn't begin to cover the cost of her room and board. But I think she feels good about contributing."

They continued down to an empty stall that Jace explained housed the horse the family had owned for years. "Mostly Carter rides him."

"Where is he?" Kayla asked, looking over the stall door.

"I expect he's out in the paddock now."

"Being on a horse might be something Nathan would enjoy," Kayla said.

"Maybe we'll give it a shot." Jace led Kayla to a wooden bench next to sturdy hooks that held bridles and bits. The area was cool and shady. They sat. He hoped he could get back the contentment of the last few minutes before the mention of Nathan reminded them both of what was at stake here. "Tell me something, Kayla," he said.

"Sure."

"Do you think you and I could go out on a date sometime? I mean a real date, just one man, one woman? Or does that even interest you?"

She smiled, looked down at her hands in her lap. For the first time since he'd met her she seemed almost shy.

"I don't know, Jace. I've got Nathan to think about. I don't want to leave him alone or with a stranger."

"You've met my family. You can probably tell that no one is a stranger on this farm."

"But I take my responsibility for Nathan

very seriously. I gave his grandparents my word that I would watch him every minute. Besides, I promised him I wouldn't leave him alone."

He picked up one of her hands and held it between the two of his. She didn't pull away. Her skin was soft and warm. "I felt a connection with you from the first time you came in the outfitter store. I've wanted nothing more than the chance to spend some time alone with you." Her reason for coming to Holly River hung over this peaceful moment like a black cloud, but heck, Jace couldn't deny he appreciated having these private moments in the barn for as long as they lasted.

He rubbed his thumb over her knuckles. "If you didn't feel it, too, tell me now and I'll stop being a jerk…about this, anyway."

She smiled again. "We'll see," she said. "I want you to get to know Nathan with the hope that… Well, I don't need to spell it out again. I don't know if we should complicate the issue with a fleeting romance that really can't go anywhere."

"You mean can't go anywhere if I don't accept Nathan into my life?"

"No. That's not what I mean at all. I mean I live in Washington. You live in Holly River. I'm going home in twelve days, one way or the other."

He curled a finger under her chin and lifted her face. Her beautiful eyes glowed with a turquoise hue in the shade of the barn's rafters. He raised his hand and took off her baseball cap, letting her hair fall to her shoulders. Shiny honey-and-wheat hair. He couldn't describe the special color with one word. He wanted nothing more than to taste her full lips, to hear if he could make her sigh a sweet murmur of desire.

He spoke in a low voice, almost a whisper. He was close enough to her ear to decide that the fragrance he'd noticed before came from her hair. He tried his best logic. "Look, forget about long-term, okay? You're more or less trapped at this home for now. You're not leaving Sweet Valley Road until you've had my mother's dinner and some birthday cake. So why don't we make the best of the minutes we have?"

He cupped the back of her head and leaned in. She moistened her lips. His mouth brushed hers, just a hint of what he wanted to give her. He was ready to deepen the kiss and risk her pulling away when a call came from the entrance to the barn.

"Hey, Jace, you in here?"

Carter!

"Dinner's about ready." Carter walked into the barn. Kayla jerked away as if she'd been stung.

"This isn't exactly what I meant by making the best of things," Jace said, helping her up from the bench. "But it's a start. We're coming, birthday boy," he hollered.

Carter grinned. "Great. Hope I didn't interrupt anything."

Jace looped an arm around Carter's shoulder and took Kayla's elbow. Together they walked out of the barn. Jace wished he could read the truth in Kayla's eyes and determine if she minded the interruption as much as he did.

CHAPTER SIX

KAYLA WAS TREMBLING when they left the barn. She certainly was no novice when it came to attention from males, but this Jace Cahill was different from the educated, social-climbing men of DC. He was almost a cross between a man and a boy. Easy, casual, yet still sure of himself. A man who didn't mind expressing his wants. And for a moment in the barn, he'd made his wants hers. And even though this first kiss had been only a touch, it held a promise that would probably keep her awake tonight wondering…

Kayla stepped into the sunlight and took a long, deep breath.

In the few minutes she and Jace had been in the barn, the long table set up in the Cahills' backyard had undergone a transformation. Large colorful tablecloths covered the sheets of plywood balanced on sawhorses. Plates were now spaced evenly, enough to accommodate at least twenty-four people. Salt and pepper shakers, wine bottles, salad dressings and barbecue sauce made up the centerpieces along the table. And in the middle of it all, a chocolate cake was the crowning achievement.

Kayla had dined in some of the best restaurants in Washington, DC, but this down-home array of country charm was as festive and mouthwatering as any of them. Taking it all in, she said to Jace, "I should have been out here helping."

"You heard Mama. She wouldn't have let you. This is your first time here, so you are officially a guest. Now, if you come again, you can expect to be given a list of chores. Besides, it looks like everyone's here, which means there are enough folks around to get under Mama's skin. She likes being the boss."

While folding chairs kept appearing from some magical place inside the house, Kayla looked around for Nathan. "I wonder where the kids went?" she asked.

"They must be inside," Jace said. He took her hand, which felt surprisingly natural, and led her to the back door. They ran into Cora, who was supervising the loading of platters and bowls. "Where are Em and Nathan?" Jace asked her.

"In the living room. They licked the beaters and asked if they could play a game. Tell them it's time to come outside. When it comes to eating at the Cahills', it's first come first served."

Kayla smiled. Nathan should be hungry. He hadn't eaten since before they went to the winery. She followed Jace through a short hallway to a large double pocket door. They stopped when they saw the kids sitting cross-legged on an old area rug, a game of Sorry spread out on the floor. Kayla recognized the game right away. It was one of Nathan's favorites, and she'd played it often with him.

"It's your turn, Nathan," Emily said.

"Oh, okay." He rolled the dice and chose his moves.

"It's a close game," Emily said. "Either one of us could win."

Without speaking, Kayla and Jace stood at the doorway, eavesdropping. "Aren't they cute?" Kayla whispered in his ear.

"They're cute," Jace said. "But so is Buster, and he's not nearly as complicated."

The large Labrador had curled up beside the children.

Jace started to interrupt the game when Kayla suddenly stopped him. "Just another minute," she said. "It's so nice just watching them together. Nathan hasn't had many moments of contentment recently."

Emily sat up straight and said, "I have two dads."

The statement was unexpected, and Kayla drew in a quick breath.

"You do? Cool," Nathan said.

"I love them both the same," Emily declared. "Papa Carter is my daddy in Holly River. He's my stepdaddy. My real daddy lives in Durham. Do you know where that is?"

Nathan shook his head, finished his turn at the game.

"Where's your daddy?" she asked.

A small pain sliced into Kayla's chest. Her hand on Jace's arm tightened. How would Nathan answer a question that should be simple for any kid?

"I don't have one," Nathan said.

"What happened to him?"

"I don't know. I've never had a daddy."

Since the turn had reverted again to Nathan, he shook the dice.

Emily, whose eyes reflected her confusion and concern, wasn't about to let the subject drop. "Don't you have to have a daddy? Doesn't everybody?"

"I guess not. But now, since my mommy died, I don't have a mommy or a daddy."

Emily thought about what he'd said for a long moment. "You win, Nathan. Let's just say the game's over now."

Kayla's heart melted just a little for the sweetness of Emily. She nudged Jace. He cleared his throat. "Kids, it's time for dinner. Grandma Cora sent me to find you."

Emily bounced up from the floor. "Okay, Uncle Jace. Nathan just won the game anyway." She gave Nathan a coy smile and waited for him to rise. "The food will be good, Nathan. Grandma Cora can really cook."

The children scooted around Kayla and Jace and ran for the back door. Kayla tried to see Nathan's face to determine if the conversation with Emily had upset him. He was walking so fast, she didn't get a good look, but he seemed okay. Maybe Emily's simple expression of sympathy did more for him than all the adult sentiments at his mother's funeral.

"Wow. That was weird, wasn't it?" Jace said.

"'Weird'?" Kayla repeated. "That's all you can say? If that didn't tug at your heart-strings, then I'm starting to wonder if you even have a heart."

She walked ahead of him, but had only gone a few steps when he stopped her. "Wait a minute," he said. "You don't get to say something like that and walk off like I'm supposed to agree with it."

"What? You do have a heart?"

Jace's breath came fast and strong from his nostrils. "Did it ever occur to you that Nathan's life might have been much different if Susan had bothered to tell me that she was pregnant?"

Kayla was battling opposing emotions—sadness at Nathan's situation, irritation at Jace's apparent lack of caring. But she had to conclude that he did have a point. She steeled herself to say, "Has it occurred to you that it's never too late to be a father?"

"No, it hasn't, Kayla. The thought never

entered my head until yesterday because the last thing I ever expected to hear from anyone was that I *was* a parent."

"And what exactly would you have done ten years ago if Susan had called you the minute the stick turned blue? You didn't want kids, remember? You didn't want Susan."

"I don't know what I would have done, but I would have had more than thirteen days to come up with a plan. Now we'll never know what that plan would have been. All I can really count on today is that I *still* don't want a kid, but now it looks like I have one. And this is only day two of the test of my fatherhood. And from where I'm standing, you seem determined to give me a failing grade."

She looked away from him, aware that coming down so hard on him might not be the best way to accomplish her goal. She wanted Jace to love Nathan. She wanted Nathan to love Jace, but that wouldn't happen overnight. Perhaps it would never happen. She sighed, stared up into his eyes. "There's still time to prove yourself."

"And plenty of room for improvement, too," he snapped at her. "I guess the only direction for me to go at this point is up in your estimation."

"Jace! Kayla!" Cora called from the back of the house. "Come on, you two. Everything's going to be cold. You'll have time alone together after we eat."

Kayla squeezed her eyes shut. "Oh, for heaven's sake. She thinks we're avoiding the crowd because we're..."

"She couldn't be more wrong," Jace said. "Let's go join the party before Mama has us married off."

"Like that would happen," Kayla muttered.

AT DINNER, KAYLA sat between Carter's wife, Miranda, and Ava, Jace's sister. Both women were as kind and hospitable as they could be, making Kayla feel welcome. They asked how Kayla knew Jace, but didn't ask for personal details. Nathan and Emily sat across from them, and Kayla was encouraged to see Nathan enjoying himself and eating a good meal.

Jace sat at the opposite end of the table. Occasionally he shot a glance her way, and though she was aware of almost every move he made, she quickly averted her gaze when she sensed him looking at her. Today had not gone well. Kayla thought that appearing at the winery, and even inviting herself to the Cahill home, would show Jace that she was as interested in his life and family as she was in procuring a good home for Nathan. The proprietor of the Mountain Laurel Inn had told her that Cora Cahill was the kindest of souls and welcomed almost anyone to her home. But still, inviting herself had been awkward.

Kayla thought of Susan and the promise she'd made to the dying woman. *This isn't going to be easy, Susan*, Kayla said in her mind. *I'm trying. I really am, but you were right about Jace and his lack of desire for children. This man does not want anything to do with Nathan. Your son is such a sweet, gentle boy. He deserves someone who loves him, supports him, guides him into manhood.* Watching Jace poke another man's shoulder over what was probably a juvenile joke, she doubted that he would ever meet her tough requirements.

Twelve more days. That was all Kayla had left before she had to return to her job, her life. Either a miracle had to happen or Nathan would return to his grandparents. *That's not the worst thing that could happen*, she said to herself. Sherry and Paul were good people, maybe not the type Susan wanted to raise her son, but Nathan would be protected, educated, provided for.

She stared at Jace as he refilled the wineglasses of the folks around him. He and his friends were laughing as if they hadn't a care in the world. Surely a life with the Wagoners would be better than one with this "flunky," a man who didn't want Nathan, and who didn't want to assume the responsibility that was rightfully his.

Dinner ended with servings of cake and the opening of presents. Since this was Carter's thirty-fifth birthday, many of the gifts were "over the hill" jokes, and he was a good sport about every one of them. The crowd broke up; Kayla thanked Cora for the meal and for welcoming them into her home.

"You bring that young fella back anytime," Cora said. "There's nothing like having a young one around the farm to make a person remember what life is all about."

Kayla promised to return, but in truth, she doubted that she would.

As she and Nathan walked to her car, Jace caught up with her. "You leaving?"

"Yes."

Nathan scurried off to the car. Kayla waited. In the growing dusk, she stared up at Jace's lips, his light brown hair catching the evening breeze. Her thoughts wandered back to the barn, to what had almost happened. She experienced an inexplicable longing—for so many things.

Jace touched her arm. "You've got to realize, Kayla. You sprang this whole thing on me without any warning. I need time to think about what it means."

"So you said Saturday night," she responded. "But frankly speaking, Jace, you thinking about your response to being a father doesn't nearly compare to the weight of responsibility on my shoulders. I've got to make a decision about this boy's future. Susan made me his guardian. You didn't ask to be a father, and I didn't ask for that. But now I've got to find a permanent place for this boy." A fierce loyalty burned hot in her veins as she said, "A wonderful boy. One who deserves…"

"I know. He deserves a father who will do right by him in all ways. I just don't think that's me, Kayla."

"I was hoping it would be."

She broke away from him and started toward her car.

"I don't have any trips tomorrow. Once a week the county dams up the Wyoga, and nobody can raft the river. But Tuesday, we'll be open." He rubbed his nape. "Maybe you can talk the kid into going rafting on Tuesday. I'll take you myself."

"His name is Nathan, Jace. Not 'the kid.'" Aware she was being overly sensitive, Kayla took a breath. "Okay, I'll see if he wants to do that."

"Good. I'll see you Tuesday morning at nine o'clock at High Mountain Rafting."

And then we'll have just ten days to sort this out, she thought.

NATHAN WAS QUIET on the ride back to the Mountain Laurel Inn. Kayla was concentrating on her GPS so she wouldn't get lost on the narrow roads.

"Auntie Kay?" he said after a few minutes.

"What, sweetie?"

"Why don't I have a daddy?"

Kayla's foot almost slipped off the accelerator. She cleared her throat, tried to appear calm. "What did your mother tell you about that?"

"She just said I didn't have a daddy. That I never had one."

Biologically that wasn't true, but how does one explain such complexities to a nine-year-old? One doesn't. One evades. "Don't you know other kids who don't have daddies?"

"Sure, but that's because they live with their mothers. Most of them have daddies. They just don't live with them." He thought a moment. "My mom just told me I didn't have one."

"I see," Kayla said. "Tell me something, Nathan, if you did have a daddy, what would you want him to be like?" Crazy, but deep inside she was hoping he would describe a laid-back, guitar-playing, basically ambitionless but good-hearted country man.

"I guess I'd want him to be like one of Emily's dads. She loves them both, and she has an extra, so maybe I'd like one of them."

"That's just not something that can happen, honey," Kayla said. "For right now you're stuck with no daddy. But you do have a nice grandfather, Grandpa Paul." Nathan stared out the window until Kayla became uncomfortable with the silence. "What is it, Nathan? What are you thinking?"

"I'm thinking I don't want to live with Grandpa Paul and Grandma. I want to live with you."

She swallowed. "I'll always be close, Nathan. We'll always be best of friends. You know that, don't you?"

He nodded. "If I can't live with you, maybe I can live with Cora. She's Emily's grandma. I like her and I think she likes me."

Kayla didn't speak. She just reached across the seat and took Nathan's hand.

CHAPTER SEVEN

THE GUESTS HAD all left. The table had been cleared. Emily was watching television with Buster. Cora, Ava and Miranda were in the kitchen storing the leftovers. There weren't many.

The backyard was blissfully quiet. Occasionally a critter ran across the roots of the shade trees. Once in a while from the barn the old horse would whinny his appreciation of the evening meal Jace had mixed into his feed bucket. Fireflies were out in full force, as if they were in competition with the hundreds of stars in the clear sky. Jace and Carter occupied the two Adirondack chairs with the thickest cushions. They each nursed one last beer.

"So, are you any closer to making a decision?" Carter asked.

"If anything, I'm more confused than ever."

Carter nodded. "Not surprising. If it helps, I thought Nathan was a good kid."

"Good? Yeah, I suppose. He didn't cause any trouble. But I can't say that I've learned enough about him to draw any conclusions. And I figure he must have issues about his mother dying. I don't know how I'd handle that."

"That's tough," Carter agreed. "But a sensitive guy like you…" He stopped, smiled.

"Right."

"And I like Kayla, too," Carter added.

Jace chuckled. "Well, naturally. Look at her. She's not hard to like."

"True, but I meant her personality. She seemed to fit right in with this odd group of people today. The girls like her, too, so if you expect a lot of empathy from Ava or Miranda, you can probably forget it. Ava's about to start her new job at the children's home, and Miranda is talking about getting pregnant again. This is a child-centered family, brother."

"I know that," Jace said. "Mama fussed over Nathan like she'd never seen a kid before." A shock of concern rippled down Jace's spine. "You're the only one I'm talking to about this. You remember that, don't you?"

"Of course. I haven't told anyone." Carter took another draw on his bottle. "So what are your biggest concerns?"

"Let's see. Where should I begin? Maybe with the undisputed fact that I know nothing about kids. The only ones I see are the screaming, whooping ones on the rafts, many of whom appear to forget my instructions the minute we get on the river. If I'm not yelling at them to sit down, I'm grabbing their arms or fishing them out of the water."

"Those are mostly kids on vacation," Carter said. "Their focus is on fun and adventure, not on paying attention. If you lived with a kid day in, day out, you'd have more control."

Jace accepted that as a probable truth. "Unfortunately my second-biggest concern is that I don't have any inclination to want to know kids better. I'm thirty-two years old, Carter. I live alone with a big dog who is enough responsibility for me."

"You know Emily pretty well," Carter said. "You relate to her without any problems."

Jace frowned. He did love that little peanut. Emily was smart and cute and funny. "She's easy," he said. "She's normal."

"And you don't think Nathan is normal, whatever that is, anyway."

"I wonder. He stands around all quiet, like a judge waiting to read a verdict on a murder case. I tried to give him a souvenir, and he wasn't interested. He hardly said a word to me last night at the restaurant. And you saw how he ignored me today."

"He's sad, Jace. He hasn't gotten over losing his mom. Besides, my evaluation is a bit different. I saw you both ignoring each other, while you paid special attention to Kayla."

"Okay. Point taken, but bottom line, I can't seem to make a connection with that kid… I mean Nathan." He smiled. "That's another thing. Kayla warned me about calling him 'the kid.' I guess I'll try to watch that."

Carter nodded soberly. "Funny how you can relate to Robert with all his problems. I've never been comfortable around Robert. And yet you can't find common ground with a boy who shares your bloodline. And you haven't known Robert all that long, either. Just sayin'."

"I've thought about that," Jace said. "But Robert needs somebody like me in his life. He's so isolated in his own world. I think I can help him."

A wide grin spread across Carter's face.

"What?"

"Are you listening to yourself, Jace?" Carter asked. "Right now I can't think of anyone who'd need you more than Nathan."

"But Nathan, if I choose to accept my responsibility—a big 'if'—would be 24/7. I see Robert once or twice a week, and I go home and live my life. That's a lot different from taking on the care of a child all the time."

"You're right about that."

Feeling philosophical all of a sudden, Jace sighed. "Funny how life throws you these curveballs. I sure wasn't expecting that few months of time with Susan Wagoner all those years ago would result in a predicament like this. Wasn't expecting it, don't know how to handle it."

Carter was silent a few moments. "I'm fairly qualified to talk about this, Jace. I've had a few curveballs thrown at me in my life."

Jace felt like a heel. His brother had been

through more in his thirty-five years than most people experienced in a lifetime. Losing Miranda, the love of his life, all those years ago; and then marrying someone else who'd suffered several miscarriages before leaving him. At least Carter's future looked happy and secure now. He'd survived, made a success of his job, was respected by everyone in town. That's what Carter had always wanted. Jace just wanted to be left alone. Still, he patted his brother's shoulder. "I'm sorry to bring up all those memories."

"It's okay, Jace. I'm just saying that the human spirit is resilient. No matter how bad our circumstances, we somehow take on challenges and adapt pretty well. And maybe we even become better men for doing so. Just something to think about."

Their conversation dropped off, each man obviously thinking his own thoughts. Carter was right. Some men became stronger, better, for tackling life's problems. Problem was, Jace didn't believe he was one of them. Some men became stronger by running—away.

KAYLA GOT NATHAN up early on Monday. They headed to the River Café before the tourists took over all the good seats at the booths. Halfway through breakfast, Kayla suggested they visit an old-time train amusement park outside town where they could ride the steam locomotive and see a shoot-'em-up between cowboys on the facsimile Western street. Nathan was all in for this plan.

Kayla was finishing her coffee when she asked, "So what do you think of Jace now, sweetie?"

"What do you mean?"

"Do you like him any better than you did a couple of days ago?"

"I like his farm."

It was a start. "He's invited us to go on one of the rafts tomorrow. Just the two of us with him as our guide. Do you think you might like to do that?"

"I don't know. I'd rather go to one of the gem mines."

"We'll do that, I promise," Kayla said. "But rafting might be a great adventure, something to tell your grandparents and friends about."

He gave her one of those typical kid you're-crossing-the-line looks that hinted that if she liked rafting so much, she should go by herself and tell her own friends. "I'm finished with my breakfast" was his answer. "Let's go to the train."

ON TUESDAY MORNING, Kayla and Nathan pulled into High Mountain Rafting at exactly nine o'clock. Jace watched them get out of their car. Since the temperature outside was warm, they were dressed appropriately in shorts and T-shirts. Kayla took Nathan's hand and walked him to the entrance of the shop.

"Good morning," Jace said. "We've got a nice day for a trip down the river." He rested his hand on Nathan's shoulder. "I'm glad to see you decided to join me today." He smiled at Kayla. "You, too, ma'am."

"Well, it is a beautiful day," Kayla said. Nathan said nothing.

"Check the bus," Jace suggested. He pointed to the official vehicle that took riders to the put-in point and indicated the double rafts on the back. "The top one is for the tourists going today. The bottom one is ours, and she's a good, strong one."

Nathan's eyes widened. "Why do we need a strong one? What's going to happen?"

Jace glanced at Kayla. A twist of her lips indicated he might have said the wrong thing. "We don't really," Jace corrected. "All the rafts are sturdy and safe. This trip today is just like floating down a lazy river."

Kayla gave him another pointed look. "Well, we're hoping for a *little* adventure, aren't we, Nathan?" She walked up to Jace and said in a low voice, "Don't minimize the activity. If he thinks there's nothing to this, and then we run into rapids, he'll be even more frightened."

"Trust me, Kayla, most folks could nap through these rapids. I've even had customers ask for their money back."

He walked over to a wall covered with safety gear. "Come on over, Nathan. Let's find a vest that's a good fit. And you'll need a helmet, too."

Nathan followed dutifully, and Jace outfitted him with the equipment mandated by the North Carolina safety board. He next chose a vest and helmet for Kayla. She tucked her hair under the helmet and slipped the vest over her shoulders. "We look like true adventurers now," she said, taking her phone from her pocket. "Come on, we need a selfie, Nathan."

The boy stood beside her. His helmet had already slipped a bit to the side. Kayla straightened it and told him to smile into the phone she held at arm's length. "When we get back, we'll get a picture of all three of us," she said to Jace.

"We're pulling out, boss," Billy called from the parking lot.

They hurried out and climbed onto the bus. Most of the seats were taken by eager tourists, and Jace took his threesome to the back. Billy started the bus and headed out toward the Wyoga River where it crossed the Tennessee–North Carolina line. As he drove, the personable young man told jokes about the coming trip. He told visitors to watch for alligators, pirate ships and the occasional elephants cooling off in the summer sun. At each preposterous warning, Nathan tugged urgently at Kayla's shirt sleeve.

"He's just kidding, sweetie," she said. "We won't see anything more than a fish and maybe a turtle."

Hasn't this boy been anywhere? Jace wondered. Alligators in the mountains of

North Carolina? Pirate ships in the twenty-first century? He made a mental note to ask Kayla why Nathan seemed so oblivious to the world around him. From what he remembered, Susan had always been ready for any adventure that came her way. She was fun loving and experimental. Didn't she pass these traits on to her son?

Thirty minutes later, the bus arrived at the entrance point. Billy and his helper unloaded the first raft, checked the safety gear on their passengers, and slid the raft into the shallow water. After he hollered "All aboard," the eight tourists settled into the raft, the teens in front, the more elderly and very young in back, where the ride was a bit smoother. Billy took his position at the rudder, and the helper pushed the raft into the deeper water before jumping on himself. In a few minutes, the raft had disappeared around a bend in the river.

"Our turn," Jace said, pulling their raft from the trailer. "Let's put 'er in."

He heard Nathan's plea. "I don't think I want to go now, Auntie Kay."

"Why not? It'll be fun."

Nathan shook his head. Watching a third

employee start the bus for the trip to the pickup point, Jace stood next to the raft, his booted foot on the side. Through the years the occasional passenger had threatened to back out at this point, but Jace or his crew had always managed to talk the frightened person into going along. Every time, the passenger was thankful he'd participated.

"Come on, Nate," Jace said. "There's nothing to this. Thousands of people do this every summer on this very river."

He gave Kayla a pleading look, hoping she would do something to move this process along, but since neither one was experienced in child rearing, he didn't hold out much hope. He imagined them getting back on the bus and driving to the pickup point, where they would have a ninety-minute wait for the first raft to arrive.

"You know what, Nathan," she said. "You just need to get to know the raft better."

Get to know a raft? What was she talking about? How does one become acquainted with a PVC welded, top-of-the-line, denier polyester Orion raft? And except for a professional, why would anyone want to? But this kid was different, and what did Jace Cahill, professional kid avoider, know about child psychology?

She took Nathan's hand and brought him to the raft. "Here, feel it. What do you think?"

He did as she told, first running his hand over the surface and eventually pounding on the solid rim. "It's hard," he said.

"Right. And strong, just like Jace said. What did you think? That we were going to be on something as light as a pool float?"

"Sort of."

"Well, what do you think now? This is more like a boat than a float."

He nodded. "I guess."

"This is the same raft they use in the Rocky Mountains, where the rivers are really wild," Jace said, joining in the pep talk.

"Really?" Nathan said, perhaps somewhat impressed.

"You betcha. Now come on. That first group is fifteen minutes ahead of us. Let's roll."

With acceptable enthusiasm, Nathan climbed in the raft. "Where do I sit?"

"Some people like to sit on the side, where it's raised up," Jace explained. "Others like to sit down inside. All in all it's less adventurous in the bottom, but less chance of falling out…"

"Falling out?" Nathan said.

"You're not going to go in the water, sweetie," Kayla said. Without another word, Nathan hunkered down on the floor of the raft.

"Sorry," Jace whispered to Kayla. "Bad explanation. I seem to be saying all the wrong things today."

"It's okay. He's in. Let's go. I'm sure he'll enjoy it."

Only he didn't. They'd only rounded the first bend when Nathan squirmed, said he was looking for something to hang on to.

"Grab any of the ropes," Jace said. "If you want, you can wrap the rope once around your wrist. Not too tight, though." When Nathan had settled again, Jace turned to Kayla, who was sitting on the edge of the raft, near the rudder Jace was controlling. "You're doing very well, McAllister," he said.

"So far, a smooth ride. When I'm behind the wheel of my car, I experience more thrills than this."

"Wait until we round the next curve."

Once they'd hit the straight patch, ripples appeared and soon turned into miniature whitecaps. Large boulders lined the riverbank on each side. The raft rode the waves with little effort, coming in close contact to the rocks. This was the part of the river where the navigator had to know how to steer the raft clear of trouble.

"You okay, Nathan?" Kayla called above the rushing water.

"No. I don't like this!"

"Just hold on," she said. "You'll be fine."

Only he wasn't. Jace watched the kid's face pale to a sickly white. "He's going to lose his breakfast," he said to Kayla.

"Oh, gosh, you're right. Let me go to him."

"Stay where you are," Jace ordered. "This is the roughest part of the river, and I can't let you move around from one position to another." He called to Nathan, "Are you feeling sick, buddy?"

Nathan leaned over and emptied his stomach onto the floor of the raft.

"Guess that answers my question."

Once the heaving ended, the crying began. "How soon can I get out?" Nathan sniffled.

The ride had smoothed. Jace knew that

only one more rough patch lay ahead. "These are only class-two rapids," he said to Kayla. "On the roughest rivers in the country, the rapids can reach a class five. A class six exists, but it's for extreme waters and is pretty rare. Nathan should be able to handle these."

She gave him an exasperated look. "Everybody's different, Jace. Obviously Nathan's stomach is sensitive to movement. Are there any more rapids on this trip?"

He couldn't lie. "About ten minutes ahead."

"Then pull over," she ordered.

"Pull over? Are you kidding, Kayla? This isn't a parking lot. It's a dang river!"

"You're steering this raft, aren't you? Why can't you steer over to the side and we can get out?"

He muttered a few choice words under his breath. The cussing couldn't be heard by the kid, but it made Jace feel much better. Using an oar, he guided the raft to a slow docking along a peaceful section of the river where a few tree limbs provided a place to tie up. Once he'd secured the craft, he stepped into the knee-deep water and tried to keep his teeth from chattering. "Not that this is cold or anything," he said to his passengers, "but the quicker you guys get out, the happier I'm going to be."

Kayla helped Nathan first. He crawled over the side and into Jace's arms. Jace set him on a grassy place under a maple tree. Next Kayla went to the side. Jace could tell she wasn't too keen on testing the water temperature herself. He held his arms out. "Come on, Your Majesty. I'll carry you."

"Thank you. That's very considerate, but I'd appreciate it if you didn't use sarcasm…"

Without waiting, he scooped her up in his arms and took a few steps to the dry bank. Before setting her down, he looked into the big blue eyes that were locked on his. Heck of a time for him to be thinking about how good she felt in his arms. He wasn't quite ready to let his anger go yet. Still, he held her a bit longer than he needed to.

When he put her down, she rushed over to Nathan. "How are you doing? Is your tummy okay?"

"Yeah."

"It was kind of fun, wasn't it?" she said.

Was she kidding? This had to have been the number one worst rafting experience of Jace's career, and he'd suffered through many mishaps. Both males gave her looks of incredulous disbelief and said at the same time, "No."

"Oh, well, I thought it was great fun…" She stopped talking and stared at them both. "I'm glad you two are finding this so funny."

For the first time Jace realized that he and Nathan were both holding their breaths trying to keep from laughing.

"Is she always so chipper about everything?" Jace asked Nathan.

"She is."

"How do you stand it?"

Nathan shrugged. "It's okay most of the time. She's my aunt."

"Okay, folks," Jace said. "Find a comfortable spot. I can't get this waterlogged raft up the bank by myself, so we have to wait for the bus at the pickup point to get the first rafters and then come by this way and rescue us." He checked his watch. "I'd say we have a good forty-five minutes until help arrives." He took his cell phone from his pocket. "I'll call Skip and tell him we're waiting, but he's got to stay at his point. Regulations."

"Then we'll just have to make the best of

it," Kayla said. Nathan had already begun to do that. He'd removed an electronic device of some kind from his backpack and was deeply involved in moving his thumbs.

Jace removed his boots and socks and lay back against a large oak tree. His cold feet reached into a warm spear of sunlight that did wonders for his mood. "Care to join me?" he said to Kayla.

She did, and they talked about safe topics for a while. What other activities were common on the river? Had Jace ever swum in the river? Safe topics. Kayla had removed her helmet, and her hair reached her shoulders, all messy and interesting looking. Jace wanted to run his fingers through it, see if the sunlight changed the look of the highlights he now noticed were almost a strawberry color.

If Nathan weren't so close, Jace might have even suggested to Kayla they try another kiss. He didn't think she would mind. She'd laughed at a couple of his answers to her questions. Maybe this rafting trip wasn't the worst one he'd ever led.

After a half hour, he said, "Shouldn't be

too long now. At least you and the k— Nathan will remember this day."

"That's absolutely true."

"Hard to believe he's my blood," Jace said, his hand partially covering his mouth.

She sat straight. "Why would you say that? Because he doesn't like bumping over big rapids in a river he's never seen before?"

"Only partly. We're just so different." Aware that he might have offended her— again—Jace backtracked. "You've got to admit that Nathan is nothing like me."

"He just lost his mother," Kayla said softly, but emphatically. "He thinks death is lurking everywhere, to snatch someone else in his life. He doesn't know where he's going to live. How would you expect him to act?"

"Like he's not afraid of his own shadow," Jace said, knowing he might be crossing a line. "Maybe someone should be talking to him."

"Someone is," Kayla said. "A professional therapist. And besides, how easy it is for you to draw such a conclusion." She breathed deeply. "You, Jace Cahill, raised on a beautiful farm with two loving parents, great siblings and all the opportunities life has to offer. I'll bet you've never known a day of true heartache in your life."

Her words cut like a knife. He stood, looked down at her. "Then you'd lose that bet," he said. "What right do you have to assume anything about my life? Have you asked anything except how much money I make, how long I've been an adventure guide?"

"Keep your voice down," she cautioned.

He did. "There's more to me than that stuff, Kayla. Don't you want to know what life experiences molded the person this precious boy over there is going to live with if he stays with me?" He tried to tone down the bitterness, but it had started flowing and he couldn't stop it. "How do you know that Nathan isn't going to end up a heck of a lot worse if he stays with me than if he returned to his grandparents?"

"That's why I'm here," she started to explain.

He took a deep breath, glared down at her. "Maybe you should start thinking about more than pawning the kid off on somebody so you can be free to live your own life and think about where he's going to end up. Paradise isn't always what it seems."

"Pawning him off?" Her voice became a harsh whisper. "You're his father!"

"I told you from the beginning, I shouldn't be. And while I'm at it, I want a strand of his hair."

She stared at him.

"For the test." He climbed the bank to the side of the road. "I'll wait here for the bus."

CHAPTER EIGHT

THE BUS ARRIVED fifteen minutes later. When she heard the horn, Kayla disturbed Nathan's game playing and told him to follow her to the road. She wasn't looking forward to seeing Jace. She had cooled off, but he'd been so angry she didn't know if enough time had passed for him.

Apparently it hadn't.

Without speaking to her or Nathan, Jace called for his two helpers to climb back down to the river and help him retrieve the raft. Kayla heard their comments when they saw the craft. "What's this on the bottom, Jace?" Billy asked. "Phew. Looks like…" He paused.

"That's exactly what it is," Jace said. "As soon as we get back, one of you guys hose it off."

Kayla glanced at Nathan. He didn't appear bothered by the comments, but just in case, she hurried him onto the bus. All the front seats were taken, so they walked to the back and took the next-to-last bench. In a few minutes Jace and the fellas boarded, one taking a seat, and the other getting behind the wheel. Jace had no choice but to sit in the last remaining spot, directly behind her and Nathan.

The front of the bus was filled with excited chatter from those who had journeyed all the way to the pickup point. But here in the back, the quiet was profound, and the ride was the longest thirty minutes Kayla could remember.

Back at the store, the crowd emptied out and went into the building to return the borrowed safety gear. Kayla and Nathan did the same, hanging up their helmets and vests on the appropriate hooks. As quickly as possible, Kayla ushered Nathan into the sunshine. "Are you feeling okay now?" she asked him.

"Sure. Why wouldn't I?"

Kids. Sick one minute, totally recovered the next. She waited until the other customers had left and then told Nathan to wait in the car for her.

After a few minutes, Jace came outside.

When he saw her still in the parking lot, he turned to go back inside. She stopped him with four words. "Oh, no, you don't."

He whirled around. "I've got another expedition to plan for. Sorry, can't stand around gabbing."

"We won't be *gabbing* for long," she said, dragging out his critical term for getting to the bottom of what had happened. "You can't run in your office and hide, Jace."

He ventured into the parking lot and stood a few feet from her. "Nathan okay?"

"Yes, actually he's fine. I think his problem had more to do with anxiety than motion sickness."

"Good. Now that we've got that out of the way, we can move on to whatever's bothering you."

She didn't appreciate his curt attitude, but she could be curt herself. So she dived right in. "I want to know what you meant when you said that paradise isn't always what it seems. Are you telling me that you didn't have a happy childhood? If so, I've met your family and I find that hard to believe. In fact, you might be using that as an excuse to get yourself out of this situation."

She paused long enough to read the concentration in his eyes. He was listening, but she sensed his anger returning. "Look, Jace, if after our time here, you decide that you want nothing to do with Nathan, I'll take him back to DC and the matter will be closed. You don't have to fabricate a miserable childhood to get out of raising your son. What did you think? That I would leave that wonderful boy with a man who doesn't want him? Do I seem that big a monster?"

He sighed. "No, you're no monster. I think you care for the kid, and you got yourself in this predicament pretty much like I have, without asking for it."

"Then what was all that nonsense about me not knowing about your life?"

"It's not nonsense," he said. "You don't know anything about it. You met the good Cahills the other day. Don't you think it's just possible that at least one rotten apple fell out of that barrel?"

Kayla could see that pain had replaced the anger she'd seen before. "So what is the story?"

"Not now," he said. "Not here. And I won't tell it in front of Nathan."

"Then when? Tonight?"

"I have a gig tonight. Gary and I are play-ing at the Muddy Duck outside of town. And don't even think about coming there. It's no place for a woman like you, and especially no place for a kid."

"Why do you play there then?"

"*Why?* For the hundred bucks. And be-cause when the customers get roaring drunk, they tend to tip better."

She frowned and wondered if he had ever been roaring drunk at the Muddy Duck. Somehow she didn't think so. "What about tomorrow night?" she asked.

"Should be okay. I'll ask Miranda if Nathan can come over to their house and be with Emily for a couple of hours." He paused, frowned. "I assume that's okay with you?"

"Of course. He'd like that."

"I should be able to get out of here by five tomorrow. I'll come over to the inn and pick you guys up."

"Fine. I'll see you then." She started to walk toward her car, but stopped and turned back. "Jace?"

His response was a raising of his eyebrows.

"I'm really looking forward to hearing your story and learning more about you."

He answered with a slight nod. "We'll see if you feel that way after you've heard it."

EARLY THE NEXT morning Jace's cell phone rang. He checked the digital screen and paused. Why would Gladys be calling him at 6:30 a.m.? He'd given her his phone number after his first visit with Robert, and she'd used it for things like confirming that he was coming. But she'd never called so early before.

"What is it, Gladys?" he said.

"I need you to come out here this morning, Jace."

"Why? Has something happened to Robert?"

"No. He's fine, but the woman who cares for him two days a week, the county worker, is coming here at nine with some other people to discuss some options for Robert." She paused. "I'm scared, Jace. I'm afraid I'm going to lose my boy."

"That's not going to happen, Gladys. Everyone concerned knows that you do a great job of taking care of Robert."

"I think I do, but I'm not so sure that everyone else thinks that. Will you come, Jace? Please?"

The timing wasn't perfect. He had two expeditions today. He was hoping to leave the shop early so he could pick up Kayla and Nathan. Still, he said, "I'll be there. I'll come out after I shower and get some breakfast." And make sure the rafting trips were set up ahead of his employees arriving. Today would not be a good day for one of them to miss work.

He arrived in Wilton Hollow at eight fifteen. Gladys had opened the door to her modest house before he'd come up the walk. "Thank goodness you're early," she said. "We can talk before they get here."

He stepped inside. Robert sat cross-legged on the living room carpet, his knees under the worn coffee table. He wore a pair of new-looking shorts and a Captain America T-shirt. His long hair had been combed, probably by the same person who trimmed it—his mother. He smelled fresh from a shower, which was a good sign. Adapting to water running from the showerhead was something Jace had been working on with him.

"Hi, Jace," Robert said.

"What's going on, buddy?" Jace said. He looked down at the numerous coins on the table. "You practicing what we talked about last time?"

They'd spent only a few minutes on understanding coins and their value, but Robert had seemed to take to the process quickly.

"Look what I can do," Robert said. He pointed to a loaf of bread. "This costs one dollar and seventy-nine cents."

Jace nodded. "Okay."

"Now watch." Robert carefully counted quarters as he pulled them from the center of the table. "One, two..." He mumbled the progression until he'd stacked up seven quarters. Then he returned to the pile of coins and withdrew four pennies, counting slowly as he'd done before.

He looked up at Jace, a smile spread across his face. "How much is that?"

"One dollar and seventy-nine cents, Robert. Perfect! You could go into the supermarket today and buy a loaf of bread." Jace felt a burst of pride. There was still so much Robert had to learn, like taxable items, specials with percentages off the regular price, the meaning of "buy one, get one free," things the rest of society took for granted. But this was an important beginning and a great morale boost for the boy.

"I can do it with Jell-O, too," Robert said. He picked up a quarter. "This is the same as twenty-five pennies. I know how many pennies each coin is now."

"I'm proud of you, Robert. The next time I visit, we'll ask your mom if we can go to the grocery store. You can get some supplies."

"Put those coins away now, Robert," Gladys said. "And go play in your room. If you're looking for your giraffe, I put it on your bed."

The stuffed animal had been like a security blanket to Robert the first time Jace had visited. Lately he'd noticed the boy didn't seem as interested in the raggedy plaything.

Robert scooped the coins into a box and stood up. "I'll see you later, okay, Jace?"

"You betcha."

When Robert had left the room, Jace said, "He looks good today. Definitely making progress."

"It's all your doing," she said. "He responds to you so well. In fact, too well. His progress is moving much too quickly."

"What are you talking about? I can't see that as a problem."

A knock on the door prevented Gladys from answering his question. "They're here," she said, walking slowly to the door.

Two women and a man came inside. Gladys introduced one of the ladies as Harriet Martin, Robert's twice-weekly caregiver. The other lady introduced herself as a social worker for the county. The man, a tall, dignified-looking middle-aged guy, announced that he was a psychologist specializing in children's problems, especially autism.

"We understand you've been working with Robert," the psychologist said.

"Not a whole lot," Jace said. "I try to visit at least twice a week, and Robert and I work on simple tasks. Sometimes he catches on real quick. Other times…" He let his voice fade away.

"We know exactly. Miss Martin keeps us informed on Robert's progress. For the longest time, there hadn't been much. But lately,

Robert has shown remarkable improvement in his basic skills."

After attributing much of Robert's success to Jace's influence, the social worker explained their reason for the visit today. "We'd like to enroll Robert in a two-day-a-week facility that would challenge his burgeoning awareness. Eventually we'll ease him into five days."

Gladys made a mewling sound as if someone had just stuck her with a sharp object.

"This is good news, Gladys," Jace said. "A chance for Robert to get out in the world."

"Absolutely it is," the psychologist agreed. "For the longest time, based on previous attempts to acclimate Robert to the school system, we didn't think he was ready for interaction with people his age. I'm confident after speaking with Harriet that now he is."

The psychologist studied Gladys's face. "You seem concerned. This won't be that much of a change, Ms. Kirshner. Robert will be brought home every afternoon by a school bus and picked up the next morning."

Gladys openly sobbed. "I told you, Jace. They want to take my baby away."

"Oh, no, Ms. Kirshner," the man said. "Robert will still be home five days a week."

The psychologist gave Jace a pointed look that suggested Gladys was responsible for her son's slow progress until now. Jace knew she was overly protective. At the same time, he realized she loved her son and would be lonely without him. But deep inside, he wondered why she hadn't considered the difference this schedule would mean to her. Maybe she could get a part-time job. That would alleviate some of the burden from his family.

"How much will this two-day-a-week program cost?" he asked. The social worker, a pleasant-looking lady perhaps in her forties, sat forward. "We charge based on the family's ability to pay. This is a state-funded program, which takes it out of the county level, a good thing since this county is the poorest in the state. We have significantly more money coming from the state than this county can provide."

She tapped her pen on a clipboard where she'd been making notes. "We are aware that Ms. Kirshner's full-time responsibility for

Robert has resulted in her having a limited income."

Jace knew that the county where Wilton Hollow and Holly River were located was struggling financially. Holly River was home to some of the richest vacationing families in the state, as well as families on Liggett Mountain who faced poverty every day. Since Miranda had moved back to the area, she'd been trying to find ways to help the people of Liggett Mountain, where she'd grown up. The fact that state money could be used to benefit Robert was a definite plus, especially for Cora.

"When would you like to put Robert in this new program?" Jace asked, trying to ignore Gladys's tearful sobs.

"The school bus will arrive at Ms. Kirshner's front door on Monday morning at eight thirty," the social worker said. "Assuming Ms. Kirshner agrees with our plan for her son." She took a form from her clipboard and gave it to Gladys. "We'll need your signature on these papers, Gladys."

"How far away is the school?" she asked.

"Not far at all," the gentleman said. "We have a lovely facility in Pine Grove in a beautiful wooded section, probably not more than a fifteen-minute drive from here. It's modern and clean and has supplies and equipment that will help Robert become self-sufficient."

"What should I do, Jace?" she asked.

"You should sign the papers, Gladys. You have to consider Robert's future, the time when you're no longer able to care for him. This is a great opportunity, a step forward in preparing him for a safe and healthy place in society."

She started to protest, and Jace held up his hand. "I don't mean to be morbid, Gladys, but eventually Robert will be on his own," he said. "The more self-sufficient he becomes now, the better for his chances in the future."

Gladys pulled a tissue from a box, wiped her nose and accepted the papers.

Jace asked the psychologist to join him on Gladys's small front porch. "So you honestly believe this will help Robert?" he asked the expert.

"Most certainly. Robert has been on our radar for several years now, but at first we only received negative reports about his ability to fit in with mainstream school. And we knew from Harriet Martin that Ms. Kirshner was taking good care of him. I hate to admit this, but I'm afraid someone at the county level let this case fall through the cracks." He sighed deeply. "It's definitely time to get this youngster out of that house and around boys and girls with similar levels of achievement."

Jace was encouraged by the psychologist's advice. He went back in the house, patted Gladys on her back and gave her words of encouragement. Now all that remained was to prepare Robert for his first steps into a more hopeful future.

ROBERT HAD TAKEN the news of the new opportunity with trepidation. His familiar anxiety had been evidenced in the twisting of his fingers, constant nodding of his head. The psychologist and Miss Martin had explained what Robert could expect come Monday, and since Robert trusted Harriet Martin, he had been willing to listen and seemed to process what they were telling him.

But the final acceptance had occurred when he stared at Jace. He didn't say anything, but his eyes remained wide and fixed, almost as if he were seeking a proper response.

"I think it's a great idea," Jace had said.

Robert thought a minute, smiled and repeated, "Great idea."

Jace took five pennies from his pocket and lined them up on the coffee table. "Starting tomorrow, not today, put one penny each day back in the box," he told Robert. "On the morning you put the last penny in, the bus will come for you and take you to school."

Robert had stared at the pennies but didn't touch them.

Now, as Jace drove back to Holly River, he thought about this opportunity for his half brother. This was good news, but he couldn't prevent the achingly familiar resentment he'd always had for their father from taking much of the joy from this small victory.

"Why couldn't you have given a little more of your time to this boy, you miserable old coot?" Jace said. "Maybe if you had paid attention to him, he might have had opportunities before now."

The situation was clear to Jace. Gladys loved her son. The boy was dependent upon her for everything. But he was also starved for attention, maybe had been for years.

Pretty soon Jace would have to swallow his hurt and his pride and tell Kayla about his relationship with his father. Maybe if he put his feelings into words, she would begin to understand why he was so dead set against marrying and having children.

It wasn't that he was afraid he'd be a bad father. It was just that he didn't have the first notion about how to be a good one. Add to that an unflinching desire to avoid the responsibility altogether, and there you had it—Jace Cahill in a nutshell. Good-time guy. Avoider of all things serious. And your basic loner.

Thinking about the conversation he would have with Kayla tonight made his palms sweat on the steering wheel. And then he saw her face in his mind's eye and he smiled. The woman was determined and obstinate. But despite all that, she was caught in this mess just like he was. He believed that both of them wanted to do the right thing. It was just that their notion of what that thing was happened to be miles apart.

All of that wasn't what made him smile

right now. The thought of spending a whole evening with her without interruption might well have had something to do with it, though.

CHAPTER NINE

JACE LEFT WORK early and was on time when he picked up Kayla and Nathan. The boy seemed more animated than he ever had before, excited, optimistic. Perhaps a chance to be with someone his own age had prompted this response. Or perhaps he was glad that in a few minutes, he would be somewhere away from Jace.

And Kayla looked fantastic in skinny blue jeans and a light pink sweater. Her hair was fastened behind her ears with two tortoise-shell clips and allowed to flow to just below her shoulders. She wore sandals, the clunky ones that were no doubt comfortable and probably cost an arm and a leg.

"Miranda has prepared dinner for the kids," he said as he opened the door to his truck. Nathan slid in first, followed by Kayla. The bench seat easily accommodated all of them.

"What's she having?" Nathan asked.

"I don't know the whole menu, but I understand it involves macaroni and cheese."

Nathan smiled. Kayla said, "Always a winner."

They arrived at Carter's substantial log cabin, which he'd renovated to a two-bedroom. Jace had always thought it was too much house for a single man, but now it was filled with love and laughter, just what Carter deserved.

Emily was waiting on the front porch. She hurried down the two steps to the gravel parking area, a huge smile on her adorable face. "Hi, Uncle Jace. Hi, Kayla. Hi, Nathan."

Jace had to give the little girl credit. She knew her manners and never skipped a cheery hello.

"Come on, Nathan," she said. "I've got Sorry set up in the living room. And after that we can play video games. My dad isn't home yet, so we can make as much noise as we want."

What an ideal situation, Jace thought, not that he'd ever thought his brother would object to a bit of noise from a couple of kids. But Emily made it sound as if she'd established the perfect play environment—no holds barred.

Miranda came out the front door and greeted everyone. "We're so happy to have Nathan for a visit," she said. "Though don't tell Cora. She'll be jealous."

"We won't be late," Kayla said, and regarded Jace. "What time do you think?"

He answered, "About three hours, give or take."

"No hurry," Miranda said. She handed Kayla a card. "Here's my cell number. Jace has it, but you should, too. Don't hesitate to call if you have a concern. But we'll be fine, I promise."

Kayla slipped the card into her purse. "Thanks so much for this. Nathan has been talking about coming over here all day."

Miranda went back inside, and Kayla and Jace got in the truck. "Are you hungry?" he asked.

"A little. What did you have in mind?"

"You like pizza?"

"Of course."

If she thought they'd end up in a noisy pizza parlor during tourist season, she was in for a surprise. He punched a quick-dial number into his cell phone. "Cheese and pepperoni okay?" he asked before the call was answered.

"Sure."

He ordered a large pizza, cheesy bread sticks and a liter of soda, telling the person on the other end that he would arrive in about fifteen minutes.

"My, you are hungry," Kayla said. "You're advance ordering the pizza."

"Takeout," he said. "It should be ready when we get there."

She gave him a curious stare. "Where are we going to eat it?"

He looked over and smiled at her. "Ah, that's the surprise. Wait and see."

THE SURPRISE TURNED out to be a small cabin in a wooded area off one of the main highways leading out of Holly River. Dusk had fallen when they arrived, so all Kayla could see was a pleasant-looking structure with a welcoming front porch and two chairs. Sitting on the porch was a large golden dog, who jumped up and bounded into the parking area when the truck pulled in.

"He's yours?" Kayla asked when the dog ran around the truck to sit at the driver's side.

"Yeah. That's Copper. He's a Labrador like his father, Buster, at my mother's place, and right now he's hungry."

Kayla got out of the truck, and Copper raced around to check her out. He sniffed her sandals and the hem of her blue jeans. Apparently finding nothing objectionable, he put his large nose on the seat of the truck and sniffed the pizza box.

"None for you," Jace said, taking the box and the Coke from the truck. "Kibbles are coming right up." Placing his free hand on the small of Kayla's back, he urged her forward. "Welcome to my humble abode."

"You live here?" She went up the front steps and waited for him to open the door.

"Yep. It's not much, but it's paid for, and it suits Copper and me."

"It's awfully remote," she said, looking around the wooded acreage surrounding the cabin. She couldn't help wondering how Nathan would adapt to this forested environment.

"I suppose, but solitude is kind of my thing. I spend all day working with people at High Mountain and this is what I look forward to at night, if I don't have a gig at one of the local restaurants."

She stepped inside to a comfortable living space with a large leather sofa, a pair of matching easy chairs, a cozy fireplace and every man's, and little boy's, requisite item, a large-screen TV. Jace put the pizza on a counter in the kitchen nook and lit a mound of logs in the fireplace. "Supposed to go down to the fifties tonight," he said. "A fire will be nice."

For what? she wondered. She didn't allow herself to dwell on all the possibilities of a warm fire on a cool night and assumed he meant the fire would be a nice accompaniment to hear some of his family's history.

After retrieving a bottle and a couple of wineglasses, Jace suggested Kayla sit on the sofa. She did. "A glass of wine before we open the soda?"

"Sure."

He poured wine for both of them.

"I figured you for a beer drinker," she said, sipping the fruity liquid.

"Can't tell a book by its cover," he said. "I had wine on Sunday at my brother's party."

Yes, that was true.

He went into the kitchen and filled an aluminum bowl with dog food. Setting the bowl outside the back door, he waited for Copper to follow him out. Then he brought napkins to his coffee table and offered Kayla a piece of pizza.

"This is good," she said, giving him room on the sofa.

"Best in town, I think." He folded his slice and took a big bite. "So what's your impression of my place?" He gave her a guarded look as if he were expecting her to criticize his way of life.

"It's nice," she said. "A bit off the beaten track, but I'm sure there are a lot of advantages to living here." Certainly there were for a man like Jace, but would there be advantages for a kid like Nathan?

"There are for me. I thought you should see it because this is my home. I'm not giving it up. This is where Nathan would live if he came to Holly River."

So, he was putting his boot down already and letting her know he wasn't altering his lifestyle. She smiled. "As opposed to a one-bedroom second-floor flat in DC where I live?"

If he'd wanted to scare her off by showing her his cabin, it didn't work. This cozy house could work for a couple of guys. Kayla looked out the large front window into the gathering dusk. The last of the sunlight shone through the highest branches of the trees, bathing the area in a soft golden glow.

"What boy wouldn't love living here?" she said, growing more accustomed to the idea as the minutes went by. "Lots of room to run, nobody to tell him to stay off their lawn, secret places for pretend adventures."

"But nobody to play with," he said.

"Maybe not in the immediate vicinity, but that is a problem easily solved. Nathan would meet kids his own age in school, on the playgrounds."

He took another slice of pizza and a generous swallow of wine and settled against the back of the sofa. "So you would approve of this little place as a home for Nathan?"

"It's not my place to approve or disapprove," she said. "I'm only here to approve of *you*. Once that happens, or should I say, *if* that happens, then, as his father, you will make the decisions about where you both live."

"I sent samples of our DNA to the lab today," he said. "Thanks for getting Nathan's."

She'd given him a sample of Nathan's hair from his safety vest. She hadn't been worried about the results. "No problem. I told you I had no objection to your sending out for verification." She thought about the wisdom of her next comment but said it anyway. "And I realize you are hoping and praying that the test proves that Nathan is not your son."

He looked surprised, maybe even a bit insulted. "I don't know about the praying part. But yes, I'm hoping that he isn't mine. Nothing against Nathan, you understand..."

"What's to understand?" she said. "You are making a decision about a person you haven't given up ten minutes to get to know."

He started to drink more wine, but set the glass back on the coffee table. "That's not fair. You expect me to bond with a child when I've never been faced with anything like this before. I'm not a kid person. Never have been."

"So you've said many times." She took a long swallow of wine to calm herself. This was an important evening for all of them. She didn't want to make Jace angry or even impatient. Especially when, deep down, she didn't believe he wasn't a "kid person." She'd seen him with Emily and wondered why he hadn't been able to establish that same comfortable familiarity with Nathan. Maybe he was just afraid. This was uncharted territory for him.

"Look, we're probably not going to decide this tonight. You brought me here for two reasons. You agreed to tell me your family situation, the one that will prove to me that the Cahills aren't as perfect as they seem. And two, you wanted me to decide that this cabin is completely inappropriate for a nine-year-old boy." She nibbled a corner of a pizza slice. "Well, sorry, but this cabin is totally charming."

"Charming?" He almost laughed. "Charming is for girls."

"Okay. Not so charming then. But fine for the two guys who could end up living here." She tucked one foot under her and placed her elbow on the back of his sofa. Giving him her complete attention, she said, "I'm listening, Jace. Since I know you can't possibly believe at this point that Nathan wouldn't be a good son, then tell me about why you want to convince me that you wouldn't be a good father. I want to hear about the Cahills."

SO FAR THE night hadn't gone exactly as Jace expected it to. He figured city girl Kayla would take one look at his cabin, imagine darkness settling over the entire area, hear the rustle of unknown creatures in the underbrush, and claim emphatically that this rustic way of life would never do for Nathan.

But no. She'd called the place "charming." She'd seen the log throne he'd built for himself on the porch. She'd set her glass on the rough-hewn coffee table and sat her pretty little backside on his distressed leather sofa. Maybe she was so desperate to have him claim the kid as his own that she'd misrepresented her feelings about the cabin. He knew the place wasn't charming. And she hadn't even seen the two small bedrooms, teeny closets and barely functional kitchen that didn't even have a dishwasher.

But assuming she was as honest as she

was tempting in the firelight, he'd tell her what she wanted to know—why the last-generation Cahill who called himself "father" never deserved the title and succeeded in making this particular offspring doubt that he'd ever be a good one.

"I'm the third-born of the Cahill children," he began. "I wasn't planned. I wasn't wanted, and I was born with health problems that dogged me for years. The doctors called it a birth defect, similar to a congenital heart problem. Bottom line, when I was about six months old, they discovered a hole in my heart."

She stared intently at him. "Wow. That's tough. But what do you mean when you say you weren't wanted? Who didn't want you? Cora seems to love you deeply, as do your older brother and sister."

"They do. In fact, my mother sacrificed her own needs by constantly making excuses for me, taking my side against my father."

"Why did she have to take sides?"

"For the simple reason that I was the fragile one. If my father could have gotten away with it, he might have drowned me as a way of thinning the herd, getting rid of the weakest link."

"You must be exaggerating," she said. "No father would look at their flesh and blood that way."

He huffed a scornful breath. "You never knew Raymond Cahill. You see, Raymond got the pot of gold at the end of the rainbow with Ava. She was pretty, smart, adaptable and a crowd-pleaser. She was everything Raymond could ask for in a child. Carter, not quite so much. But even though Carter's star didn't shine as brightly as Ava's, he still had admirable qualities. He was strong, likable, a good athlete, a plum in the Cahill family tree. As far as my father was concerned, it was time to quit while he was ahead."

"You must have had many good qualities, as well," Kayla said. "I mean, aren't all children special in their own unique ways?"

Jace shook his head. "Apparently that is a great misconception. I was sickly, awkward, whiny and slow. And that was just the first two years. After several surgeries I became stronger, but I added a few not-so-pleasant characteristics to my makeup. From the first time I could express myself adequately I became belligerent, rebellious, the one who shirked his chores and seemed hell-bent on failure. At least that's the way my father saw me."

He thought a long moment. "And you know what, Kayla? That wasn't such an inaccurate description. I did everything I could *not* to please the old man. I talked back, dared him to challenge me, ran away from home and my responsibilities at least once a month." He smiled. "Usually just to a friend's house, and my mom came and got me. But generally speaking I was a pain in my father's butt. And the more he called me weak, the worse I became."

"Didn't he try to correct your behavior?" Kayla asked.

"Oh, sure, in all sorts of ways, most of which I will remember all my life."

He watched Kayla's eyes narrow, her brow furrow. Perhaps she didn't want to think of Jace enduring those punishments. "He wasn't physically abusive, was he?" she asked. "That would have been beyond cruel. I mean you already had health problems."

"He could swing a pretty good right hook, and he tried it a couple of times, but my mother always stepped between us. I don't know how she managed to be there every time I needed her, but she was. I called her my shadow protector."

"And your father never abused her?"

"Heavens no. He adored my mother. In an odd sort of way she grounded him, made him a somewhat ethical man, though many who knew Raymond Cahill didn't believe that he actually had any morals. She used to stand right up to him and say, 'If you want to get to Jace, you'll have to go through me.' That put an end to it—for that time at least."

Under her breath, Kayla mumbled, "How horrible for you. Thank goodness Cora was there."

Jace put a finger under her chin and lifted her face. "Hey, don't feel sorry for me. All the good qualities had gone to Ava and Carter. I was the problem child from the beginning. I was no picnic to live with."

"But you were a child," she protested. "All children should have a healthy, supportive, loving environment around them as they grow up." She wrapped her hand around his wrist. "You were denied those things, the very things I want for Nathan."

He reached up and smoothed his hand down her hair, stopping to toy with the strands brushing her shoulder. "I know, Kayla, and believe it or not, I want those things for Nathan, too. I just don't know if he can get them from me. I've had no practice at being a dad, and my role model in the father department was a man I hated."

She blinked hard, banishing a tear from her eye. "We are in quite a situation here," she said. "I'm not sure how we'll ever resolve it."

"I don't know, either," he said, letting his gaze settle on her face and wondering if she could see the desire in his eyes. His relating of his childhood had opened up a kind of honesty inside him that soon became his passion for this woman who seemed to understand. She looked so sweet, so vulnerable at this moment.

He realized he wanted to make her happy, but the one thing she wanted he couldn't promise. So he gave her a warm smile and said, "But as I see it, we're in two situations. The one with Nathan, which is undoubtedly complex. And the simpler, more elemental one, the one that involves one man and one woman." His hand moved from her hair to her nape, and he gently massaged her tense muscles. "I'm attracted to you, Kayla. I want to please you, but not by promising you something that might not be good for that boy."

His face was so close to hers, he could feel her breath on his lips, warm and seductively spiced with wine.

"I want you to please me as well, Jace," she said, moving her mouth even closer to his. "Maybe we will come up with a solution for Nathan, but for now..."

The moment he had fantasized about for days, if only in his dreams, became a reality. His lips settled over hers in a gentle, persuasive kiss that soon became insistent and hungry. She gave in to his passion, kissing him back with a desire that was unmistakable, and perhaps had been building since they met and was now blossoming because of the closeness, the honesty, the reality of his life.

When he broke away, she breathed heavily, looked into his eyes. "We probably shouldn't be doing this. It doesn't simplify our primary situation."

"But it sure as heck addresses the second situation, and the way I'm feeling now, with you, that can't be all bad." His mouth covered hers for another mind-blowing kiss, and this time he wasn't so quick to part from her. This time he thoroughly enjoyed every sweet, wonderful moment.

CHAPTER TEN

SO MANY EMOTIONS raced through Kayla's mind. The loneliness of her small Washington apartment. The grief she'd felt when Susan died. The burden she'd accepted for Nathan, the bitterness that her ambition had denied her the wonderful sensations she was experiencing now. She'd never found enough time for a lasting relationship, always telling herself that she would make up for the emptiness in her life when her goals had been reached.

Now she was simply left wondering how she had lived without these feelings Jace stirred in her for all of her carefully planned life in Washington. Suddenly she wanted it all—success, a secure future for Nathan, a magical, passionate life for herself. But was it possible? This was a man who didn't want kids, didn't want to marry... She refused to think about that now, when his kisses made her dizzy, his hands made her skin tingle with awareness.

Soon enough the practical side of Kayla McAllister surfaced. She hadn't come here for this. She didn't need an entanglement of this kind in her life. She'd traveled to Holly River for Nathan, and to complete one last promise to Susan. Any enjoyment she'd experienced with Jace's kiss was temporary. Nathan's future would be permanent. The kiss was emotionally selfish, and Kayla wasn't selfish. She pushed Jace away.

"We shouldn't be doing this," she said.

Jace dropped his hands to his lap, looked down. He cleared his throat. "Once again we have two directly opposite points of view on the same situation. I was doing exactly what I thought was right."

"It's not right, not when the next years of Nathan's life rest in our hands."

"Isn't that *your hands*, Kayla?" he said. "Aren't you the one Susan entrusted with the fate of her child?"

Anger threatened to bubble from somewhere deep inside. Again he was shifting the responsibility for his son to her. "No more than she entrusted me to search for the boy's father to see if he would assume his role in Nathan's life." After a long, calming breath, Kayla continued. "I would leave town right now, Jace, if this weren't such a crucial issue, if Nathan's life weren't at stake. I would take Nathan away, and..."

"And what, Kayla? Keep him yourself?"

"I can't do that. You know I can't. A life with me wouldn't be fair to Nathan." She stood, paced the small space that was Jace's living room. "You live in this cozy forest wonderland, remote yes, but perhaps perfect for any young boy."

"'A forest wonderland?'" He chuckled. "Come on, Kayla. It's a dinky cabin on a mountain road, far from town, far from the schools." He shook his head. "Do not, and I mean *do not* romanticize this situation. I have to drive three miles to get a bottle of milk. It's eight miles to the nearest park. And I can't even imagine trying to navigate this area on a bicycle." He shook his head. "Every boy needs a bicycle."

"You could move," she said impulsively, knowing how Jace would react. He didn't disappoint.

"So could you."

"He would adapt to this environment," she said, "much easier than he would living in a cramped city apartment with me."

"You think so?" Jace let several moments pass before adding, "With a man who doesn't want to be, and never wanted to be, a father?"

She walked to his window, looked out on the pitch-dark landscape, only broken by the scant rays of light from his porch fixture. "I could put Nathan in his grandparents' care," she said, her voice barely above a whisper. "They will take him."

"That's a good idea then," Jace said.

She tried hard to keep a sob from escaping, but it did anyway, a trembling rush of air that brought tears to her eyes. She couldn't fold. Not now. This was too vitally important. "It is also the last thing Susan wanted," she said. "And the last thing you should want, as well."

"I don't even know those people, Susan's parents," he said. "They could be kind, and considerate, with all the nurturing skills a child needs."

She spun around. "They're not! Susan didn't want that."

He stood, crossed his arms over his chest and stared at her. "Do you really believe she wanted me to raise him? Come on! She hadn't seen me in ten years."

"I don't know what she would want now, and I can't ask her." Kayla took two steps toward Jace and stopped. "But I think I know this much. *I* want you to raise him. I think that despite your own upbringing, you would be good to him. I think you could introduce him to things he's never experienced..."

"Like that rollicking ride down the river?"

Ignoring the reference, she said, "But if you are certain you could never love him, that you would only regard him as a burden, then I will take him away and put him in the care of his grandparents."

"Nothing quite like emotional blackmail, Kayla."

She didn't say anything because she couldn't disagree. He rubbed the back of his neck, shook his head sadly. "Come sit back down, Kayla."

"Why? So we can confuse this already disastrous moment with more emotion?"

"No. Sit down because there is still something about my family that you don't know. You might as well hear it all."

She refused to move. He held out his hand to her. "I have a younger brother," he said. "I need to tell you about Robert."

YEARS AGO JACE had decided several things about his future. One, he wouldn't marry. Instead he would enjoy women when he wanted to, always be as considerate as possible, but never commit. Two, he wouldn't have children. If that meant he would die alone in this cabin, then so be it. There were worse things. Three, he would never ever complicate his life. He would live each day for himself, help out his mother when she needed him but basically do only those things that he wanted to do.

And four, and this was the biggie, he would never discuss his father with anyone and try his hardest to put the old man out of his mind as if he'd never existed. So much for this decision. He was about to tell this woman everything.

And as far as the other decisions were concerned, he now had a needy half brother, a mother with an inherited Christmas tree farm who wanted more from him than he would ever give, a son who, despite Kayla's wishes, probably didn't even like him, and a life that could become as complicated as he'd ever imagined.

As he sat next to Kayla on the sofa, he leveled his gaze on his clinched hands, one thought running through his mind. *How did I get myself into this mess? How did the fate of even one other person become so entwined with the choices facing me today?*

He thought about taking Kayla's hand. Not for her, but for himself. But he didn't. Instead he switched his attention to her hand as it lay on her lap and imagined the long, slim fingers wrapped with his, her palm soft against his calloused one.

"There is one more black spot on my father's reputation," he said. "It seems that as much as he loved my mother, and I believe he did, he couldn't remain faithful to her."

Kayla's eyes widened. "He cheated on Cora?"

"I don't know how many times, but the proof that he did it once lives in a small town about forty-five minutes from here. His name is Robert. I learned about him just over two months ago. He is my twelve-year-old half brother. And he is autistic."

"That must have been so hard to learn, Jace." Kayla raised her hand as if she might touch his arm, but she dropped it back to her lap. "How involved are you in his life?"

He told her about Gladys Kirshner, the small home she and Robert shared together. He told her about the first time he met Robert. How the boy didn't speak and even seemed frightened of him. He explained about the research he'd immediately done to determine the extent of Robert's problems.

"I try to visit him at least twice a week," Jace said. "I'm not a psychologist, but I think I've helped him. I won't abandon him now, not when he has so recently experienced a breakthrough."

She questioned him about Robert's progress and he told her about the boy going to a school where professionals could help him succeed. "I have hope for Robert that I hadn't seen for weeks," he said. "Someday I imagine he can even live a fulfilled life. But I won't abandon him. Because he has continued to relate to me, I won't stop whatever support he gets from my visits."

"Nor should you," Kayla said. "It's truly a wonderful thing you do for your brother. Does he get equal attention from Carter and Ava?"

He smiled. "Not so much. They've met him, but their reaction to Robert is wrapped up in some financial difficulties my mother is having." He didn't know whether to fill Kayla in on the most intimate details, but what the heck? He'd gone this far. "My mother has been supporting Gladys since my father died. Raymond contributed to the boy's care as a way to avoid physically being around Robert. And my mother didn't have the heart to stop."

He laughed softly. "We're an odd bunch," he said. "Basically we're all good people who want to do the right thing. Even me, though I wonder if you'll ever believe that. Unfortunately we can't all come to a consensus about what that right thing is. Carter and Ava ask about Robert occasionally, while the brainy child, Ava, tries to figure out what to do about the money drain. Mama keeps paying Gladys, and I keep showing up for Robert, who, of course, has no idea he's at the center of such drama in the Cahill family."

Kayla shook her head slowly. "Wow, this is incredible." She shifted on the sofa so she could look directly into his eyes. What he saw in her eyes was only sympathy and understanding, and the emotions calmed him, made his breaths come easily. "Of course Robert has to continue as a priority in your life," she said.

He nodded. "Kind of strange, isn't it? That a twelve-year-old boy would become a priority in a man's life whose only list of priorities was that he never have priorities in the first place."

She smiled. "Yeah, it's strange, but it's also revealing. What I need to know is how your obligation to Robert might affect any relationship you could have with Nathan."

The big question. Jace had been wondering the same thing for almost a week now. He raked his fingers through his hair and gave her the most honest answer he could. "I don't know. I wouldn't be able to keep the boys apart forever…"

"You shouldn't keep them apart. They are related. Robert is Nathan's uncle."

"But they are so different. I can relate to

Robert. I can speak plainly and he gets it. I don't feel like I can even do that and relate to Nathan at all."

"How hard have you tried?"

"What? I took you on that raft ride…"

"That was making Nathan relate to you? When have you tried to relate to him? When have you spoken plainly to your son?"

"I just don't get the feeling that we're on the same wavelength," he said, raising his hand and holding it flat high above his head. "Nathan's up here, and I'm, well…" He thumped his chest. "You get it."

"Nonsense," she said. "Nathan is bright, but he doesn't know one-tenth of the things you know. He's gentle and sensitive. That may scare you, but after what you've just told me about Robert, I firmly believe that you exhibit these tendencies yourself."

Sensitive? Jace had always thought he was about as sensitive as a tree branch that gets caught in a windstorm and crashes through a roof.

"Spend some time with Nathan, just the two of you. Show him this part of the country, the places that you knew as a child."

"Oh, yeah, he'd love that."

She chuckled. "Okay, so the first attempt didn't go so well. But I'll talk to him, prepare him for an outing with you."

Panic gripped Jace's chest. "You're not going to tell him…?"

"No. He's not ready to hear that. Go out as friends, get to know him, Jace. It's what you should do and frankly, it's the least you can do."

He smiled at her. "You're an impossible dreamer, you know that?"

"I'm not. I'm a realist, through and through. I don't dream things that are so big they can't possibly come true. Trust me."

He paused, took a deep breath and let it out slowly. "Okay. We don't have a busy day tomorrow. I do have a gig tomorrow night, but tell Nathan I'll pick him up at the inn tomorrow around two and we'll do something, maybe try fishing at the trout farm where kids catch fish without even trying very hard. I'll bring sodas and…what do kids eat?"

"They are humans, Jace. They eat what anyone eats."

"Okay. It's just that if I'm going to do this, I don't want to screw it up."

"You won't." Then she surprised the heck out of him. She placed her hands on each side of his face, leaned in and kissed him. "Let's end this way," she said. "I don't want you to think I didn't enjoy that earlier."

CHAPTER ELEVEN

THE NEXT MORNING Kayla's phone rang before 9:00 a.m. Recognizing the name on the digital screen, she answered quickly. "Good morning, Beverly."

The voice on the other end was as it had been on two other occasions since Kayla had arrived in Holly River—a combination of panic and impatience. "Kayla, I can't find the congressman's file on the clean water project in Virginia Beach. And—"

"Beverly, calm down," Kayla said. Beverly Hodges, the middle-aged woman who had been temporarily brought over from the office of another congressman who was currently out of the country, had been chosen for her ability and knowledge of the workings of Congress. In addition to those qualifications, Kayla had given her a quick but thorough walk-through of Russell Meyers's office procedures. Despite the preparation,

Beverly had seemed to encounter many obstacles to her running of Russell's office.

"The file is on the computer under Stilton Water Systems," Kayla said. "Check the *S* folder."

"Oh, yes, I found it," Beverly said. "I'll print it out for the congressman to look at when he gets back." She emitted a long-suffering sigh. "Russell didn't have time for his morning coffee, and he blamed me for not alerting him to his first meeting today."

As well he should, Kayla thought. She always gave the congressman a list of the next day's appointments before he left the office for the evening. Often she presented him with nuggets of her own research that might ease him into his day. Russell had approved Kayla's absence, however, and he should have expected a few glitches in the smooth running of his office.

"Where is Russell now?" Kayla asked. She wanted to remind him of his Monday-morning meeting with the Armed Services Committee and the argument he would be required to present on extra funding for the Virginia Naval Air Station.

"He's with a group of high school sophomores from his district. He's giving them a tour of the Capitol building."

Kayla smiled. And he's doing it without his second cup of coffee—quite a feat for Virginia's oldest and most respected House member. "Okay. Well, is there anything else, Beverly? If not, I'll call in later. I need to speak to Russell anyway."

"I wish you'd hurry back," Beverly said. "I didn't know your boss could be so demanding."

"You just need to work out some kinks, Beverly. And I hope you do, because I can't see my mission here wrapping up any sooner than I'd planned. But by the time I get back, I imagine you and Russell will be fast friends."

Beverly scoffed. "I truly cannot see that happening."

"Hang in there, my friend," Kayla said. "Remember, Russell's bark is much worse than his bite."

She disconnected, thinking about the relationship she and the congressman had established over the two years she'd worked in his office. Weeks had gone by before Kayla had the office running in a way both she and

Russell were comfortable with. But now they worked together like a well-tuned race car. Still, he would have to break in a new assistant if Kayla's ambitions came true. She'd always wanted to be on the decision-making side of a political desk, even if she had to start with a small one, and she would take the first opportunity to advance her position in government. Her dream had always been to enact laws that helped people live better lives.

Nathan, still in his pajamas, padded out of the bathroom. "Was it Beverly again?" he asked.

"Good guess." Nathan had overheard more than one conversation between the two women. "Get dressed, honey. We'll go into town and do our laundry this morning and then stop at the River Café for lunch. Okay?"

And over a couple of grilled cheese sandwiches, she'd tell him about his outing with Jace. And hope he was up for it.

THE FIRST HIGH MOUNTAIN expedition returned to the store early. The river had been running swiftly. No one had fallen in or complained. Billy called from his cell phone at eleven and said they were on their way back.

At eleven forty-five, Jace left High Mountain in Billy's capable hands and headed over to the River Café. He'd grab a quick bite, load up on snacks for him and Nathan, and be at the Laurel Mountain Inn by two with time to spare. He wanted Nathan to be eager to go, but maybe that was too much to hope for.

As usual, a couple of cop cars sat outside the café. One belonged to the chief of police, so Jace went inside expecting a leisurely conversation with Carter. Maybe he'd even tell Carter that he was taking Nathan out on his own today. His brother would like that.

Instead he found Carter and Sam McCall sitting at a table, their heads bent in conversation, their sandwiches barely touched. Jace ambled over. "Can anyone join this party?" he asked.

Neither man looked enthusiastic, but Sam dragged a chair from a nearby table and indicated Jace could sit.

"What's going on?" Jace asked. "I'm assuming this serious atmosphere isn't because there has been a rise in the crime rate or you guys wouldn't be sitting here. So I figure somebody died."

Carter gave his friend Sam a sideways glance. Sam shrugged, suggesting it was okay for Carter to let Jace in on whatever calamity had these guys so upset.

"You remember Allie, the waitress who used to work here in the café?" Carter said to his brother.

Jace definitely remembered her. "Who could forget? The cutest Most Wanted gal we've seen in Holly River for a long time. She was Bonnie to Dale Jefferson's Clyde."

Both men gave him a warning look. "She was also the love of Sam's life," Carter said. "You could try to be a bit more sensitive."

Jace knew all about the interest Sam had shown in the petite blonde who'd arrived in Holly River with a mysterious past. Sam had fallen hard for her, believed they had the makings for a future together. And then she'd slipped over to the dark side, working with an old family friend from her previous hometown as well as partnering up with Holly River's most notorious bandit, Dale Jefferson. The whole bunch of them had eventually been caught by Carter and

Sam when Allie and her friend were discovered tending Dale's acres of flourishing marijuana. Dale was picked up soon after.

"I'm sorry if I wasn't sensitive enough," Jace said. "I know Allie got bail and ran off into the night never to be seen again." He stared hard at Sam. "Good grief, Sam, with every woman in town hot on your trail, I figured you'd have gotten over Allie by now."

"It's only been a couple of months," Sam said. "Haven't you ever been in love, Jace?"

"Only about a hundred times," Jace said. "But maybe it was never the real thing because I can't remember ever needing more than a month or so to mend my broken heart."

"That's because you were always the one breaking hearts, brother," Carter said. "Not the other way around."

Jace ordered a ham-and-cheese sandwich with extra pickles and mayo and turned his attention back to Sam. "I promise to be sensitive from now on," he said. "I'm figuring whatever you guys are talking about has something to do with Allie."

"I heard from her," Sam said. He punched some buttons on his smartphone and handed the instrument to Jace. "I got this text from her this morning."

Jace read it. Dear Sam. I'm so sorry for disappointing you, and I feel just horrible about running off. I'd like to come back and I'll accept whatever punishment I deserve. Even time in jail would be better than the life I'm living now. I miss you, Sam. I hope you'll forgive me someday.

Jace handed the phone back to Sam. "Sounds like she means it to me."

"I suppose," Sam said. "But if she thinks she'll get a break from me, she's wrong. She'll have to face a judge and probably jail time. There were robberies, and she was an accessory. And then she was up to her knees in the whole marijuana-growing thing."

"But the big question is," Jace said, "can you ever forgive her? That's what she most wants to know."

Sam's face showed the scars of love lost and the weight of a difficult decision. He paused a few moments and then said, "I loved her, Jace. Can't turn that off like a darn spigot."

"Then I'd say your decision is made."

"That's what I told him," Carter said. "I

suggested he text her back and tell her he'll be here when she returns. He'll help her any way he can, but she's got to pay her debt to society."

Sam nodded. "That's what I'll do." He got up from the table and walked to a quiet corner of the restaurant. His hands immediately became busy on his phone keypad.

Carter took a bite of his sandwich. "Somehow I don't think that's all that's going on here," Jace said. "You suddenly look like a guy who isn't Holly River's happiest newlywed. Everything okay, bro?"

"Yeah, it's just that Miranda's upset about something."

"Want to tell me about it?"

Carter thought a moment and said, "I would. You know how she moved here wanting to be this county's greatest social worker ever?"

"Well, I thought she moved here to marry you and become the greatest wife ever, but okay, I get where you're coming from. This county could use some assistance." Miranda had come to Holly River several months ago to help her cousin Lawton when he was released from prison. She'd taken time off work in Durham as a social worker to help assimilate Lawton into society again. She'd done a great job with Lawton and even managed to capture the heart she'd broken years ago and marry her first love, Carter. Now she was doing her good works locally. Jace had thought she was content with the move.

"She's trying to do too much too fast," Carter said. "She wants to help everyone on Liggett Mountain, even the ones who don't want to be helped."

Jace didn't get to Liggett Mountain often, but he knew Miranda had been raised in poverty like all the other residents of the depressed area outside Holly River. It was like the county they all lived in was divided down the middle into the haves and the have-nots. Miranda and her cousins and family had always been part of the have-nots, though Miranda had overcome the limitations that life on Liggett Mountain had instilled in her. Jace could understand her inclination to want to help the people on Liggett.

"What's she trying to do?" he asked.

"She wants state and federal funding to improve the folks' lives up there. Better housing, more job opportunities, road improvements, easier access to the schools and businesses in Holly River."

"What's wrong with that?" Jace asked. "Maybe Miranda just wants everyone to be as happy as she is."

"Nothing's wrong with it," Carter said. "But Miranda doesn't know a whole lot about how local government works, especially the skeleton government we have here in Holly River. She needs someone to guide her through governmental red tape. She needs to meet the right people..." Carter stopped talking and stared over Jace's shoulder.

Before Jace could figure out what had commanded his brother's attention, a familiar voice said, "Hi, guys. What's this about Miranda needing a connection with government agencies?"

Just the sound of that voice brought a pleasant quiver to the pit of Jace's stomach. He turned around, a smile already plastered on his face. "Kayla. Nathan. I was just getting ready to come see you guys."

What was it about this woman that made Jace temporarily forget that the biggest problem of his life still loomed like a dark cloud wearing cargo shorts and a Superman T-shirt? And that he was about to spend the rest of his afternoon trying to get to understand this cloud better?

Kayla had brought complication into his life, and Jace didn't like complication. He should be cringing at the thought of spending a couple of hours at the trout farm with a kid who should have been anyone else's son but his. And he should be ducking under the table to keep from having to face the woman who was determined to make him into something he wasn't and never wanted to be. And yet here he was, pulling up a couple of chairs and insisting that Kayla and Nathan sit down.

The waitress came and took orders for hamburgers, fries and milkshakes, and Carter filled Kayla in on Miranda's hopes for the people of Liggett Mountain. Amazingly Kayla seemed fascinated. She asked questions about local politics and the most influential citizens in positions of authority. The list wasn't long—there weren't many.

"Who makes the decisions for the town and outlying areas?" she asked.

"We have a council meeting every month," Jace said. "If anybody needs anything, they come to the council and ask. Then there's a vote. If there's enough money in the coffers we try to satisfy the request. If not, then things go back to the way they were."

"Do you go to the meetings?" she asked Jace.

"Me? No. I get all my information from Carter." He smiled at his brother. "As police chief, he has to go."

"What Miranda is trying to do is admirable, but it's obvious there isn't a great amount of funds to accomplish this." She tapped her fingernail on a menu as she thought. "Too bad I work for an out-of-state congressman. If I worked for a representative from North Carolina, I might be able to help."

"She would appreciate your help anyway," Carter said. "But don't sell her short. Miranda is sure determined. I wouldn't be surprised if she went door to door asking for donations." He smiled. "I remember how hard she worked to get her cousin Lawton accepted by the people in this town."

"Maybe I'll give her a call," Kayla said. "I can offer a few general suggestions that might lead her in the right direction. The first thing she'll need to do is work with the town council."

Jace chuckled. "Obviously you've never met them."

The food was delivered to the table, and Nathan dug in to his burger "What are we doing after this?" he asked Kayla.

She passed a sheepish glance at Jace. "I haven't had a chance to tell you yet, sweetie, but Jace has a big surprise for you today."

Oh, great. She hadn't told the kid yet. Now he had to sit here and watch a nine-year-old's face fall to his chest when he learned he'd have to spend a couple of hours with the awful man who'd caused him to puke on the raft.

Nathan set his sandwich on his plate and stared at Kayla with huge round eyes. "What?"

"You and Jace are going to a trout farm," Kayla said. "You're going to go fishing."

Nathan looked from Kayla to Jace. Jace slapped the smile back on his face in hopes of making Nathan think this was exactly what he wanted to do with his day.

"I don't know how to fish," Nathan said.

Kayla gave Jace an eyebrow-raised glance as if to say "you take it from here."

"Nothing to it," he said. "I'll have you catching trout before you know it."

"Are you going with us, Auntie Kay?"

Kayla shook her head. "I have some things to do, like folding all that laundry. I didn't think you'd want to do that."

"No...o...o."

"Tell you what," Jace said before Nathan could express his total dislike of the plan. "We'll leave from here and stop at my place to pick up Copper. I think you'll like him."

Nathan suddenly seemed interested. "Who's Copper?"

"He's just about the friendliest, shaggiest, licking-est dog you've ever met."

"Friendlier than Buster at Cora's house?"

"Well, Buster's pretty darn friendly, but I'd say it's a draw. Not surprising since they're father and son." The irony of what he'd just said didn't escape Jace. Sons should be like their fathers, shouldn't they? Although he wasn't anything like Raymond.

Kayla smiled down at Nathan. "Okay, Nathan? Sound like fun?"

"You won't be too lonely without me, will you, Auntie Kay?"

"I'll be fine. You go and have fun."

She nudged Jace's leg under the table with the toe of her sneaker. When he looked at her, she mouthed, "So far so good."

CHAPTER TWELVE

"THIS TRUCK IS KINDA COOL."

Jace glanced over at his passenger. Nathan sat on the truck's bench seat, his short legs swinging because they didn't quite reach the floor. So far he'd consulted Nathan about snacks and packed the cooler he had in back of the truck. One thing he hadn't expected was for Nathan to compliment his vehicle.

Jace liked his truck, a sturdy 1976 Ford that he'd restored one summer eight years ago. But the eight years had taken their toll on the trusty Ford. The vinyl on the bench seat had started to crack. The headliner drooped. The steering wheel was shiny from the oil on Jace's hands. And no one in recent memory had ever said that the truck was cool.

"You rode in this old truck last night, remember? Did you think it was cool then?"

"Probably, but we were going to Emily's

house, and I wasn't paying much attention to how we got there."

No doubt because going to Emily's was a lot more important than getting a ride in the famous Yellow Bomber, Jace's affectionate name for his wheels.

They pulled into Jace's drive and Copper came running from behind the cabin.

"That's your dog?" Nathan asked.

"That's him. I should warn you that he's messy and his manners are terrible." As if illustrating the description, Copper stood at the front of the truck and barked excitedly.

"I think he's neat," Nathan said, opening the truck door. Before stepping to the ground, he looked over at Jace. "He won't bite me, will he?"

Jace smiled. "I don't know. I don't think he's had a bite of kid today, so I can't be sure. Want me to see if his stomach's growling?"

Nathan's eyes widened, and then he laughed. "He won't bite me. I know it." He climbed out of the truck, got down on his knees and let Copper lick his face. "He likes me!"

"You get him into the truck," Jace said. "I'll go inside and get his leash."

Nothing much had happened by the time Jace came out of the cabin. Dog and boy were still on the ground getting acquainted. Jace whistled. Copper broke free and jumped into the truck.

"Wow, he's really smart," Nathan said.

"In dog IQ, he's a genius," Jace said. "Climb in, Nathan. I'll bet the fish are jumping at the bait right now and we aren't there to catch them."

Nathan settled beside the dog and draped his arm over Copper's neck. When they'd pulled onto the road, he turned to Jace and said, "What will we do with the fish if we catch them?"

Jace thought a moment. He knew the trout farm let kids keep their catches, but Nathan's expression told him that probably wasn't in the kid's game plan. "Here's how I see it," he said. "There are only two reasons to go fishing. The first one is for the fun of it. The second is because you need a fish to make dinner. We've already eaten, and we have a cooler full of snacks, so we're just doing this for the fun. We'll throw our fish back in. How's that?"

"That's good," Nathan said. "And the fish will like us if we do that."

This boy is certainly concerned with creatures liking him, Jace thought. "You bet they will."

Jace was feeling confident as they rode down the country lane that led to the trout farm. The windows were down in the truck, the radio was blaring a bluegrass song—they were just two guys out for an adventure. Of course this didn't mean that Jace wanted to be a father, but he could at least see himself getting through the next couple of hours without damaging the kid too much. And he was starting to imagine himself seeing the boy every so often, once the cat was out of the bag about Jace being his dad. What kid wouldn't want to spend a few weekends with a guy who knew how to fish and had a cool truck and dog?

They entered the pond area and parked, and Jace went up to the fella who ran the hatchery, a man he'd known since childhood. "Hello, Gus. We need a couple of poles and some bait."

Gus looked at both males. "Got just what you need, Jace. Received a new batch of brown PowerBait dough yesterday. Fresh and fragrant as it gets. The fish are loving it."

"We'll take a bag," Jace said, pulling a five-dollar bill from his wallet. "How much for the poles?" Jace had plenty of poles, but he'd decided to leave his at home and give Nathan the whole experience, including helping out a neighbor who needed the business.

"Not charging for the poles today," Gus said. "Instead I'm asking six dollars a pound for the ones you catch. We'll clean them for you, naturally."

"We're throwing ours back," Nathan said.

"Oh, well, in that case, give a holler when you catch one and I'll weigh it on the spot, and you can do what you want after that. Go on and pick out a couple of rigs."

Jace chose a pair of six-foot poles with number eight hooks, just the size needed for a one-to-four-pound trout. He handed one rig to Nathan and gave him the bait pack, and carrying the cooler and his own pole, and holding tight to Copper's leash, they marched to the edge of the pond—a quiet spot where not too many folks had already gathered.

This activity was a favorite of tourists in the mountains. The hatchery supply made it easy for kids to catch fish. Jace figured a lot of the kids here today had never fished before in their lives, just like Nathan.

"Just a couple of first tips," Jace said when they'd set down their gear and he'd tied Copper to a nearby tree. "This bait comes in all colors, some of them real pretty like a rainbow. But we're using brown because it's the same as the pellets the trout are fed by Gus when they're born. The trout see the color and think it's a pellet, and they bite."

"Okay. What do you do with the bait? Throw it in the water?"

Throw the bait in the water? Jeez, this boy had never fished, that was for certain. "No, Nathan, you put it on the hook and drop your line in the pond. We'll do that in a minute. First I have to tell you to watch your line very carefully. Hold the rod still when you cast in, and then keep your eyes on the line. If it moves, that means a fish is interested in what's on your hook."

"So I might catch him?"

Jace smiled. "Not *might*, buddy. You will.

I'll bet you catch one before I do." *And I'm going to make sure that happens.*

Nathan walked to the edge of the pond and leaned over. "Wow, look at all the fish! There's hundreds of them."

"Sure are. And the temperature is just right today, so they're swimming near the surface. You only need to drop your hook a few inches." Jace opened the bait pack and took out a dough ball. "Let's get you set up."

He selected a nearby boulder and they both sat down in the shade of a maple tree. Jace put the hook in the palm of Nathan's hand and told him to hold on to it while the rod dangled by his feet.

"Isn't this sharp?" Nathan asked, staring at the hook.

"Yep, it's sharp, so pay attention to what I'm telling you." Jace kneaded a dough ball between his thumb and forefinger until it was soft. "You need to rub the dough ball like this each time you get a new bait from the pack." He thought of a reference Nathan might understand. "You've used Play-Doh, haven't you?"

"Sure. But not anymore. It's for babies."

"Okay, but you're going to treat the dough

ball like Play-Doh. Keep squeezing it until it's soft." Jace lifted his own hook from the grass and pressed the dough ball onto the tip. "Carefully now, you squeeze the dough around the hook—all the way so the hook is completely covered. It's okay to even get some bait on the line." He held up his hook so Nathan could see. "Now this rig is ready to fish. You try it. And don't worry if you mess up the first time. We've got lots of bait."

Nathan stared at the hook he was holding between his thumb and finger just as Jace had done. "It won't stick me, will it?"

"Not if you're careful," Jace said. "Besides, you know which is the sharp end." He handed Nathan a dough ball. "Go ahead. Squeeze the dough around the hook. Press carefully but firmly."

Nathan attempted to do as he was told, and Jace watched him until he was convinced he'd make a fisherman of the kid before the day was done. But then something happened. Jace wasn't quite sure what, since he was checking his own pole, but Nathan suddenly screamed, dropped his hook and began shaking his hand.

"You said it wouldn't stick me," he cried.

"Yeah, if you were careful." Jace took his hand. "Let me see." A pale pink spot had appeared on Nathan's fingertip, but it was no big deal. "Didn't even break the skin," Jace said. "You're okay."

"But it hurts."

"It'll stop in a minute. I'll fix your rig for you this time. When you do it again, watch what you're doing."

"I was!"

"Okay." Jace handed him the rig. "Go to the edge and kind of fling your line in, like this…" Jace expertly cast out his line. Nathan did as well as he could. With the number of fish in the pond, he definitely did well enough to catch a trout. "See how your dough ball is floating just below the surface? That's perfect. I'll bet a bunch of fish are eyeing it already."

True enough, the boy hooked a trout almost immediately. Jace stuck his pole in some soft mud for safekeeping and stood beside Nathan. He knew he had a fish on his hook already but he wanted Nathan to haul in a catch first. "You got him, Nathan. Bring him in," he urged.

Before he knew what had happened, Nathan had jumped into the water and waded out a few feet.

"What are you doing?" Jace hollered, going in after him. Jace didn't know when the pond level deepened.

"I'm going to bring him in like you said," Nathan answered.

"Not like that! Just pull on your rod. That's how you bring in a fish." He hooked his hands under Nathan's arms and lifted him from the soft muck of the pond bed. Then he slogged back to the shore where an obviously angry Gus waited.

"You know better than that," Gus said. "Nobody's supposed to go in the water. I'm not insured for that."

"I know," Jace said, setting Nathan on the ground. "It was a mishap. Won't happen again."

"We got rules, Jace."

"Okay, I get it."

Gus wandered off and Nathan stomped his feet on the grass. The muck clung to his sneakers like thick glue. Jace had rushed to get Nathan so fast that he'd left his expensive hiking sandals stuck in the pond bed during the rescue. He wasn't about to go in the dirty water again and risk Gus's wrath, so he would be barefoot the rest of the day. Not to mention out a pair of shoes.

"Auntie Kay is gonna be mad at me," Nathan wailed. "She just bought me these sneakers before we left home."

The end of Jace's patience was evident in a throbbing of a vein at his temple. *Be cool, Jace,* he told himself. "It'll be okay, Nathan. I'll tell Kayla what happened. She won't be mad." He said the words, but he knew he might be ponying up for a new pair of sneakers. "The important thing is that you still have a trout on the end of your line. Don't you want to catch it?"

"I guess so."

"Okay, now listen. Pull back on your rod. Give it a quick jerk. You'll feel the weight on the line. That's the fish. After you give it a jerk, turn the spinning reel…" He stopped, showed Nathan what to do. "And bring him on shore. You ready?"

This could still turn out okay. Nathan was listening. His eyes were on the prize. His mouth was set in a firm line. He was prepared to do what was necessary to bring in the greatest catch of all time. *Please let this go well*, Jace thought to himself, wondering who might be listening.

"Okay, jerk the rod," he said.

And boy, did he ever! He jerked the rod with the force of a superhero. The tip and hook reared up into the air, leaving the rod vertical to the ground below. The end of the short line shot out of the water like it had been propelled with a bottle rocket. The fish flew through the air and sailed over Nathan's head.

Obviously not a smooth move, but maybe this catch could still be saved. But no. The worse thing that could have happened occurred in the blink of an eye. The little six-inch trout landed on the ground with a thud several feet behind Nathan. Copper barked excitedly and sprang for the flailing creature. Copper's front paws had the fish in a death grip seconds before his powerful jaws clamped down on the gills behind the trout's head.

Nathan screamed, "He's killing my fish!"

Jace hollered at his dog, and Copper backed away. But it was too late. Pale water-infused blood seeped from the fish's torn scales. Gus walked up with his scales. "Let me get a measure of this one. Can't be more than a half pound or so."

"Can you come back later, Gus?" Jace said, his attention fixed on Nathan's horrified expression. "We need a minute here."

"Oh, sure," Gus said. "Call me when you're ready."

Gus walked off and Jace watched Nathan's face crumple like cellophane wrapping around a basket. Nathan sobbed like his heart had been torn out.

Jace got down on his knees in front of him, took his arms in his hands and forced the boy to look straight into his face. "Nathan, I'm sorry. Copper didn't know. It was instinct. You know what instinct is, don't you? Copper didn't mean anything by it. He saw the fish flying through the air, and…"

"You said we'd throw our fish back, that we wouldn't kill any." The words were hardly discernable through Nathan's sobs.

"I know, but things happen. We can't always predict…"

Nathan stared at the fish as if his best friend had just been mowed down by a gang of bikers.

"Nathan, buddy," Jace said. "It's just a fish."

A simple concept, Jace thought. Easy enough for anyone to understand. But not Nathan. The boy sniffed, rubbed his finger under his nose and said, "Not to another fish it isn't. This could have been somebody's mother."

Oh, wow. This moment was cutting too deep, too profound for Jace to handle. Some poor fish's mother had just died.

"I know how the baby fish feels," Nathan said. "You don't! You still have your mother, and she's a great one."

"I know." Jace's hands gripped more tightly on Nathan's arms. He didn't know where to go with this one. He waited for Nathan's sobs to subside, and he said, "I don't think fish feel what we do, if that's any consolation. This momma's babies probably have already forgotten about her."

The look Nathan gave him could have melted ice. "I want to go home."

"Sure, we'll go home." Jace put his hand on Nathan's shoulder and pointed the boy toward the truck. He stopped and untied Copper from the tree. The dog bounded behind Nathan as if he wanted to play. Taking the fishing gear and the cooler, Jace passed Gus and handed him a ten-dollar bill. "This should cover it," he said. "Ten dollars worth of fun."

"Come back anytime!" Gus called.

The ride back to the Mountain Laurel Inn was morbid—the worst possible kind of sadness hung over the creatures in the truck. Halfway back, Nathan put his arm around Copper's neck. "It wasn't your fault, boy," he said, and buried his face in the thick, soft fur.

Yeah, right, Jace thought. *It was mine. All mine.*

When they reached the cottage where Kayla and Nathan were staying, Nathan jumped out of the truck and ran for the door. Kayla came outside, tried to speak to the boy, but he sidestepped her and scurried to get inside.

"Hang on, Nathan," she said. "Don't go in like that. What happened to your sneakers?"

He quickly toed off the shoes, ripped off his socks and disappeared into the cabin.

"That was fast," she said to Jace. "Did something happen?"

"You might say that."

She glanced down at Jace's bare feet. "What happened to your shoes?"

"I'm donating them to the fishing hall of fame," he said.

"Oh, dear. That doesn't sound good."

Jace figured that was the preamble to a lecture he was sure to get. How could he be so insensitive? How could he have let this happen? Didn't he know how fragile this child was?

Instead she took Jace's arm. "Let me check on Nathan and then I'll come back out. Go sit on that bench and wait for me. We'll talk."

Her voice was kind and gentle, as if she'd already forgiven him. Jace wanted to kiss her right there, but deep inside he wondered if it was all an act. Anyway, he went to the truck to let Copper out and they both went to the bench to wait.

CHAPTER THIRTEEN

KAYLA CAME OUT of the cottage a few minutes later and sat beside Jace on the bench. "He'll be okay," she said. "He's watching TV and just told me a bit about what happened. Something about a dead fish being somebody's mother."

"I didn't mean to screw this up, Kayla," Jace said.

"I know that. It's just that his mother's death is fresh on his mind. It still hurts and will for some time."

"Who would have thought a simple trip to the trout farm could have ended up like this, with Nathan reliving his mother's death?"

She laid her hand over Jace's wrist. "Everything in his life right now reminds him of his mother's death," she said. "Or the fact that she's no longer with him. He needs to relearn how to live without her in his life."

"I guess it's obvious now that I'm not the one to help him do that."

She smiled. "It's one setback, Jace. Your heart was in the right place. You only meant to show Nathan a good time. After all is said and done, having a heart in the right place is the most important aspect of raising a child."

Her words cut deep into his chest, and he sucked in a painful breath. "I'm not going to raise him! Don't you see that, Kayla? I'm only going to ruin him, make him hate me. If you don't even tell him he has a father, that's fine with me. Let him go back to his grandparents and have a normal life."

Jace stood, walked away from the bench and stared over the manicured lawn of the mountain inn. Each breath was an effort. For heaven's sake, he wasn't going to cry, was he? It was sad, sure, but he was right. He had no business raising a kid, especially one with these delicate problems. He hadn't asked for this. He didn't want it. Hell, he had enough problems raising a dog, and he prayed often enough for guidance in that arena.

"Who can say what a normal life is, anyway?" Kayla said, coming to stand beside him. "Susan didn't think a life with her parents would be normal for her son." Soft hands came to rest on his upper arms, and suddenly his breathing eased. "Jace…" Her voice was calm and comforting. "This was a bad experience. I wish it hadn't been, but no one said this would be easy. You've lived your life as an independent man, and suddenly you're faced with a needy child, your son. We've got another full week. Let this play out."

He crossed his arms over his chest. Her hands massaged his tense muscles, running up and down his arms until he relaxed. The tension melted from his body until he suddenly leaned back against her.

She turned him, looked into his eyes. All at once, it was as if the problems of the world, and especially of this little corner of it, could be solved by trusting in the wondrous blue of those eyes. Jace wrapped his arms around her and drew her to his chest. They stood that way for several minutes, her cheek against his chest, his chin on the top of her head. "Tell me about his grandparents," he said.

"If I gave you the impression that they are bad people, I was wrong," she started.

"They're fine, upstanding, moral folks. They have friends, business associates. They lead a busy life. And they certainly hadn't planned on having a nine-year-old in their home at this stage of their lives."

Jace felt a lightening of the awful weight on his shoulders. "But they'll take him?"

"Yes, they will. They will treat him kindly, give him what he needs, manage his trust fund…"

She gave Jace a sharp look. "Oh, I hadn't meant to…"

"Don't worry," he said. "I'm not interested in whether or not Nathan inherited any money."

"I know that. I never thought for a moment that you were. Anyway, the Wagoners will provide for Nathan, see him through his education, instill proper values, I would think."

"Then what's the problem?" he asked. "Nathan already knows them. He's comfortable with them. They are his grandparents, for heaven's sake. It's the perfect solution." He paused, waiting for her facial expression to change from worry to acceptance. There was no change.

"The problem is…" She continued, "is that Susan didn't want that. She made me promise to find you and determine your suitability as a father."

He exhaled a long breath. "I guess today showed you just how unsuitable I am."

"No, it didn't. You're new at this and you're scared. That's understandable. But I believe, in the end, you will be entirely suitable." She placed her hands on each side of his face. "You're a good man, Jace. Crazy as it seems sometimes, I could see myself…" She stopped, bit her bottom lip.

"See yourself what?" he asked.

"Never mind."

See herself with him? See herself giving Nathan over to him? What did she mean?

"The point is," Kayla continued, "Susan did not want her parents to raise Nathan, primarily because they aren't open, outgoing people. They wouldn't introduce Nathan to the joys of childhood, the exhilarating experiences he could have in life." She sighed heavily. "One of Susan's greatest regrets, which she expressed to me on her deathbed, was that she had always been too busy being a working woman, being a responsible mom, to teach Nathan how to have fun. She'd always hoped for the time to take Nathan to wonderful, exciting places, but she didn't have that chance.

"If Nathan goes with the Wagoners, he will live a protected, secure life, but it is doubtful he will ever enjoy the undiluted joy of being a carefree boy. He will be cheated out of the best parts of life, the things Susan wanted him to know to become a happy, normal young man."

She smiled. "He doesn't need you to teach him math or manners. He knows that already, or he will. He needs you to teach him to be a boy first and then a man. The Wagoners can't do that for him. They will be so concerned about raising him with proper structure and etiquette, that they will never love him enough to let him be the person he could be. I can't do that for him, either. But you, Jace..." Her hands grasped his arms again. "You're his father. You can introduce him to the parts of his personality he doesn't even know exist yet. The little boy parts."

He frowned. "Why? Because I act like such a dumb, stupid little boy?"

"No. Because you are a man who, despite

the problems in your early life, found the little boy in you and didn't let it die."

He scoffed. "Ask my mother what she thinks about that. She wants nothing more than for me to run the family Christmas tree farm, and I disappoint her every time she brings it up. She never gives up hoping that I will be a man, one she can be proud of."

Kayla smiled. "I can't advise you about that. But as far as Nathan is concerned, let's give this another shot, okay? When do you want to see us again?"

He cupped the back of her head, smiled at her warmly. He was feeling better, thanks to her. "That's a leading question, lady. When are you free?"

"You know what I mean. I'll take Nathan tomorrow to get new sneakers. Are you playing anywhere tomorrow night?"

He was. A decent place where kids were as welcome as adults. "The pizza place at Sawtooth Center. You know where it is?"

"I do. We'll be there."

"I'm playing solo so make sure your applause is loud and enthusiastic."

"Of course."

He leaned down and kissed her, a quick

but passionate press of his lips to hers. And he was entirely satisfied to feel that she kissed him back. Then he whistled for Copper and headed for his truck. When he left the inn driveway, he was starting to wonder if he wasn't in real trouble this time—and not just about a kid who'd suddenly walked into his life.

CHAPTER FOURTEEN

SINCE THEY HAD plans for pizza on Friday night, Kayla and Nathan stayed in on Thursday night. No cook, Kayla had managed to put together a feast of grilled cheese sandwiches and canned spaghetti. Ice cream for dessert was the perfect ending.

"That was really good," Nathan had said. "Grandma never lets me have grilled cheese for supper."

Kayla smiled. "I'm not in favor of lying, you understand, but I'm thinking we might *avoid* telling Grandma about all the ways we've altered your diet since you've been with me."

"I know what you mean. My mom used to say things like, 'Why open a can of worms?'"

"Exactly." Kayla pulled down the covers of Nathan's bed and began fluffing the pillows. "I guess you've been missing your mom a lot today."

"Yeah. That fish made me think of her." He giggled. "Not that she was anything like that fish, but…"

"I get it," Kayla said. "Maybe we should talk about the fish and what happened today?"

He sat on the bed and crossed his legs. "You're mad at me, I guess," he said. "I ruined my sneakers and got mad at your boyfriend."

Kayla almost choked on her soda. "Boyfriend? You think Jace is my boyfriend?"

"Well, isn't he? You're always making plans for us to be together. You make those funny eyes when you look at him. And he's always touching you even when there's no reason to."

Kayla couldn't quite look Nathan in the eye. "I don't know where you come up with this stuff. I like Jace, sure. He's a nice man, but he's not my boyfriend." She laughed, a nervous sputtering sound.

"Then why are we always with him? This was supposed to be our vacation."

She should have anticipated this question. Nathan was so bright and inquisitive. But she wasn't ready for it, and now was stumped for an answer. "I don't know," she said. "We met him the first day we were in town when we went into his store. He seemed like a neat guy, one who could tell us about what there is to do around here."

Nathan didn't say anything. Uncomfortable, Kayla finally looked him in the eye. "What?"

"You could have Googled that."

"Okay, that's true." She searched the recesses of her mind for a plausible explanation. "Here's the thing, Nathan. Jace is someone your mother and I used to know way back when we were in college." Not exactly true, but it was a better reason for Kayla wanting to see him today. If only Susan had known him, why would Kayla seek him out now?

"So he was your boyfriend in college?"

"No. He was never my boyfriend. Not even remotely so. No way." *That's enough denial, Kayla*, she thought. *He gets it.*

"Then he was my mom's boyfriend?"

"Kind of. She did talk about him sometimes. Your mom liked Jace. She thought he was fun and interesting. And kind. And I just thought that maybe she would have wanted you to meet him. I had already decided to take you on a little vacation, and the mountains seemed like as good a place as any. And so, well, we're here, and we're having fun, aren't we?" *Please, Nathan, don't read more into this than what I've told you.*

"Yeah. It's fun, if you don't count fishing."

"I think maybe we should talk about the fishing. I know you were angry with Jace when the fish died."

"Only because he said we would throw our fish back."

"Yes, I understand, but you realize that it wasn't Jace who killed the fish."

His face fell. "It was me. I jerked too hard on the fishing pole, and the fish went flying to Copper."

Kayla put her hand on Nathan's shoulder. "Oh, no, sweetie. You didn't kill the fish. He would have been fine. Jace would have taken him off the hook and thrown him back in. He…or she…would have gone back in the water and swum happily away."

"But Copper got him before that could happen."

"Yes, he did. But Copper didn't do it because he was mean. He did it out of instinct. He saw something moving, possibly something unfamiliar, and he went after it. It was an instinct that has been with him since his earliest puppy days." She waited for the story to sink in, and then said, "Think about putting your finger above a lit candle. You wouldn't do that, but what if you did? What if the flame was too hot? Would you leave your finger there?"

He gave her a typically preadolescent look. "That would be stupid."

"Yes, but the movement that would make you draw your finger away quickly is an example of instinct. You don't think about instinct, it just takes over. Sometimes it keeps you from getting hurt. Sometimes, instinct can even save your life."

"Copper was using his instinct today?"

"Yes. I don't know why exactly. Maybe he thought the thing flying through the air was a toy, and he wanted to play. Maybe he thought he was protecting you. The point is, he did what dogs do in the only way dogs know how to do it, with their paws and their jaws.

"And here's the main thing I want you to think about," she added. "You told me that you forgave Copper. When Jace was leaving today, you even ran outside and hugged Copper."

He nodded. "That's cause I knew about instinct before you told me."

"Maybe you did. Or maybe you just realized that what happened today wasn't anybody's fault. Not Copper's, not Jace's and certainly not yours."

After a moment, Nathan said, "Jace ruined his shoes today, too."

"I know he did."

"Maybe that happened because his instinct made him go in the pond and pick me up and bring me out."

Kayla felt the grin spread across her face and doubted that she'd ever had a bigger smile in her life. Maybe she had some mothering instincts of her own. She sat on the bed next to Nathan and gave him a hug. "I do love you, you little wiseacre. You're smart and adorable and clever beyond words..."

"It's okay, Auntie Kay. You don't have to keep saying things like that."

"Oh, yes I do." She drew back and tapped the end of his nose. "So can you forgive Jace like you forgave Copper?"

"Yeah, I know we're seeing him tomorrow night. I'll tell him then. What do adults say? Bygones are bygones?"

"That's exactly right. And you know what, Nathan? I'm sure Jace will be really glad to hear it."

THE NEXT MORNING Kayla's phone rang at eight o'clock. She recognized the name of the caller and the Virginia area code. "Hello, Sherry, how are you?"

Susan's mother answered in her typical calm, exact manner of speaking. "We're okay, Kayla. I was just calling to check on my grandson."

"He's right here. Would you like to talk to him?"

"No, that's not necessary. You can tell me what has been going on with the two of you. I can't imagine that there is much left to do in that area that you haven't done already."

"Oh, we're finding new things to do every day." Kayla glanced at Nathan, who was still in bed. She hoped he wasn't upset by his grandmother's unwillingness to talk to him. Since an open comic book lay next to him, she assumed he was okay with it. "I suppose you are missing Nathan," she said. "That's easy to understand."

"It's not just that we're missing him, Kayla. School starts in a week and we need to have him measured for the Page Academy uniform. And he'll need supplies and new shoes. And goodness, he'll have to have that hair cut!"

Kayla watched the sun come through the blinds and reflect on Nathan's mop of golden hair. She loved the fact that his hair had grown since they'd been in the mountains. But she supposed a shorter cut would be preferable to the folks at Page Academy. There was no doubt Nathan was going to receive an exemplary education, one his mother could never have afforded.

"We'll be home on Friday night," Kayla said. "That gives you time to get to the uniform shop and get his clothes and shoes."

"It's pushing our timeline, but I suppose it will work. I thought you might bring him back early."

"I don't think so, Sherry. I told you how long we'd be gone, and I truly believe that Nathan needs this time to adjust to his mother not being around. He seems relaxed and ready to enjoy life again."

"Wouldn't we all like that, Kayla? Well, all right. It will just be more difficult for Paul and me, but we'll manage somehow."

"Thank you, Sherry. I guarantee you that Nathan is fine, and he's having a good time."

"Tell him hello from his grandfather and me."

"I will."

Kayla disconnected and experienced the recurrent pang of guilt she'd suffered because she hadn't told Susan's parents of their daughter's request that Kayla be guardian for their grandson. The Wagoners had assumed, and rightly so, that they were going to be responsible for Nathan and be his legal guardians. Kayla had retrieved the legal documents from Susan's deposit box and transferred them to her own bank's vault without showing them to the Wagoners.

She'd hoped, and still did, that Nathan's future would rest with loving grandparents or a caring, nurturing father. Only when that decision was made would Kayla tell the Wagoners about Susan's final wishes for her son. She anticipated only a minor problem with Sherry and Paul. If Nathan remained with Jace and not the Wagoners, she didn't think they would object too strongly. But, on the other hand, might the Wagoners see this decision with regard to Nathan as a personal afront? She hoped they wouldn't fight to keep him if he was happy with her.

A HAPPY AND hungry crowd gathered at Marco's Pizza on Friday night. Jace had prepared the hostess for the arrival of his guests, and a table for two by the stage awaited. When Kayla and Nathan came in, Jace nodded to the hostess and she brought them to the table.

Nathan was decked out in a plaid shirt and nice shorts, a step above his usual attire of cargo shorts and T-shirts. Jace couldn't help noticing that he had on new shoes. He'd obviously tried to tame his hair into some sort of style, but mostly the do fell every which way. For some reason Jace liked the kid's hair. Maybe it reminded him of his own pre-haircut days when he'd had the ponytail.

But it was Kayla who brought the smile to his face, or made the one he'd already plastered on grow even bigger. She had on a black-and-white-striped sleeveless top and black jeans. Something on her sandals sparkled from the overhead lights. There was an element of the exotic or maybe European about her appearance, especially since her hair was pulled back on one side and fell loose from the other in soft waves to her shoulders.

They both waved at Jace, and he continued his song, a Zac Brown Band favorite that usually got the crowd clapping along. He remembered that he had three more songs in this set before he could stop and go to the table. Maybe he'd skip a couple of verses and hurry the set along. But maybe he shouldn't. He was performing really well tonight and didn't mind these two hearing the best of Jace Cahill.

As soon as he was able, he went to their table. Kayla had been served a glass of red wine, Nathan something fizzy in a red plastic glass. "How you guys doing tonight?" Jace asked as he turned a nearby chair around and sat backward.

"Great," Kayla answered for both of them. "We ordered a pizza, a large, so there's plenty for you if you have time to sit with us for a while."

"I might just take you up on that."

"You sound great," she said. "I really liked every song in the set. How about you, Nathan?"

"Yeah, they were good."

"Most people like country rock," he said. "There's something about being in the mountains and cnvying Zac Brown having his butt in the sand." He focused on Nathan, hoped the kid was no longer irritated with him. "Have a good day, Nathan?" he asked.

"Yeah, we went gem mining. I got lots of quartzes."

"Great. You can have them cut and polished if you like. There are a couple of places in town that will do that for you."

"Maybe." Nathan paused. Jace could feel his toe tapping against the table leg. Finally he spoke again. "Can I talk to you, Jace? Just the two of us, man to man."

Jace passed a quick glance at Kayla. She shrugged. "Well, sure." He stood. "Want to go outside for some privacy?"

Nathan stood, and the two of them exited by the front door and chose a bench on the sidewalk. "What's this about, Nathan?" Jace asked him.

Nathan's leg pulsed back and forth under the bench. "It came to me yesterday…"

Jace smiled. Suddenly Nathan seemed older than his years. "What's that?"

"I owe you an apology," he said.

Jace felt his eyes widen. "You do?"

"For that whole fish thing. I don't know what got into me, but it wasn't your fault."

Again he sounded like a little man, giving a heartfelt apology without any excuses.

"It's okay, Nathan. We can all act kind of strange in tough times. Truth is I felt as bad about it as you did. Wish the whole incident had gone another way."

Nathan nodded. "And another thing. Even though I lost a pair of shoes, I'm glad you picked me out of that pond. I suppose I could have drowned. And I know that you lost a pair of shoes, too. Good thing Auntie Kay didn't yell at the two of us."

Wow, had they just experienced a moment of common bond here? Jace smiled. "Yeah, we were lucky there. Women don't usually get the mud excuse too well."

"I'm going to save my allowance money,"

Nathan said, "and buy you some new sandals."

"You don't have to do…"

"I want to. It's the right thing to do. And maybe we can try the fishing thing again, but go barefoot when we do. Copper can come with us again. He was just acting on instinct, you know."

"Yeah, I knew. Okay, Nathan, that would be great." Sensing the conversation over, Jace said, "I bet the pizza's at the table by now. Want to go in?"

"Sure. I said what I came to say."

Jace thought about thanking Nathan for his honesty, for the apology. But he didn't. Somehow he figured it would only ruin this moment of manliness for the kid. Jace simply put his hand on Nathan's shoulder and they walked back into the pizza shop.

The pizza had been delivered to them. Jace noted right away that before he sat down, Nathan turned his own chair around backward, just as Jace had done earlier, until he realized he'd have trouble reaching the pizza. It was a sign of solidarity, however, that Jace didn't miss.

SUNDAY WAS FAMILY day at the Cahill farm. Though Carter and Miranda had taken today for themselves, a shopping trip to Hickory to pick out furniture. Kayla envied doing something so simple, so mundane as selecting a new sofa and chairs. The couple had dropped Emily off at Cora's, and she immediately went to Jace, then ran to find Nathan.

They were a cozy group this sunny green Sunday. Jace went to the barn to tend to the animals. Ava stayed in the house checking some family records, she'd said. Emily and Nathan played in the yard, and Kayla and Cora, holding glasses of lemonade, sat in a comfortable pair of lawn chairs in the backyard while the beef roasted in the oven.

"So tell me, Kayla," Cora said, "how are you and Jace getting along?"

Though the directness of the question surprised her, Kayla responded with a vague answer. "Fine, Cora. We've become good friends. Jace has suggested some interesting things to do in the area."

"That's nice. How do you know Jace again, Kayla? I can't believe you just walked into High Mountain Rafting and started up a conversation with him that has led to you two seeing so much of each other."

Kayla could have stuck to the original story, but she figured Cora already figured out that she and Jace were more to each other than friends who'd met in an outfitter shop. "Honestly, Cora, I knew of Jace before I came to the High Country."

Cora nodded. "I thought so. Did you know him in your past, perhaps when you were in college?"

"No," Kayla answered honestly. "Jace was a friend of my best girlfriend, a girl named Susan. They dated for a while, and Susan used to talk about him."

"I remember that name," Cora said. "Jace never tells me much, but I recall him saying he was seeing a girl in college named Susan. Because he mentioned it at all I thought something might come of it. Whatever happened to her?"

Kayla explained about Susan's death. "Actually Nathan is her son, and I'm his godmother, so I guess you could say that there is a connection there." Kayla paused to make certain she didn't reveal too much. "Susan had kept up with Jace's life and she knew he lived here in Holly River. When I tried to come up with a place to bring Nathan to escape his grief, I thought of this spot right away."

"Nothing like the mountains and the beauty of nature to calm a person's soul," Cora said. "Still, that poor little boy. Where is his father?"

"He's not in Nathan's life," Kayla said. "It's possible that Nathan will go to live with his grandparents."

"I guess that's good. These people will take care of him?"

"They are very conscientious," Kayla said. "They'll see that Nathan has whatever he needs."

"So I guess Jace knows that this boy is an orphan? I hope he's been sweet to him while you've been here."

"Yes, he's been very nice."

Cora stood from her chair. "I'd better go check the meat. Maybe you want to check on the kids."

Kayla watched Cora go into the house. Then, from the far recess of the backyard where she'd gone to visit the children, she saw Jace enter the house shortly after his mother did.

JACE WALKED UP behind Cora as she popped several potatoes into the oven. "Smells good in here," he said.

She whirled on him. "I swear, Jason Cahill, if you ever opened up to me about anything, I'd fall over in a dead faint."

Plainly she was overreacting about something. "What are you talking about? What haven't I told you this time?"

"About your past with Nathan's mother, Susan. Why didn't you tell me? It just breaks my heart to think of that boy without his mother. Especially since you could do so much to help."

"Who told you about me and Susan?" he asked, though he knew the answer. "She had no right to tell you anything." Especially about the baby Susan had nine months after they'd broken up.

"Well, she did, and thank goodness for her honesty, at least. Now maybe we can do something to make that boy's life better."

A few choice words for Kayla jumped into Jace's mind. How could she? She'd promised not to say anything. "Mama, you're jumping way ahead of the game here. You know how

I feel about being a father. I've never wanted to be one, and I don't now."

"A father? Who said anything about you being a father?"

Cora stopped, stared at him. Jace's heart pounded against his rib cage. Was it possible that Cora didn't know and he'd just spilled everything? Movement at the back door caught his eye, and he stared over Cora's shoulder. Kayla stood in the entryway, her head slowly shaking. Her mouth silently formed the word "No."

In a quivering voice, Jace said, "You didn't tell her?"

"I didn't," Kayla said.

Cora glared at Kayla and then at her son. "You're that boy's father," she said. "It all makes sense now." She stood there breathing heavily while he and Kayla watched. "Admit it, Jason. And then step up and do the right thing."

CHAPTER FIFTEEN

KAYLA WATCHED THE muscles in Jace's face tighten one by one. A hot flush came to his cheeks. She wanted to reach out and touch him, to calm him as she'd done in the past.

"Well…" Cora wrung her hands on her apron. "You're obviously not denying it."

His voice was barely above a whisper. "No, I'm not denying it."

"Oh, Jace…" Cora's words were fraught with emotion. "What are you going to do about that sweet angel out there who suddenly is without his mother? And where have you been for these first years of his life?"

"I just met him," Jace said. "The truth is, I just found out he even existed." He shook his head several times before adding, "I… I don't know yet what I'm going to do."

Cora turned to Kayla. "And what about you? I understand you're the boy's godmother. I suppose that gives you the right to have a say in his future. And that's why you're here, isn't it? To find someone who will love that child? Could it be Jace? What have you decided?"

Kayla shook her head as Jace had done. Neither one of them had an answer for Cora. "I...haven't yet."

"Someone had better come up with a plan," Cora said. "Because this issue isn't about the two of you bickering over who will care for this boy."

The shock had left Jace's face to be replaced with a spark of anger. "We haven't bickered, Ma. We both want what's right."

"I hope that's true, because this is about a lonely child who needs love and guidance."

Jace's voice raised another notch. "We know that. We understand what's at stake. Kayla and I are trying to come up with a solution that works for Nathan."

Cora stared at the floor, then she straightened and looked at him in the eye. "Why am I dreading the very thought of what that solution will be, Jace? I know you. I know how you've avoided responsibility your whole life. I suppose I'm partly to blame for that, but I'm afraid this will be just another in a long string of decisions you've avoided."

"I'm not sure what you're talking about, Ma, but it's pretty obvious that I can't avoid a decision about this matter."

"I don't know, son. You're thirty-two years old and still haven't decided what to do about your future."

"But we've been through all of this."

"I'm not done. Guiding those rafts down the river a couple of times a week, playing your guitar. That's not responsibility, Jason Edward. That's having it your way, all the time.

"I've made excuses for you throughout your life because you had a tough beginning and a father who didn't treat you fairly. And as long as you didn't hurt anyone else, I was happy to stand up for you. But now you're a big, healthy, strapping man, and your father is dead, so no more excuses." She glared into his eyes. "This time it's different. This is about another little boy—your son."

Jace pulled out a dining chair and sat heavily. "Ma, you're coming to conclusions that haven't been decided yet. Conclusions that must be reached by Kayla and me. Don't you think we both want Nathan to be happy and well cared for?"

Suddenly Cora's eyes widened. "What did you mean by you've only 'just met him,' Jace? Do you swear to me that all these years you haven't been content to lollygag around Holly River while that boy was raised solely by his mother?"

"No, Ma, of course not. I didn't know anything about Nathan until Kayla showed up at High Mountain."

Cora looked at Kayla for confirmation. "That's right, Cora. Jace didn't know."

"I guess I'm relieved to hear that," Cora said. "But what it really means is that you've got a lot of making up to do."

"I'm aware of that," Jace said. "And how to make up for the fact that Nathan grew up without knowing he had a father is what I need to work out. I can't do anything about the fact that Susan kept him a secret."

"Does Nathan know?"

"No, he doesn't, and Kayla and I aren't telling him until something definite has been arranged. Nathan has only just recently decided he likes to hang around with me. At first we didn't seem to connect on any level."

Cora's eyes softened, and she went to her son and put her hands on his arms. "There's still time, Jace. You just have to keep trying. You're my baby, and I guess I've spoiled you. But sweetheart, you have a heart as big as all of North Carolina. Don't sell yourself short. You can give this boy exactly what he needs."

Jace stepped away from her. "Stop it, Ma. You have no idea if what you're saying is true. I don't know if I can give Nathan what he needs, so how in the world could you know it? You're right about me. I'm self-centered, a live-free-or-die hermit who doesn't even get his mail delivered. I have a small cabin and one dog for a companion. I live week to week, and sometimes I wonder how I'm going to keep Copper in dog food. The way my life is now I certainly can't afford to raise a kid, to educate him, help him grow into his future."

Jace's tirade made Kayla's heart ache for him. Jace Cahill didn't know or appreciate his own potential.

"Then change, Jace," Cora said. "That's what parents do. They sacrifice. They do what is necessary for their children."

"Is that what my father did, Ma? Did he

sacrifice for me when I was sickly? Did he ever sacrifice for Robert?" He clamped his lips shut and shook his head. Perhaps he knew he'd gone too far. "I'm sorry. I didn't mean to bring that up. But now that I have, you know darn well it's you who is sacrificing for Robert, not my father. Raymond Cahill made no provisions for the son he refused to acknowledge."

Kayla backed toward the door. She suddenly felt uncomfortable, almost like a voyeur caught in the middle of intimate Cahill family details. Though she knew the love between mother and son was strong and would survive this rift, she ached for both of them. This man, now dead, this Raymond, had certainly done a number on both of them. "I should go outside," she said.

Jace held up his hand. "No. It's all right. My mother and I are done for now. I'll be…" He waved his hand vaguely, pointing to no place in particular. "Somewhere out there." He pivoted quickly and went into the main part of the house. A moment later, Kayla heard the front door slam just before she became aware of Cora's sobs.

Kayla put her arms around the older woman.

"We'll work it out, Cora. I care deeply for Nathan, and Jace is coming around."

"He's a good man, Kayla," Cora sputtered between sobs. "He just always had such a hard time. And he certainly didn't have a good role model for a father."

Kayla gave Cora a squeeze.

"He probably won't even come in for dinner," Cora said. "I've made him so angry."

"I'll go talk to him. He'll come in. And I have a hunch his appetite will be as strong as ever."

Cora smiled, tried to chuckle at that remark. "That beautiful boy, Nathan, is my grandson," she said, her voice rising with the sheer wonder of the knowledge. "Now that I know the truth, I realize how much he looks like Jace did at that age. I hope Jace decides to keep that child as part of this family."

Me, too, Kayla thought as she left the kitchen.

HE WATCHED HER come toward the apple orchard. He hadn't tried to hide, instead picking a large tree laden with ripening apples and sitting with his back against the bark and his arms wrapped around his knees.

Kayla had come into his life like a whirlwind, determined to shake up everything about the way he lived. And she'd done a bang-up job. The day she told him Nathan was his son, the fundamentals of his existence began to take new shape and meaning. Suddenly his work at High Mountain didn't seem good enough, and he no longer had a clear definition of who he was as a man. And today he'd disappointed his mother, who wanted nothing more than to be proud of him. Well, maybe she did want something more than her son running the tree farm now. She wanted a grandson.

Without speaking, Kayla sat next to him in the shade of the tree. After a moment, she said, "How are you doing?"

He focused on his knees. "Just dandy."

"Don't be upset with Cora. She doesn't know how difficult this situation has been for you, how hard you've tried to form a bond with Nathan."

He turned to stare into her eyes. "How about how hard I've tried to feel like a father to Nathan? That's the crux of this whole thing, isn't it? How to make me into a father? How to make me want to be one with all the trimmings that come with the position?" He refocused on his knees. "By the way, the biology of my parenthood is established. I got the report from the DNA testing lab yesterday."

"You did?" Kayla touched his arm below the short sleeve of his plaid shirt. "Was there ever any doubt?"

"No. The biology is the easy part. I guess I could tell from the beginning that Nathan is part Cahill. Curly hair like my mother's, and I suppose a few characteristics of mine. But how am I supposed to feel like a father in spirit, in dedication, in caring?"

"All of this might come to you…"

He noticed that she didn't say the instincts *would* come to him. Now she said they *might* come to him. She was beginning to doubt, to see the inadequacies in his makeup, the ones he'd always known existed.

"Each day is a new beginning, a chance for you to be with your son," she said.

"Stop it, Kayla! That's hogwash and you know it. There have been small changes, but nothing to make either one of us believe that a miracle could be just around the corner. It's time we both stopped kidding ourselves."

The hurt in her eyes was almost his undoing. Just by one simple look she could make him feel like less than a man. He didn't want to be that person he saw through her eyes, but he couldn't become what was never in the cards for him.

"Kayla," he began, with the intent of salvaging what he could of her opinion of him. "I don't think you have any idea what the last week and two days has meant to me." He took her hand and held it tightly as if it were a lifeline. "You are the last person I want to disappoint. You've tried so hard, and you've believed so strongly that I could be the father you want for Nathan."

His eyes clouded. Her face blurred. He cleared his throat. "You have shown such faith, almost enough for me to believe I can pull off this parenting thing. But I can't be the person you want me to be. I've thought it through every which way. I've thought of nothing else for days. What's the best for Nathan? For me? For Kayla? And I've come to the conclusion that what is best for Nathan is to go back to the people he knows, the familiar life that will comfort him and prepare him for what's ahead."

Her voice was soft and gentle. "And what is best for you, Jace? To forget I ever came here, because I'm ready to admit that maybe it was a mistake…"

He slipped his arm around her shoulders and pulled her close. "That's not possible," he whispered into her hair. "I will never forget you came into my life. It's not just that I can't forget you. It's that I don't want to. I want to remember your determination, your drive, your unending hope that a family could be made from the mess I created ten years ago."

She looked up into his face. "Oh, Jace, don't give up. You're so close to becoming what Nathan needs."

He cupped her face. "I'm not, Kayla. And as much as I want to be what that child needs, I want to please you just as much. I would do anything to be the man who will make both of your dreams come true. Kayla, I can't stop thinking about you. I've never felt…" He paused, leaned down and kissed her.

The kiss was long and deep and wonderful. And when she drew back, her eyes were moist, her breath uneven. "Your mother is right, Jace. This isn't about us."

"No?" He tried to smile. "Then why when I kiss you does everything else in the world suddenly seem possible? That the worst of my problems can be conquered and everything will turn out okay? Why does being near you make my palms sweat and my heart pound? And why when I know I can't make you happy and proud, do I feel like less of a man and twice a failure? I know Ma means well, but she was wrong when she said this situation is only about Nathan. This week has been about us, Kayla, as much as it has about Nathan. I can't separate the two."

She bit her bottom lip, slowly nodded her head. "I know. When I came here I didn't intend to have sympathetic feelings for you. That certainly wasn't fair to you. In fact, I even resented that you didn't know about your son, as if it were your fault."

He started to speak, but she held up her hand. "That was Susan's fault, only hers. And even though she kept this secret for so long, and that was wrong, I tried to keep my promise to her. But nothing now is what I thought it would be. I thought I would make arrangements for Nathan, ones his mother hoped would work, and I would go back to my real life…"

"And that life is in Washington," he said. "Do you think I haven't considered that? Can you for one minute imagine living in Holly River?"

He searched her face for her answer and read in her sad eyes the truth of her conviction to her position in Washington.

"I can't accomplish my goals in Holly River," she said.

"I know. You should go back to your life," he said, "and pick up where you left off. And Nathan will be happy being near you, even if he lives with his grandparents."

"You will never convince me of that, Jace," she said. "I'm sorry. Maybe I'm the original foolhardy optimist, but I can see that boy with you for years to come. I just believe…"

"I know you do, but honey, you're wrong. I can't do this. I can't tear that child away from what he knows, from a solid chance for a good future, for an uncertain life with me. My mother is right about one thing. I'm a flunky and a failure, and a man who has avoided serious responsibility his whole life."

"No, you're not."

"Yes, I am. Do you know how I met Susan? Why I was in college in the first place? I did just well enough in my PE classes to avoid flunking out. And why? So I wouldn't have to work in that dang paper mill next to the man I hated. I'd confronted him enough times in the past to realize I'd do anything, hide out anywhere, to avoid confronting him again."

He smoothed his hand down her hair, letting the soft silkiness drift slowly through his fingers. She was so much more than pretty. She was honorable and caring. She even cared about him. God help him, if he didn't know that he was Jace Cahill, ne'er-do-well bachelor and family disappointment, he'd swear he loved her. He could almost believe she'd started to change him. Almost.

"I promise you this, Kayla," he said. "You can tell Nathan I'm his father if you want to. If you don't, I understand. But either way, I will support him. I don't have a lot of money now, but I'll get it some way. I want to contribute to his life." He stopped, took a breath. "No, I *need* to. I don't care if he knows where the money came from. It's enough that I know. And maybe someday, you and I..."

She stood. "I'm not leaving until Friday," she said. "I'm not giving up until then, either. On Friday, if you haven't changed your mind, Nathan and I will go." She bit her bottom lip until the delicate flesh turned pink. "We will manage without you."

She stood straight, with determination and resolve. He rose, took her in his arms again. "I'm sorry, so sorry."

She pushed gently against his chest and turned away. Over her shoulder she said, "Please come inside for Cora's dinner. She's actually worried you might not forgive her for what she said. Silly, isn't it? We all have to forgive." Then she walked back to the house.

CHAPTER SIXTEEN

JACE WAS UP early Monday morning. Truth was, he didn't think he'd slept at all, so the six o'clock hour wasn't difficult to face. He had coffee on his porch, watched the sun rise over the mountains and dressed for his trip to Wilton Hollow. He hadn't promised Robert he would be there for his first day of school, but somehow it seemed the thing to do.

There were no river trips as usual on a Monday but he could be at High Mountain for the scheduled zip-lining adventure. Heck, maybe he'd even drive the bus out to the mountaintop himself. Perhaps a bit of honest work was just what he needed.

The Kirshner household was in a state of near chaos when Jace arrived at seven thirty.

"Thank goodness you're here," Gladys said. "Robert won't come out of his room."

Jace glanced at the coffee table where he'd

left the five pennies. They were all gone, so Robert knew what an important day this was for him.

Jace went to the boy's room and knocked lightly on the door. No response.

"Robert, it's Jace. I'm coming in."

He stepped inside the door and stared into his brother's frightened eyes. Other than the stark terror etched in his face, he looked pretty good. He had on a pair of chino pants, a nice solid-color shirt. His hair had been combed back off his forehead and maybe even trimmed some. Robert's shoes lay by his bed.

"You look pretty slick, buddy," Jace said. "Let's get your shoes on." He walked toward the sneakers, but Robert stopped him with a high-pitched sound of warning.

"I'm not wearing them," Robert said when the keening stopped.

"You have to wear shoes to school, buddy," Jace explained. "And these are way cool. This brand's the best."

"I'm not going."

Those were the last words Robert spoke for the next fifteen minutes while Jace cajoled, teased, argued and pretty much did everything he could think of to motivate the boy. "This is a great opportunity for you, Robert," he said. "A chance for you to be with other kids, to show off your skills."

"No skills," Robert said, staring at his feet, which were covered in white socks.

"Of course you have skills," Jace said. "I've seen you do lots of things that make you very special."

Jace realized his mistake as soon as he'd said the words.

"Don't want to be special."

"Too late for that, Robert. You are special, but in a good way. You're clever. You learn fast. You have a wonderful memory." He got down on his haunches in front of Robert and said, "What happened? Why did you change your mind about school?"

"People will make fun of me."

"If they do, your big brother will have something to say about that. But I doubt that will happen. Besides, you might be the smartest one in the class. Maybe not today, but after a few weeks. You're going to learn and grow so fast. I hope I still recognize you when I come to visit."

Robert thought a few moments and then said, "You come to school with me?"

"Today?"

Robert nodded.

And that's how Jace spent the morning of his brother's first day out in the world. Riding on a yellow school bus, bouncing along country roads for nearly twenty minutes. There were a half dozen other children on the bus. Each one seemed to occupy his own world, as did Robert. Finally the bus arrived and Jace walked Robert into the building, which actually looked very little like a traditional elementary or middle school. The paint colors were subdued, the lighting soft, voices mostly hushed. A calming environment.

A staff member came into the hallway, a plump lady who looked like she'd been made sweet by too many cookie recipes to count. "This must be our newest student," she said with a smile. "You're Robert."

He nodded.

"Come and meet the others." She took his elbow and led him down the hall. Once, he turned around and looked back at Jace. Jace waved, but never even had the chance to remind Robert that the bus would take him home this afternoon.

Jace reboarded the bus and settled in for a repeat bumpy ride back to Wilton Hollow, just as the driver had promised him. He didn't know how this day would end, but for now he believed he had accomplished something that wasn't all about him. Maybe by giving his time and energy to Robert, he wouldn't feel like such a heel for refusing to accept his own son. Probably not.

Jace arrived at the outfitter store a little before 11:00 a.m. One lone employee manned the premises, a young woman he'd hired a few weeks ago to fill in when all the guides were out on tours. She looked up when he came in, smiled and returned to her reading of what looked like a textbook. He remembered she was enrolled in the local college.

He took a bottle of water from the glass cooler, sat on a stool behind the counter and looked at his messages. There weren't many, but one stuck out from the others. "Harry Pratt," he said. "I wonder what he wants."

After chugging half the bottle, he dialed the foreign number that would connect him to Harry. The man had been gone for five years. Moved to Costa Rica after selling his outfitter business in a nearby town. Claimed he wanted to get away from it all, which he obviously did.

"CR Adventures, where thrills await," the voice answered.

"Is this Harry?"

"Sure is. This you, Jace Cahill?"

"It is."

"Thanks for getting back to me, son."

The familiar use of the word *son* seemed odd since probably only fifteen years or so separated the two men. Harry had to be pushing his late forties by now. "No problem. I'm kind of surprised to hear from you. I figured you guys who went off into paradise didn't remember us mountain folks."

"But I do remember you, Jace, that's why I'm calling. How would you like to experience a bit of paradise for yourself?"

"What are you talking about?"

"Look, Jace, I don't know how well you keep up on what's happening in Central American countries…"

Not at all.

"…but there has been a real boom in these

small countries. I got to Costa Rica at just the right time. I set up my first adventure business and now I'm getting ready to open my fifth branch."

"That's impressive, Harry," Jace said. "What activities are you offering?"

"Pretty much the same as I did when I operated in the mountains. Raft trips, kayaking. But I've added rock climbing and ziplining." He chuckled. "Might even branch out into bungee jumping. Your hard-core adrenaline junkies like that."

"It all sounds good," Jace said. "I'm happy for you. But I still don't see how any of this relates to me."

"I'm getting there." He took a deep, audible breath. "I need help, Jace. This business is growing faster than I can keep up. Tourists are pouring into Costa Rica, enjoying the cheaper vacation costs, but wanting the excitement my businesses offer. Right now it's just me and another guy who manage all four sites with the help of a handful of employees. I have assistant managers at each location, but I need someone on-site who can make decisions." He paused. "I'm running myself ragged, kid."

"Are you saying you want to hire me?" Jace asked.

"That's exactly what I'm saying. For a managerial position, not as an assistant. You've got experience. You know what you're doing. You've had all the safety training and lifesaving drills. Jace, you could step off the airplane and right into a manager's position at CR Adventures. And it's Costa Rica, buddy."

Jace's imagination whirled. "I don't know if it's true that I could manage a property, Harry. I haven't been as hands-on as I used to be."

"You telling me you don't know what to do if a passenger falls in the river?"

"Well, yeah, of course."

"You know CPR?"

"I do. Haven't had to use it in…well, ever."

Harry laughed. "Probably won't need to use it here, either. You can navigate a river?"

"I can navigate the Wyoga well enough. I don't know about what may be long, intricate rivers where you are."

"It's all the same, Jace. Trips may run an hour or two longer but the process is what you're familiar with. Pull in sixty bucks a ride, load up the rafts and drive a bus to the drop-off point. Appoint one of your staff to be guide and you wait at the pickup. It's just what you do now, isn't it?"

Jace had pretty much stopped listening after he heard the rate Harry charged. More than what he got for the same trip at High Mountain. "I suppose so, but Harry, why can't your guides do all this? Why do you need a manager?"

"Are you kidding? Jace, these boys do a good job for the six bucks an hour I pay them, but they don't know how to keep records, apply for licenses, keep the safety gear up to standards. They can't communicate with local officials. And worst of all, they can't sell a trip. I need a second-in-command, a guy who's got smarts and a personality. A salesman who has run a successful business stateside. And that's you."

True enough. Jace could do all that. He was a good detail man. He'd been doing it for years. And he wouldn't have to participate in trips every day, the part he disliked most. There were a couple of important questions he needed answered.

"When do you need someone?" he asked.

"Yesterday," Harry quipped. "Say yes and get your butt down here."

Jace thought of Nathan, his plans to see the boy occasionally in Virginia if Kayla decided to tell him he had a father. He didn't want to give that up. And he sure as heck didn't want to give up Kayla. He had hopes for a future with her, someday... But in the meantime, he had promised to support Nathan, and right now he didn't have the means to do that.

"I've got to ask, Harry. What's the pay for this position?"

"I can start you at fifty a year."

Fifty thousand? That was almost twice what Jace had reported on his last tax return. Granted, the money from a couple of his guitar gigs had gone right in his pocket, but most of them were reported on the proper legal forms. Wow. Fifty thousand dollars a year.

"I sense your hesitation, Jace," Harry said. "You're thinking why should you give up a sure thing like you've got in Holly River. Well, let me tell you...you can live like a king in Costa Rica for half what it costs you in the States. I can set you up in a nice beachfront apartment for under a grand a month. A few trips to the local markets, and your refrigerator is stocked for a month. When you said this area is paradise, you weren't kidding. But my advice is to get in on this deal before everybody else discovers what we've got down here."

Jace couldn't stop thinking about Nathan and Kayla. What would they think if he suddenly left the country? Nathan might not be the wiser if he didn't know of his connection to Jace in the first place. But Kayla. Would she think he was running away?

He couldn't consider that now. Yes, he would be leaving, but this was an opportunity for him to make things right for Nathan. With this job he could pay the grandparents whatever they wanted to keep the boy happy and well cared for. And Jace would feel like he was doing what he should for the child he'd fathered. At least as far as finances were concerned, he would be a responsible father. And because he was doing what was best, Kayla could tell Nathan about Jace and he could see the boy when he wanted to. But he would be in Costa Rica...

"There's one other thing," Jace said.

"Fire away," Harry said.

"I have connections here. My family. There's my mother, who's not getting any younger." Without mentioning that he had a son, or a half brother who depended on him, Jace said, "I wouldn't feel right leaving her without knowing I could come home if she needed me."

"So go home. Just give me a couple days' notice so I can fill in during your absence. After that, fly stateside when you need to. Hopefully not during the heaviest tourist season, but within reason, I don't see why you couldn't leave when your mother wants you to come."

Was this too good to be true? Jace had started thinking of this phone call as a sign, a gift from fate that would get him out of this horrible dilemma. He could take care of his son, at least financially, which would maybe make Kayla a little proud of him. At least she wouldn't think he was a complete washout. And she might even come to Costa Rica sometimes. And he wouldn't have to give up his freedom.

"I'll need some time to take care of High

Mountain," he said. "Maybe I'll lease my cabin."

"Take a week, Jace. But no longer. I've got to have someone here. If not you, then it will be someone else. But you're the guy I want."

"Give me a couple of days to sort things out," Jace said. "But this looks like a go as far as I'm concerned. It's a good offer, Harry."

They disconnected. Jace took a few deep breaths to calm his pounding heart. The hard part was still to come. He had folks to tell about his decision.

CHAPTER SEVENTEEN

HOLLY RIVER WAS abuzz the next morning with news about the return of Sam McCall's girlfriend, Allie. Jace ran into Carter at the River Café, and they sat down for a cup of coffee together.

"I heard about Allie. So she came back?" Jace said.

"Yes, she did. She turned herself in to Sam. He arrested her and she's sitting in our holding cell for right now."

"Wow, that has to be tough on Sam."

"It is, I suppose, but he's managed to get the judge to approve bail."

"Is she admitting to everything she and Sheila did with regard to Dale's marijuana activities?"

"Yes, as well as her knowledge of the thefts Dale committed. Allie is in a good bit of trouble."

Jace nodded. "But Sam is standing beside her?"

"Looks like it. He doesn't want her staying in the cell for long."

"Where is she going to go?" Jace asked.

"Beats me." Carter stared at the entrance to the café. "But we might as well get answers from the man himself. There's Sam."

Looking better than he had in weeks, and almost brimming with his old confidence, Sam strode up to the table. Jace figured that being reacquainted with his old love had brought about the change. For sure, Allie's return was a good sign that she wanted to make amends.

Sam pulled up a chair. "Just saw Allie and told her the bond should be effective in a few hours. She should be out this afternoon."

Without thinking what this whole process might have cost Sam, Jace bluntly asked, "Where'd she get the money for collateral?"

"I put it up," Sam said. "It was just a few thousand, and I could scrape that together. I mean, she didn't commit a capital crime or anything."

"No, she didn't," Jace said. "Good for you,

Sam. You've definitely done your good deed for today."

"Allie is really sorry," Sam said. "She said getting mixed up with Dale and Sheila was the worst decision she ever made in her life, and that includes sticking with an abusive boyfriend for a couple of years."

"By the way, Sam," Carter broke in. "Where is Allie going to stay? She can't go back to Sheila's cabin."

"That's the best news," Sam said. "I talked to Cici over at the Lovin' Leash. She said she'd hire Allie to work a few days a week, and Allie can set up an apartment in the back of the store. It's good for Allie. She loves dogs. And the fact that she has a job will look good to the county judge."

Jace's ears perked up at this good news. He was probably as happy as Sam was that Allie was back and employed. That meant Sam wouldn't be going anywhere, and the plan Jace had been working on this morning might just work.

"You know, that reminds me," he said. "I'm going to be leaving town in a few days," Jace announced.

Carter swallowed a huge gulp of air. "What are you talking about?"

"I'm moving, actually," Jace said. "Don't know if I'll be back, but of course, I'll visit."

Neither man spoke, probably letting the surprising news sink in. "Anyhow, I have to rent out my cabin and get someone to look after Copper until I can bring him along." He stared hard at Sam. "You still living in the studio apartment above the chiropractor's shop?"

"Yeah... Why? Not that I believe you are really planning to leave Holly River, but if you were, are you thinking of renting your cabin to me?"

"Why not? Copper loves it there, and though it's small, it's more room than you have now. Bet you can't even have company up in that small studio."

Sam gave him a sideways look. "I've always managed."

Jace chuckled. "But think about what I'm offering. Peace and quiet. No nosy landlord. Freedom to roam in the mountains behind the house. Just pay your utilities and a flat four hundred a month, and the place is yours." He set his face in a serious scowl. "And take good care of my dog."

"Now wait just a minute," Carter said. "This is going too fast for me. I don't know what's happening, but I don't like the sound of it."

Ignoring for the moment his brother's outburst, Jace said, "Think about it, Sam. I need an answer pretty quick."

"I don't need to think about it. I'm in, if you're serious," Sam said. "I've always liked your place."

Jace stuck out his hand. "Gentlemen's agreement?"

They shook on the deal.

"Maybe you'd better give me some time with my brother here, who looks like he's about to burst a blood vessel."

Sam stood. "Sure thing. See you guys later."

As soon as he'd left the restaurant, Carter whirled on his brother. "What is going on, Jace? Where are you moving to and why? You've never been interested in leaving Holly River."

"True, but now I am. I've got an opportunity in Costa Rica."

"Costa Rica! That's in Central America. You're not going to Costa Rica! What did you do, Jace, commit a crime and you're running away? Are you in witness protection or something?"

"Calm down, Carter. I'll tell you everything." And he did. He explained about the phone call from Harry Pratt, the generous offer that, according to Jace, he'd be a fool to turn down. The decent living arrangements the job provided, the frequent chances to come home. "It's a darn sweet deal," he said. "You've got to admit, Carter."

"I'm not admitting anything," Carter said. "Does this have something to do with Kayla showing up here with Nathan? Are you running away from your responsibilities to the kid? Because not only would that be wrong, but you told me that you didn't have to take Nathan if…"

Jace held up his hand. "I'm not running from anything, Carter. I'm leaving so I can take responsibility for my son." He leaned over the table to be closer to his brother. "Don't you see? Before that phone call from Harry, I had no resources to take care of Nathan. Now, with what Harry's paying me, I can afford two hundred a week, even more, to support Nathan."

"Pardon me if I point out one very significant resource, brother, that has been yours for the taking for a decade now, a flourishing Christmas tree farm not five miles from here that needs a strong hand to expand into something pretty terrific."

"Don't bring up the tree farm again. We've been over this a thousand times. I don't want to be pinned down to a nine-to-five job. And I'm not particularly pleased with the thought of Ma looking over my shoulder."

"So you're planning to take the boy to Costa Rica? Kayla is never going to go for that."

The same recurring pang of guilt that had been plaguing Jace since yesterday stabbed at his heart—the one part of his plan that wasn't ideal. No plan was perfect, right? There were always flaws.

"No, I'm not taking Nathan to Costa Rica," he said. "He'll live with his grandparents in Virginia, but I'll send money weekly. I'll make sure the grandparents don't have to assume any financial responsibility for my kid. And I'll visit him. I'm hoping that

Kayla will let me tell him I'm his father and that he's not alone."

"That's what you think being a father means, Jace? Providing financial aid? That's how you think loneliness is avoided? By visiting once in a while and sending a check?" Carter shook his head. "You've got a lot to learn about being a parent…"

"Cut the lecture, Carter. I've thought this through. I can't provide for the boy without giving up everything I value. By taking this job I don't have to do that. Besides, the kid doesn't even like me. He acts like I'm some sort of freak of nature. We may be able to work that out, but it will take time—time I don't have with my present circumstances. I've got to provide for Nathan now."

"And what about Kayla?"

"What about her?" Jace had to pretend as if he hadn't given a thought to Kayla's opinion. To admit the truth was to admit too much.

"I thought you two were getting close. Maybe I'm wrong, but you seemed to like her—a lot."

Jace shrugged. "She's all right."

"Miranda really likes her. They've talked

on the phone a few times and get along great."

"Isn't that nice?" The sarcasm in his own voice was enough to make Jace wince.

"What's with these answers?" Carter asked. "You're acting like some hard-nosed jerk who doesn't care about anything or anybody. And I know that's not you, Jace."

"That's where you're wrong, brother. I'm not acting. This is me trying to do the right thing. As far as Kayla is concerned, okay, I thought for a while that maybe…" He stopped talking, took a deep breath. "But forget it. She lives in Washington, DC. I live in Holly River, soon to be Costa Rica. Either way, there's not a lot of hope for a relationship spanning several hundred miles."

"You don't know that. You would just have to try harder."

"Right. Like I could compete with the drive of a political junkie who lives in the center of the action. I don't think so."

"We have politics in North Carolina, if you haven't noticed. I know Miranda and Kayla have talked about some of the needs the people in our community have. You were in on the discussion when we talked about improving the lot of folks on Liggett Mountain."

"Look, Carter, I appreciate what you're saying, but you're so far off base, you can't even see the base anymore."

"You don't think Kayla cares for you?"

"She may, a little. But I guarantee you she doesn't admire me. All she knows about me is that I got her best friend pregnant ten years ago and I'm not much to brag about now. And she's right. Ma's disappointed in me. You're disappointed. And Ava—good grief, she thinks about as much of my abilities as she would the leprechaun on a box of Lucky Charms."

Both brothers were silent for moments, leading Jace to believe that Carter had no argument against the truth. Finally Carter said, "Speaking of Ma, have you told her?"

"Not yet. Telling her and Kayla will be tough. I figured I'd tell Kayla on Friday. That gives me a couple of days to firm up my plans."

"I thought she and Nathan were leaving on Friday," Carter said.

"They are, and before you say it, I guess the coward in me chose that day because they would be gone soon. I'll go over in the morning and we'll work out the details of child support and whatnot. Ma? I figure I'll drive out to the house on Sunday and let her know. I've bought a plane ticket for the next day."

"Mama is going to freak," Carter said. "Hope you're ready for that."

Jace frowned. "I'll never be ready for that."

"I wish I could talk you out of this," Carter said.

Jace sucked in a quick rush of air that seemed to burn in his lungs. He sort of wished his brother could talk him out of it, too. But then he'd just be the same old flunky Jace with no plan, and no possibility of doing for Nathan what he should.

He stood, pushed his chair under the table. "I've got to go. You can imagine I've got a lot to do, especially now that I'm turning my cabin over to Sam. I'm working all day for the next two days. Got some major bookkeeping to do. Plus, I have a gig here at the café Thursday night." He raised his hand and studied the calloused fingers that had strummed a guitar for years. At least he'd been good at something.

Carter looked up at him with sadness in his eyes. "I'll miss you, little brother. You've always been there for me."

Jace patted his back. "I'll still be there, Carter. Only now I can offer you a sunny, warm vacation spot in the middle of a North Carolina winter." Before he could get ridiculously emotional, he turned away and left the café.

JACE DIDN'T SEE or hear from Kayla the next day. Maybe she was giving him time to think. If so, it was working. Even though he was busy at High Mountain, going over his records and assuming the responsibilities of one of the boys who'd gone out of town, he still felt like his day was missing something vital. He'd gotten used to seeing Kayla almost daily. He'd gotten used to the way she encouraged him, the way she made him feel.

Jace never used to worry about the way he felt about himself, but Kayla had changed that. Before, he'd been content to be Jace, the guy who lived like a hermit with his dog, the guy who could get a date when he needed one, the guy who was never called upon to fill a vacancy in a volunteer pool. The Happy Loner. Jeez, he could write a song with that title.

But now that a son had come into his life, he'd started to think about what kind of man he was. And he missed Kayla's input on important matters that affected him. He liked her touching him when he needed it, arguing with him when he needed that, too. He liked that when he thought about her, he never thought about where his next date was coming from.

So the following day, after working hard and being Kayla deprived, he ambled into the River Café around six o'clock to entertain the tourists who remained in town. He wouldn't have a big crowd, so if he only put out half effort, who would really care?

He was nearly through with his first set when she walked in and took a seat at a table for two near the stage. Did she know he would be there? Or was this a coincidence? And where was Nathan?

She smiled at him, the gesture so sweet, so natural, a pang seemed to split his heart in two. She had on a pair of denim jeans and a turquoise scoop-neck sweater that showed off the tan she'd gotten since coming to Holly River. Turquoise was her color, one of the earthy, genuine gemstone colors that made her seem like she was part of nature, especially with her hair loose about her shoulders. The candle in the center of the table burnished her hair a soft auburn, a beautiful fall color. He couldn't picture her in an office in Washington, DC. He could only picture her here in Holly River. But that didn't make any sense. He wouldn't be here much longer.

He finished his set, put his guitar in a rack and went to her table. "Is this seat taken?" he asked, nodding at the empty chair across from her.

"No. You're welcome to it."

He smiled. "You knew I would be here tonight or are you just out looking for fun?"

"I knew."

The simple admission made him feel warm inside. He pulled the chair out and then changed his mind. The last thing he wanted was to sit three feet away from her and dredge up chitchat. He wanted to hold her, kiss her, burn her sweet image into his brain. So at the risk of scaring her to death, he reached across the table, took her hand and hauled her upright. "Come with me. My break is twenty minutes." He grinned at her. "And if I go over, who cares?"

Her eyes widened, but not with fear. With a sense of adventure, the thrill of the unknown.

He walked her to the back of the restaurant, out the rear exit and into the park across the street, decked out with twinkling lights.

They sat on a deserted bench. Before reaching for her, he said the first words he'd thought of. "Nathan okay?"

"Yes, he's with a sitter."

"Good."

"I've missed you." He kissed her then. A full-on, never-wanting-to-stop kiss. She made a slight gasp of surprise and then leaned into him, giving of herself completely. He cupped the sides of her face, parted her lips with his and explored every inch of her mouth. She tasted spicy and sweet, sweet from being Kayla.

When they finally stopped, she breathed deeply and rested her forehead on his chest.

He could barely make out her words when

she said, "What are we doing? We can't keep on like this. I think your twenty minutes is up."

"Probably so. But I don't care. Let's go back to my cabin."

"Jace, we can't. I'm leaving tomorrow. I have to get Nathan home in time for school. I have to get back to my job."

"But we have tonight." And he would tell her about his plans tonight, before they… But this was supposed to be the new, improved Jace Cahill, the one who valued honesty, integrity. At least, he hoped he was.

"Yes, but if we…" She stopped, took a long, quivering breath. "I can't have one night with you and then leave as if nothing happened." She blinked hard. "How can we have this night and then nothing more? What if you forget me?"

He smiled. "Kayla, I could never forget you. Two weeks ago I didn't even know you, and now I believe with all my heart that you'll always be a part of me."

"But Jace, you sound like we're parting for good. Is that true? Are you giving up on Nathan?"

He raised her face and kissed her again,

a profound expression of his longing. "No, I'm not."

"Tell me, Jace?" She swallowed, her eyes glistening. "What about Nathan?"

Suddenly her words were the crashing-into-the-rocks moment he'd feared. Why had he been thinking to satisfy his own urges when the problem between them still existed? What a jerk he'd almost been. "I have a plan," he said.

She stared up at him, waiting, looking vulnerable and beautiful.

Even if she'd been willing, if he had talked her into going back to his place, he couldn't have gone through with what was on his mind and in his heart.

When had Jace Cahill become so committed to playing fair, he asked himself?

He took her hand and they stood. Then they headed back toward the café. "I'll tell you tomorrow," he said.

CHAPTER EIGHTEEN

THE DRIVE FROM the River Café to the Mountain Laurel Inn wasn't nearly long enough for Kayla to gather her thoughts and make sense of what had just happened. When she pulled in the drive to her cottage, she had decided two irrefutable facts. Why had she gone to the café tonight? Simple. Because she couldn't stay away. Was she sorry she had gone? As she moistened the lips that had been so thoroughly kissed, she knew the answer was no.

"How is everything?" she asked the college girl who had stayed with Nathan.

"Fine. Nathan is an angel."

They both spoke in a whisper since Nathan was fast sleep. The television, turned low, was a soft accompaniment to the boy's steady breathing.

Kayla smiled. Yes, Nathan was an angel. She paid the girl and watched her leave in her car. Then Kayla went to the edge of the bed and sat down. The urge to touch Nathan, to soothe his forehead, stroke the mop of blond curls, was almost more than she could bear. But she didn't want to wake him. Friday would be here soon enough.

"So what is your plan?" she whispered as if Jace were in the room. "Are you going to go on with your life as if we'd never come to Holly River? Have you come up with a compromise that you believe is fair to Nathan and that will ease whatever guilt you may feel? Or have you decided to be the father this child needs? Because I know you can do it, Jace."

In her heart, Kayla admitted the last choice was not the one Jace had decided upon. And how would she live with his decision?

She rested her palm lightly on Nathan's arm. "We'll make it right for you," she said. "If I have to leave you with your grandparents, I'll come see you every week. We'll have fun, we'll…" She couldn't go on because she knew that her words were empty, her promise not nearly what Susan wanted for her son. If Kayla gave Nathan to his grandparents, she would relinquish her rights as his guardian. His grandparents would make decisions about his life and future.

She stood and walked to the window overlooking the parking area of the inn. "No matter what he decides," she said, "I will forgive him. I have discovered what Susan must have known. Jace Cahill is a good man. He would have made a good father. But deep inside he doesn't believe that, and I don't think he's willing to try."

Kayla raised her face so she could stare at the stars. "I tried, Susan. You know that. Maybe I failed you, maybe I failed Nathan. But I won't be leaving this town without some scars of my own. One of those scars will be opened again and again, every time I think of him, because I understand now why you gave yourself to him, why you loved him."

She walked back to the beds, took her pillow and curled up on the sofa. She didn't need the bed tonight. She wouldn't be sleeping much.

THE NEXT MORNING Kayla woke up early. She decided to let Nathan sleep as long as he could. They had a lot to do and a long drive ahead of them. Jace texted her before she'd finished her coffee. He would be here at nine, hoped that would give them enough time to talk.

She'd stared at the text with a callous humor. There would never be enough time to talk about the last two weeks, the next few years.

A few minutes before nine, Jace arrived.

Kayla checked on Nathan before closing the door behind her and going outside. Jace greeted her with a quick, wonderful kiss—a sweet morning kiss that couples share. Only they weren't a couple.

Pointing to the two Adirondack chairs in front of the cottage, she said, "We'll talk here. Nathan is still sleeping, but I'll be able to hear him if he wakes."

Jace pulled his chair closer to hers, sat and took her hand. "I have something to tell you."

"I assumed that." She swallowed. "You might as well begin."

He cleared his throat, looked down at her hand in his. "I've made a decision about Nathan's future...and mine."

A quick sharp pain pierced her chest. She took a deep breath, and it subsided. *You knew this was coming*, she said to herself. "Oh?"

"I've had a job offer from an old friend, a guy who used to own a business like mine, but in Boone. I guess he was my competitor." Jace paused, rubbed his hand over the stubbled jaw that proved he hadn't shaved this morning. "He wants me to come work for him, doing basically what I do here in Holly River, but…in Costa Rica."

"Costa Rica?" She hadn't meant to utter the words so loudly, but her shock had taken over the moment he said them. "You're going to Costa Rica?" Of all the scenarios she'd thought about last night, a move to another country certainly wasn't one of them. "But we'll…" She stopped herself. "I mean *Nathan* will never see you."

He looked into her eyes. She was sure he could read the hurt and disappointment in them. She'd often been told she had expressive eyes, and knew now that it could be a curse.

"That's not so, Kayla. I can see Nathan almost whenever I want or need to. Not every day, of course, but if he needs me, I can come to him."

"By flying six hours, renting a car, driving to his home in Virginia? Come on, Jace, how many times will you do that?"

"You have to trust me, Kayla. I've thought this through from every angle. Do you think it's easy for me to leave my home, my family?"

"Sorry, but I'm thinking it must be." *Just as Costa Rica must be a most convenient way to avoid your parental responsibilities.* Kayla choked on a sob. *Oh, Susan, I never thought he would do this...*

"I can assure you it's not. And this decision is not one I made lightly.

"There are so many advantages to this move," he went on.

She tried to listen, but many of his words were lost in a fog of disillusion and disappointment. She heard him mention "financial responsibility," "significant pay raise," "lower cost of living," "booming tourist economy." He went on about the difficulties and benefits of leaving everyone he held dear and fleeing the country, but only one thought kept repeating in Kayla's mind. *You are running away, Jace. You can't face your fear of owning up to the results of your passion years ago.*

He laid his palm against her cheek. She jerked away from him.

"Kayla, think about it. I can send whatever Nathan's grandparents need to take care of him. I can't do that if I stay here. And I won't have to relinquish my connection to him. By law, I will be supporting him."

"Your *connection to him*?" she repeated, her words bitter and angry. "You are his father. There is no stronger tie than that. He is you. He is yours. Spiritually, biologically, genetically. It's not like someone just glued you together for a couple of weeks and now the glue is wearing off."

"I don't think that. Please, see my side of this. I only want to do what's right for Nathan."

"No, Jace, you want what is right for you. You don't want to give up your freedom, your lifestyle." She paused, collected her thoughts. His facial expression was glacial. She was hurting him, and it didn't make her feel any better.

"And you know what?" she said in a much

calmer voice. "I get it. If sending money to Nathan's grandparents every month makes you feel better, makes you believe you are meeting your responsibilities, I understand. You didn't ask for Nathan and me to come to Holly River. You didn't ask to be a father."

"No, I didn't. A lot of guys would have simply brushed off the whole idea of raising a kid. But I didn't. I want to contribute to Nathan's future. I want you and me to see each other..."

"What? With you in Costa Rica and me in Washington? Don't let your delusions of beautiful futures carry you away to the impossible, Jace. Support your son financially if you want to, but there is no you and me."

"There could be—"

"Stop it, Jace. I came here with my heart on my sleeve. I came here with a gift, the most important gift anyone can get. A child. But that's not for you. I get it." She sighed. "Maybe you are living with the idea of a future only a fool could dream up. But I've been living the last two weeks the same way. I kept believing, hoping, that you would see Nathan as the treasure he is. It's time we both stopped playing fools and faced reality."

She turned away from him. "You can go. You've said what you needed to say. I will tell Nathan's grandparents about you, and I will text you their phone numbers so you can deal directly with them from now on."

His hand pressed on her back. She stiffened. "Kayla, don't end it like this. Surely you can see what you mean to me, what the last two weeks have meant. I've fallen for you..."

"I said you can go. I have packing to do. Nathan and I have to get on the road."

He stood, took a few steps away from the chair he'd been sitting in. The front door of the cottage slammed, startling both of them. Nathan stood just a few feet away in his pajamas, the overly large ones with colorful rocket ships on the fabric his grandmother had bought him, saying he would "grow into them."

This morning, in his too-big pj's he looked like a little boy, rumpled, confused. How long had he been standing there? What had he heard?

"Ah, hi, Nathan," Jace said.

Nathan sniffed, ran his finger under his

nose. "We're leaving today. You know that, don't you?"

Jace looked away. "I know."

"You were going away without saying goodbye."

"You were sleeping," Jace said. "I'll see you again."

"But we had a talk, a man-to-man talk. That means you don't leave without saying goodbye. I said I would buy you new shoes. That was a promise from me to you. Men keep promises."

Jace shook his head, closed his eyes against every emotion that must have been bombarding him at this moment. Again Kayla thought, *He's a good man. He hurts.*

Nathan took a step toward Jace, stopped. Jace got down on one knee. "Come here, kid."

Nathan ran to him and hugged him fiercely, his arms wrapped around Jace's neck, his cheek against Jace's face. Jace's hands came slowly upward, enclosing his son in the most natural of human embraces, one that Jace had probably never received from his own father.

"You're a good kid," Jace said, the words

almost unintelligible. "I'll see you again. That's a promise you can believe in."

"When?" Nathan asked.

"Soon. As soon as I can."

And then Jace stood, took a long look at Kayla and headed for his truck.

THE DAY LOOMED long and unsettling for Jace as he drove to High Mountain Rafting. Perhaps he would go out with the first expedition and leave one of his boys to man the store. Physical activity seemed the only solace for the ache in his gut, the emptiness he was feeling. Nathan's hug, so sweet and genuine, had been spontaneous and surprising. If Jace weren't the cold, insensitive jerk Kayla believed him to be, he almost could convince himself he still felt the press of those little hands on the worn denim of his shirt.

No decision was irreversible, he told himself. For now, he believed he was doing the right thing, the only thing that would truly benefit Nathan and secure his future. Maybe someday he could establish a more traditional relationship with his son and with the woman who had brought him into his life.

Ah, Kayla…beautiful, determined, ambitious woman. She had turned his comfortable world upside down while at the same time opening his eyes to the possibilities of finding real love. He couldn't forget her, so he would, in time, try to prove himself to her. He would keep the promises he'd made— send money, visit when he could, and maybe before too long, Kayla would see that his actions had been self-sacrificing, principled and the best he could offer his son.

Jace parked and went into High Mountain. Billy was there already, probably demonstrating to the boss that he was worthy of the responsibility Jace had placed on him. Billy would be the one to keep High Mountain afloat through the winter months when kayaks were replaced with toboggans, and inner tubes with skis. The two men had discussed the future of High Mountain yesterday and since Billy would soon graduate from Taylor-Crowe College, he was anxious to show his abilities as caretaker of the business.

"Morning," Jace muttered as he came in the door. "I'm going along with the first busload today, Billy."

Billy waited until the customer he was

helping had gotten his change and then turned his attention to Jace. "Are you sure? I mean, you've been working so much on the books, I figured you'd keep at it today."

"Probably should," Jace agreed, "but I'm antsy, couldn't sit behind that counter if I had to. And besides, I'm leaving Monday and this is probably my last chance to join a tour. It's like taking a sentimental journey in a way."

"Okay. Well, Joe and Sandy are the official guides for this first one. You can switch places with them or drive the bus and wait at the pickup point for the rafts to come in."

"Yup, that's what I'll do," Jace said, looking out at the beautiful late-August morning. "I'll drive the bus and hopefully clear some of the cobwebs from my brain."

Both rafts had been loaded onto the trailer. Eager tourists had taken seats on the bus. So fifteen minutes later, Jace steered the vehicle onto the highway, headed for Tennessee. Three kayakers had also joined the group at the last minute, so the bus was transporting a large load. Joe kept them all entertained with tales of river monsters and mountain lore.

A half hour later the men went to work

dislodging the rafts from the trailer and setting the kayaks on the riverbank.

"Kayakers go first," Jace said. He helped the group of one father and two sons into their individual crafts. The irony of assisting in a family outing didn't escape him, and he tried not to think of the time he'd taken Nathan on this river. He'd pushed the kid too hard that day, expected too much. He hoped this father didn't make the same mistake. The youngest of the boys seemed to be about twelve, but unlike Nathan, he was eager to set off.

"Dad, let your sons go ahead of you," he shouted as the group prepared to leave. "This is a safe river, but that doesn't mean there aren't hazards along the way. Be aware of where your kids are at all times. If you have a problem, remember, the rafts will be along behind you, so stay calm." With a stern look at the boys, he said, "Have fun but no hotdogging. I'll see you at the pickup."

The kayaks had disappeared around the first bend when the High Mountain crew slid the two rafts into the water. Eight passengers each and one guide, a typical safe number for the basically smooth-flowing river. Jace watched the rafts float down river until the passengers' life vests were only specks of orange on the sparkling water.

"I'm going to miss the Wyoga," Jace said to himself. From what Harry had told him when he called to accept his offer, Jace knew that the river in Costa Rica had class-four rapids, much different from the easy-flow two-classers of the Wyoga. Jace would have to study up on his lifesaving techniques and his cautionary speeches to adventurous rafters.

He returned to the bus, took a bottle of water from his cooler and had a long swig. It would be almost two hours before the kayakers reached the take-out point and only a fifteen-minute drive by bus. Time to kill. Time to think. He fussed with his cell phone, trying to find a radio station that would keep him occupied, but when he noticed a failing charge he turned off the instrument. Couldn't be caught without enough power to make a phone call if need be.

After a half hour, Jace decided to head on down to his destination. Might as well wait there as here. He pulled onto the road, the now-empty trailer rattling behind him on the rough blacktop. The trip to the take-out point ran alongside the river, but trees and vegetation mostly hid the water from sight. Jace enjoyed watching the current when he had a view. After a few minutes, he caught a glimpse of the full rafts. Everything seemed fine, didn't appear as though one of his guys had been forced to jump in and save some-one.

And then he rounded a curve, and the calm peace of his morning was suddenly shattered. The kayakers had made great time, usually the case with young men or boys anxious to show off their prowess. As instructed, the kayaks holding the sons were ahead of the father. The first kayak, navi-gated by the youngest of the boys, the one Jace figured to be twelve, was significantly in front of his brother's.

The log jumped into Jace's vision almost as if it were a living thing. A large, glis-tening birch log that hadn't been reported yesterday when one of Jace's employees did the customary run along the river looking for obstacles. Must have rotted from the in-side out, and without enough pulp to hold it upright, crashed into the current last night.

River water flowed over and under the log, crashing into its weight and even creating a small waterfall.

At least the log was on the far side of the river. The flow of the side closest to Jace was no more than a class two, though where the water met the log, the force had become much greater. Jace pulled over, determined to watch the kayakers safely maneuver the obstruction. With commonsense planning and even minimum skill, all the kayakers should be able to stick to the calm side of the river and avoid a problem.

With common sense and minimum skill… The thought echoed in Jace's mind as the youngest boy neared the log. He should be steering his kayak away from the danger, but no. With a holler of anticipation he headed right for the log.

Jace jumped out of the truck, ran to the river's edge. Waving his arms, he yelled, "Hey, kid! Over here! You're heading for trouble."

The boy turned his head to look at Jace, and he tried to correct his trajectory. But it was too late. Either he panicked or the river caught him in a vortex of its own making, but the kayak headed right into the log. The front end crashed into solid wood, bounced back a few feet, dipped and went under the log. Jace's heart raced. With luck the kid would know to duck, and the kayak would keep upright and come out on the other side of the obstacle. But it was a skilled maneuver for even the hardiest of river riders.

After a few heart-pounding seconds, Jace realized the kayak was not correcting. The tail end of the craft was sticking up as if the front were stuck in the mud of the riverbed. He tore off his shoes and waded into the water, each second hoping, praying, the kid's helmet would show above water. But no. The kid had disappeared, and each second meant the difference between life and death.

CHAPTER NINETEEN

A DISTANCE OF perhaps one hundred yards separated Jace from the upended kayak. Not so much, especially for an experienced river swimmer like Jace. But today the current was running fast, even more so because of the fallen log.

Jace's strong arms cut through the water. He was only minimally aware of the chilly temperature, the debris catching on his jeans. He persevered, finding extra strength to fight the rapids created near the log. When he reached the kayak, he held on to the log, took a deep breath and dived under the water.

His vision was blurred, the water murky from silt churned up from the riverbed. Keeping one hand on the log so he wouldn't be washed downstream, Jace reached out for the boy. He swiped at water, flailing about in panic as seconds ticked away. Finally he grasped something solid and spied the bright orange of the kid's life vest. Why hadn't the vest kept him above water? He tugged on the vest, finding it immovable, as if trapped.

His lungs burned as he fought the impulse to surface and grab more air. But there was no time to take a breath now.

Grasping the vest strap, he followed it with his hand to where it had become snagged in the bark of the log. Jace pulled but couldn't free it. He remembered the knife in his pocket, the one he always took to work or on rafting adventures just in case. Thankfully he had remembered to bring it this morning.

Needing two hands, Jace wrapped one of his legs around the boy's body to maintain stability and flipped the knife open. He sawed through the nylon fabric of the strap and felt it give way. The boy's natural buoyancy lifted him to the surface. Jace followed him up.

When his mouth broke the surface, Jace gulped life-affirming air. His throat ached; his eyes burned from being open under water. But he spied the boy, floating unconscious, his face above the water. Now was the true test of strength. He would have to fight the current to get them both safely to the nearest shore.

He grabbed the boy by the chest and began swimming backward, long, deep, one-armed strokes to cover the fifty or so feet that remained between them and dry land. When he reached the bank, he dragged the boy up the slippery incline.

The urge to collapse next to the body and give his own labored breathing a chance to stabilize was strong, but Jace turned his attention immediately to the kid. He knew he should call for medical assistance, but his cell phone had been in his pocket when he entered the water. For now at least, the boy's chances rested with Jace.

He began CPR, pressing and releasing the heels of his palms on the kid's chest. His efforts were relentless. He wouldn't quit until either the boy stopped breathing or a medical expert told him he'd been too late in his rescue.

"Come on!" he shouted to the boy. "Breathe, Nathan, breathe! Don't you die on me." Water ran down Jace's face and mingled with tears streaming from his eyes.

Everything was a blur, the surrounding

vegetation, the rushing water, even the boy's father, who had managed to paddle near the log and had jumped in. The father was shouting, asking questions, demanding to know what had happened. Jace never stopped pumping the boy's chest even when he hollered to the dad and the other brother, "Call 911. Tell them we're at the Baker Bridge curve on the Wyoga. Tell them to hurry. And don't try to cross this river yourselves!"

Never stop trying. Life is too precious. Those were the two thoughts that kept running through Jace's mind until finally, with a choke and gasp, water spewed from the boy's mouth. He puked up at least a gallon of the foul stuff, but when he was finished, he was breathing. His eyes were open.

"Wh-what happened?"

"Hush," Jace said. "Don't talk. Your throat has to feel like it's made of sandpaper."

"It does."

Jace fell to the ground beside the kid, his chest heaving.

"Did you save me?" the boy asked.

Jace tried to smile, realizing for the first time that everything on his body ached. "It was nothing."

"Thanks."

Jace stared at the boy and realized his mistake from a few minutes before. He had called the kid "Nathan" just as naturally as if he'd been rescuing his own son. Suddenly his emotions were so near the surface that they hurt in his chest, Jace lifted the boy's head, settled it on his shoulder and gave him a fierce yet gentle hug. "You're welcome."

And at that moment he realized that he would have given his own life for this boy, a stranger, who deserved to live his life until he became a doddering old man. And there was no difference between this kid and the one who was Jace's own son, who needed him, too. They could have been one and the same. As Jace held on to the boy, he suddenly knew that he might have what it took to be a dad after all. He could swear to sacrifice, to protect, to love. His instincts would guide him where he needed to go.

He lay quietly, his arms around the chilled youth, his hands rubbing his skin over his clothing while all around them activity buzzed. A motorized canoe, fit to maneuver the swells of the Wyoga, brought a rescue team of three EMTs. Jace abandoned his position to allow the men access. By then the kid was talking, telling them what had happened.

The canoe then went back for the father, who rushed to his son's side. He reacted with expected fear and panic, constantly questioning the paramedics, needing constant reassurance that his boy was okay.

"The guy who drove the bus today saved me, Dad," the kid said.

That's me, Jace thought. Not the owner of High Mountain Rafting. Not the newest employee of CR Adventures, soon to make his mark and his fortune. Just "the guy who drove the bus." But now Jace added another qualification to his list of accomplishments. Jace Cahill, father.

He said goodbye to the dad, the kid, the medics, and started down the gentle slope into the river. He was already soaked. He was chilled to the bone, so he refused a ride back on the canoe. "I got here, didn't I?" he quipped. "I can get back the same way. Besides, I've got folks to pick up downriver."

The swim back was a piece of cake once he was free of the rapids caused by the log. He walked out on the other side, assured his employees on the rafts who had stopped to watch that he was fine, and got into the bus. He needed to make a call but would have to wait to use one of his employees' phones at the turnout point. Yes, as soon as he could, he'd make one call and then another and hopefully his life would feel like a missing piece of a puzzle had just been found.

As he drove down the bumpy road, he realized he hadn't even gotten the kid's name. Nathan, that was good enough for now.

THE REST OF the expedition went smoothly, with the exception that three who had started this morning returned to town in an ambulance. The rafts arrived at the pickup point towing empty kayaks behind them. Once Jace assured everyone that he was fine, and actually beginning to dry out a bit, he borrowed Joe's phone. His first call was to Harry Pratt in Costa Rica.

"What? You're not coming?" Harry said when Jace explained his change of heart.

"Something's come up," Jace said. "It's a family matter, but I just can't leave now. I'm sorry, Harry. It was a great opportunity."

"You're not kidding it was," Harry said.

"I've got to have someone, Jace, so this is it. No second guesses. I'll have hired someone else by this time tomorrow."

"I understand," Jace said, anxious to get on with his next phone call. "Thanks for thinking of me, Harry."

Almost three hours had passed since he'd left Kayla and Nathan at the Mountain Laurel Inn. They still had to pack, probably have breakfast. With a little luck maybe they hadn't even left town yet. Although, now that Jace considered the last hour of his life, he wondered if he hadn't used up his share of luck, at least for this day.

Kayla answered on the second ring. "Hello?" Her voice was clipped, controlled. He wasn't using his own phone so she had no idea who the caller was. Maybe she was already back in Washington mode. He hoped not.

"Are you still in town?" he asked.

"Jace? No. We left about an hour ago."

His hopes plunged. An hour ago, but the first of any journey out of the mountains meant a slow go on the narrow, twisting roads. "Are you out of the High Country yet?"

"Not quite. What's this about? I really must concentrate on my driving."

"I need to see you." An hour…an hour. Where was she? "Have you passed the apple tree farm yet, you know, the one with the big red barn?"

"Maybe five minutes ago. We've got about a half hour's drive to get to the town of Marion."

"Pull over. Stop. Wait for me."

"Where are you?"

"I'm in Tennessee, but I'm heading back to Holly River soon."

"Then are you kidding me? You've got to be two hours away, and already Nathan and I will be lucky to reach Virginia by nightfall."

He heard her take a deep breath. "Besides," she said. "There's no place to pull over. We're in the Pisgah National Forest, Jace. It's not like there are rest areas every few miles."

She was right, but where there were forests, there were campgrounds, and he thought of one now. "Look, Kayla, I know this sounds kind of crazy, but I've got to see you. There's a place called Big Black Bear Campground. It's close to where you are now, on the right. You can't miss it. The sign has a huge bear on it."

"A campground?" Her voice was wary.

"I'm not suggesting you camp, honey. Just stop there. The camp store is about a half mile up the turnoff. I know the guy who owns the place. His name is Rick. When I get off the phone with you, I'll call him, tell him to expect you."

"Why are you asking me to do this, Jace? I thought we'd discussed everything there was to discuss this morning. What else is there to say?"

"More than you know. Please, Kayla, just do this for me. As soon as I get the bus back to my store, I'll leave in my truck and be there sooner than you think."

"What is this about? Can't you give me a hint?"

"No. I can't. Trust me. How's Nathan?"

"He's fine." She paused, sighed. "I suppose he'd get a kick out of a campground with the name Big Black Bear."

"He definitely would," Jace said. "It's a little slice of heaven, with majestic mountain views and hot showers."

"Huh? I don't think either one of us needs a shower, Jace."

He chuckled, feeling exhilarated. She was going to stop. Lifting the front of his long-sleeved T-shirt, he sniffed the damp fabric. Whew! "Speak for yourself, sweetheart."

"What does that mean?"

"Gotta go. I have to turn this bus around. Got people to see in a campground."

He disconnected. "Let's get moving!" he shouted. "If you're late getting on the bus, you'll have to walk back."

CHAPTER TWENTY

THIS WAS CRAZY. The road to the campground, though only about a half mile, was a challenge of rutted gravel road and occasional low-hanging branches. Kayla was driving a midsize automobile; she wondered how motor homes navigated the road at all.

And what was even crazier was that she was doing this without knowing why. Jace hadn't told her anything. If she delayed her trip and her own plans to hear more of his Costa Rica dreams and financial arrangements for Nathan, she was not going to be happy—even though seeing Jace at all, even for a short conversation, was making her heart pound with anticipation.

"Stop it, Kayla," she reprimanded herself.

"Stop what?" Nathan said.

"Nothing, sweetie." She needed to divert his attention. "Oh, look, there's the camp store. We can get a soda and snacks in there."

Kayla parked near the entrance to the log structure. Thankfully the actual campground was quite spacious, with large lots for motor homes and grassy areas around small fishing ponds. Drivers might have a difficult time getting here, but once their RVs were set up, tourists must find the Big Black Bear quite beautiful and serene.

"Is Jace here?" Nathan asked, craning his neck to see out the car window.

Kayla hadn't told him they would have a wait. She'd just mentioned that Jace wanted to see them before they drove too far out of the mountains. "No, he's not here yet. We can have our snack, and then he should arrive."

Nathan got out of the car and met Kayla at the door to the camp store. "This place is neat. Look, Auntie Kay, there's a playground over there. Can I go play?"

"Sure, in a few minutes." She wanted to make certain that Jace had called ahead and she and Nathan weren't unwelcome guests.

The screen door to the store opened wide and a large bearded man in a flannel shirt and khakis came outside. "I'm Rick. You must be Kayla," he said, extending his hand.

"Yes, that's right. And this is Nathan."

"Jace told me to make you all comfy. The special today is hot dogs with potato chips. We have a shady patio out back with tables and chairs where you can wait in the cool breeze."

Nathan's eyes lit up. "Can I have a hot dog, Auntie Kay?"

"Sure. I think I will, too." She started to take her wallet from her purse.

"You won't be needing that," Rick said. "It's on the house."

"Thank you, Rick."

Well, Kayla, there are certainly worse places to be on a sunny late-August day, she told herself minutes later when she and Nathan were devouring their hot dogs. Truthfully only Nathan was devouring his. Every bite Kayla took settled like a river rock in her stomach. She couldn't see the road they'd just taken, so she didn't know if Jace was pulling in. But he would be here soon, and that thought alone was enough to make digesting food a challenge.

After lunch they played a game of I spy, which took twenty minutes or so, and then

Nathan asked if he could go to the playground.

Kayla remembered how he was their second night in Holly River at the barbecue restaurant. Even when Jace took him to meet some local kids, Nathan had hung back, reluctant to join in the game of corn hole. These past two weeks had made a difference in Nathan. He seemed happier, more self-assured, more like a little boy who didn't carry the weight of the world on his small shoulders.

Kayla smiled at him. If only…

"Be careful," she said. "And stay where I can see you." She imagined every parent who allowed their little ones to go off on their own said the same words. *Stay where I can see you. I wish I could see you every minute of the day.*

Nathan trotted off toward the playground. Watching him, Kayla's eyes blurred with tears. *How can I do what must be done?* she asked herself. *How can I come this far and then abandon this child?* Sherry and Paul Wagoner weren't bad people, but nor were they loving and caring. Kayla had witnessed their practical and emotionless ways of trying to communicate with Nathan, and it made her heart ache. She had loved and cared for their grandson in the last two weeks more than his grandparents ever had. And that was terribly sad.

How can I do what must be done?

"Kayla?"

She turned at the familiar voice. She'd last seen Jace a few short hours ago, but at the sight of him, she felt as if she'd been missing him forever. He was still unshaven, but now rumpled and wrinkled like he'd hurried to catch her without giving a thought to his appearance. And still he was handsome and solid and a much better man than he believed he was. And as good a man as she'd left behind this morning.

She quickly wiped her eyes. "Jace, that was fast."

"I didn't fool around," he said. "Grabbed a new High Mountain T-shirt so I'd be at least partly presentable and was on my way." He came up to her, leaned over her chair and kissed her. "You look beautiful."

"Jace, you stink!" She pulled away from him, waving her hand in front of her nose.

"Sorry. That's river water. And muck. And maybe some fish guts."

"But your pants are damp. And your shoes. They're wet, too. You went swimming in the river in your clothes?"

He stomped his feet, creating a squishy sound, and then toed off his work shoes. "Not swimming exactly, and I didn't have my shoes on this time, but I guess they suffered anyway."

"What happened?"

"It's a long story. I'll tell you later."

Using the tips of her fingers, Kayla gingerly picked up one of his expensive Rockports. "Another pair of shoes, Jace? That's two in two weeks." She paused before adding, "Oh, right. You can afford new shoes now. You're making so much money in Costa Rica."

He smiled, sat in the chair next to her. "That's where you're wrong, honey. Shoes will be a continuing problem for me."

"And why is that?"

"Not going to Costa Rica." His smile widened.

For a moment Kayla didn't think she'd heard him correctly. Her heart was hammering in her ears. She gulped for air. "What did you say?"

"Not going. I've made other plans."

"So that's why you wanted to talk to me? Are you going to Colorado now? Or maybe New Zealand? I've heard there are impressive rapids in those places."

"There are, but I'm not going there. I'm staying in Holly River. I plan to be a poor man with a loyal dog and an amazing son. The dog already loves me. I hope the son will, too, in time."

She didn't know whether to laugh at his ridiculous turnabout or slap him across his face. Did he really think she was going to buy this story?

"This isn't a game, Jace. You can't toy with peoples' emotions like this. You can't possibly expect me to believe that you suddenly love Nathan and you want him in your life."

His expression sobered. "To be fair, Kayla, I never said I couldn't love him. I never said he didn't belong in my life. I did say having a child wasn't a responsibility I looked forward to. I did say that I probably wasn't in a position to raise a child financially, and I might not be the best one to bring him up. But I know now that he's my son, and I do believe that he belongs with me."

She couldn't stop a sarcastic laugh that burst from her lips. "I'm not buying it, Jace, not for one minute. There's no way I would turn this child over to you when you've radically changed your mind in only—" she looked at her watch "—five hours."

"I have changed my mind about Costa Rica," he said. "But I don't think I changed my mind about Nathan. I've finally accepted what my mind was trying to tell me all along."

"Which is?" She waited, knowing that nothing he could say would lead her to believe that he was suddenly father material.

He scraped his hand over his jaw. "Which is, that Susan and I made this baby ten years ago. It was an act of fate. I didn't know about it, and truly, two weeks isn't a lot of time to get used to the idea. But I have. Nathan is here—he's part of me. He deserves a parent who will take care of him, guide him, love him. I can do that. I know I can."

Kayla vigorously shook her head. "No way, Jace."

When further words failed her, she waited for Jace to say something.

"I'm his father, Kayla. I believe he needs me. And I believe I need him. I don't want him to be alone. I don't want him to live with his grandparents even though they can give him things I can't. But they can't give him a father. Only I can do that."

Kayla stared across a parking lot to the playground. Nathan was involved with some kind of game with the other children. He didn't even know that Jace had arrived. He was safe and secure because she was close by. How would he feel with Jace? Suddenly she wondered why she ever started this quest in the first place. It had been a ridiculous idea from the beginning—trying to make two strangers accept each other as family. Had she been thinking of Susan? Of herself?

It was time to put all the motives behind her and realize that other people didn't matter anymore. The only one who mattered was Nathan.

In a voice calmer than she believed possible, she asked one serious question. "What brought about this sudden change, Jace?" If he could convince her that the change was real, that he was dedicated to this boy, well, even then...

"I guess the realization that I want my son with me came about in that smelly river today."

"What?"

"I told you it's a long story. And I'm happy to tell it to you someday, but for now, just believe that something happened that made me realize that a man is worth what his deeds prove him to be. The best he can do is care for what's his—his family, his children."

He stared at his hands clasped between his knees. "I know it sounds corny, like I'm some kind of deep thinker..." He smiled. "We both know I'm hardly that. But I gave of myself to someone else today, and it made me realize that the best life is the one where you give of yourself to help another person. I want to help my son through good times and bad. I want to be part of his life, to watch him grow, and maybe, someday, earn his respect."

Her throat burned. She felt it start to close as her breathing became more difficult. Her eyes filled with hot tears. She and Jace had both come to a realization today. She didn't know how she would leave Nathan with his grandparents. And Jace knew that he could step up and be the father Nathan needed. So now what?

She reached over and laid her hand on his thigh. He didn't move except to cover it with his own hand. "Oh, Jace, why didn't you realize this before?" she said in a tortured, scratchy voice. "Why did you wait until now?"

He lifted her hand, brought it to his lips. "Does it matter, Kayla? Does it really matter? It's all working out the way you wanted it to from the beginning. And maybe there's hope for you and me…"

Her sob stopped him. She looked into his eyes. "This is not the way I want it now," she said. She swallowed, found the breath to say, "Because I can't give him up, Jace. These last two weeks with him… I've decided, well…just since I got to the campground, that I would raise him myself. It will break my heart to give him to you."

He didn't speak for what seemed forever. As the seconds ticked by, Kayla's fear grew. Would he be angry with her? Would Jace consider that these whole last two weeks were a trick? Would he believe anything she said ever again? She threaded her hands to keep them from trembling. She felt like her body would crumple if she tried to stand, to move.

Finally he said, "You can't mean this, Kayla. All this time… You made me feel like I was lacking something in my character. And now I've found it, and you're yanking away the very thing that has made me the man you wanted me to be."

"I know. I didn't expect you to change your mind. You seemed so positive this morning. And I started thinking about leaving Nathan with his grandparents. I couldn't do it, Jace. He has been like a different child these past two weeks. I can't ignore the gains he has made and leave him with people who are cold and indifferent."

She reached into her purse and withdrew a tissue. She wiped her eyes and blew her nose. The simple gestures helped her regain some calm. She stared up at Jace hoping to find sympathy, compassion. What she saw was disbelief, skepticism. "I love him, Jace," she said. "I'm willing to change my life for him, so he will be my top priority."

Jace slowly shook his head. "How thoughtful of you...now."

The icy chill in his voice raised the hairs on the back of her neck. "I'm his guardian," she pointed out, as if that would provide a conclusion that would end further discussion.

"I'm his father." Jace's features were immovable, as if made from stone. "We know which one of us has the best claim to Nathan."

She choked back a sob. "I don't want to fight you on this."

"Then give me my son. It's what you came here for. Everything you've done since arriving in the High Country was designed to make a father of me. Now you've done it."

"But I didn't think I'd done it," she said. "When I left Holly River this morning, I believed I had failed. But I was determined not to fail Nathan again. How do I know that you would even be a good father to him?"

"Because I'm telling you I would be. After what you and I shared that should be enough." He raised his eyes to the sky before settling them on her face again. "I've never lied to you, Kayla, never once. And

I'm not lying to you now. I've become what you wanted me to be. Surely you can see that. In two weeks you have come to know me better than anyone else on this earth."

He was right. She knew it. She'd never once thought he wouldn't be a good father. She only believed that he didn't have the confidence in himself to take on the job. But now he did. She couldn't question his resolve. She only knew that hers was as strong. She'd known Nathan since the day he was born. She'd always cared for him. But only in the last two weeks had she come to love him. Surely the same was possible for Jace.

She needed time. "Jace, there is paperwork. I need to speak to a family court judge, to Nathan's grandparents. The decision must be legal. It's not like we're deciding on which car to buy. This is a child's life."

"Then let him live it with me, his father."

"We'll sort it out," she said, not knowing if that could ever be true. Maybe once she and Nathan were gone, Jace would go back to the life he loved, the one where he lived as a loner. A mountain man with a dog, and happy to be just that. But then, what would happen to her? What about her feelings for Jace, the ones that had blossomed the day she met him and had continued to grow with each passing day?

How had this all gone so wrong? She wanted to blame Susan for putting her in this hopeless situation, for letting both of these males into her life, her heart. But how could she find fault with a dead person? How could she give up any hopes she might have had for her and Jace by sacrificing Nathan?

Out of the corner of her eye, she saw Nathan heading toward them from the playground. He was smiling, his eyes bright and alert. "Jace, you're here!" he called.

"We can't tell him anything yet," she said to Jace. "Let me take him home to Virginia today. I'll call you in a couple of days with what I've found out. I might have trouble with Susan's parents. I don't know."

"I'm not going away, Kayla. As much as I've come to care for you…" He paused as if admitting anything further might be a mistake. He turned just as Nathan flew at him. "Hey, buddy, you had fun over there on the playground?" He was amazed his voice sounded so normal.

"Yeah, it was great."

Nathan had been playing hard. A hot flush covered his cheeks; dirt smudged his hands. Kayla's heart melted. At this moment, he was a typical little boy.

"What did you want to talk to us about?" Nathan asked, taking Jace's hand.

"Oh, that," Jace said. "I forgot to get your auntie Kay's address, and that's really important. I mean all of us are pals now, right? Got to know where to send your Christmas present. Who knows? Maybe I'll even send you a tree."

Nathan grinned, obviously pleased with Jace's excuse.

Jace ruffled Nathan's hair. "And besides, I just wanted to see you both again and figured this campground was the perfect spot."

Kayla stood. "Nathan, we'd better get going. We have a long drive."

"Okay. Bye, Jace. You can come to see me anytime you want."

"I'll take you up on that offer," Jace said.

Nathan walked ahead toward the car. Kayla held back. She hoped Jace could see the emotions she was feeling by looking into her eyes. But maybe that was asking too much. Could he see her determination to do what was right for Nathan? Could he see her love for Nathan? Could he see her love for a man who'd chased her down the mountains to show her he had changed?

Jace reached up, cupped her face in his hands. "Like you mentioned earlier, we'll work this out, city girl. But maybe one thing should be said, one more piece of honesty for this remarkably honest day." Looking directly into her eyes, he said, "I'm pretty sure I love you."

CHAPTER TWENTY-ONE

NAVIGATING THE REMAINING miles down the mountain, Kayla was barely aware she was behind the wheel of a car. Oh, she was careful. The roads were narrow and twisting so she paid attention to the asphalt in front of her, but her mind, her thoughts were back at the campground.

"How could you say something like that at a time like this," she said aloud. "What did you expect me to say?"

"Say to what?" Nathan asked her.

She glanced at him, conscious that she had spoken the question so he could hear it. "Nothing, sweetie. I was just thinking about Jace."

"Me, too," he said. "It's sad leaving him, don't you think? I wish you could have been his girlfriend."

I'm wondering now if maybe I am. But how could she take anything he said seriously? He'd told her often enough that responsibility and relationships were practically alien to him. And now he claimed he loved her…or, as he put it, he was *pretty sure* he loved her. What was she supposed to do with that information?

She had to protect her heart. But still, miles later, her heart hadn't returned to its normal rhythm. Her eyes hadn't completely cleared from wanting to cry with some sort of feminine emotion that was uncommon to her. Her mind hadn't stopped jumping to a time in the future—a cabin in the woods, a husband, a family.

She didn't want those things.

Kayla McAllister would never want to sit on a front porch and watch fireflies in the night sky. She'd only just decided to take Nathan into her life on a permanent basis. That one choice would require her to make many changes in her life. But she could still be the activist she considered herself now. She could still be a part of the country's political spectrum.

A husband, a family, a cabin in the woods. She'd never thought of those things as a priority in her life, though she supposed that since she'd decided to raise Nathan, she had already committed to a family of sorts. But what about her own dreams? She wanted to be someone who made laws that made a difference.

She'd almost forgotten Nathan was in the car. But he soon reminded her by saying, "So what about being his girlfriend, Auntie Kay? I saw him kiss you once."

"You did?"

"Yeah, out the window of our cabin. It looked like you liked it."

She sighed. "You'll understand when you're older, sweetie, that there is much more to being someone's girlfriend than just enjoying his kiss. Being a girlfriend requires commitment. It means you should think about the other person as much as or more than you think about yourself. It means putting someone else's needs above your own."

"Okay."

Okay? This nine-year-old boy had just agreed with her as if he'd understood the concept and found it easy as pie. Well, hadn't she just committed to Nathan? Wasn't she putting his needs above her own? Maybe it wasn't really so hard. At least she was will-

ing to try with Nathan. And she was determined to make it work.

But that was far different from being a
girlfriend—to a man whose only commitment in life so far had been to a dog, an only
moderately successful company and a guitar. She wasn't willing to give this man the
responsibility of raising his own son. How
could she give her heart and her very life
to him?

Her head was spinning. He might love her.
She might love him. He would never come
live in Washington, DC. For heaven's sake,
what would he do in Washington? What kind
of a job would he get? But on the other hand,
how could she leave a successful career to
live in quiet Holly River?

"One thing at a time," she said, again
aware that she was speaking aloud. In a
few hours they would be in Virginia, and
Kayla would have to tell the Wagoners that
their daughter had made her, not them, the
guardian of her child. It was all legal. But
Kayla could legally refuse the guardianship
if someone else wanted to take over the responsibility.

In fact this whole trip had been predicated

on the belief that refusing was exactly what she'd do if she discovered Jace Cahill wanted his son. And if Jace turned out to be a disappointment, she would simply leave Nathan with his grandparents and visit him when she could. Simple, right?

Boy, what a difference two weeks could make in the lives of three very different people. Her eyes on the road, her thoughts turned to the miles that still lay ahead before reaching the Wagoners' home. *One thing at a time, Kayla. Drive.*

"I MUST SAY I'm not really surprised," Paul Wagoner said. "We never could depend on Susan to do the right thing, the sensible thing."

Sherry Wagoner grabbed her husband's arm and shushed him. "Lower your voice, Paul. Nathan is just upstairs."

Thank goodness. Sherry and Paul had greeted their grandson when he and Kayla arrived shortly before eight o'clock. After asking if Nathan wanted something to eat, Sherry had suggested he go up to his room. Neither Paul nor Sherry had asked about his vacation. Kayla had seen Nathan's room. It was beautifully decorated with rocket ships and astronauts and had more than an adequate array of toys and electronics. Everything a kid could want, right?

"This just isn't possible, Kayla," Paul said in a hushed tone. "Why would Susan leave the care of her son, our *grandson*, in your hands?" Definitely the king of his castle, Paul looked around the massive great room overlooking a lake and added, "We have a large home, plenty of help, the finances to raise the boy. And you, Kayla. Not to be demeaning…"

No, of course not…

"But you have a full-time job that pays a middle-class wage at best, a small apartment. Your neighborhood is in the center of Washington, DC, no room for a boy to run, no good schools…"

"Excuse me, Paul," Kayla said. "But I'm taking Nathan on Monday to the Briarwood Academy. I may be able to get him enrolled even at this late date. It's only a half mile from the Capitol building and my office, and even you must agree the credentials are more than acceptable."

"But we're Nathan's family," Sherry argued, her voice almost a moan. "We are the logical ones to take him in. I've already arranged for a full-time housekeeper to be here when Paul and I cannot be. Nathan will never be alone."

It depends what you mean by "alone," Kayla thought. "You can't believe that I would leave Nathan alone, either," she said. "I will make arrangements for afterschool care. Lots of working mo…" She stopped herself before allowing a comparison between herself, an adopted aunt, and a biological mother to further aggravate the situation. "Nathan will always be taken care of," she said.

"I want to see this so-called guardianship agreement between you and Susan," Paul said.

"It's not exactly an agreement," Kayla clarified, knowing she had never agreed to the decision. "But it is a legal document. It was drawn up by an attorney, and I had its validity checked by someone on the congressional legal team. I'm sorry if this upsets you, but it is what your daughter wanted."

"Did Susan hate us so much she would do this?" Sherry asked her husband.

"She didn't hate you," Kayla said. "She was grateful for all you did for her. And neither Susan nor I would want to keep Nathan from you. He can visit on weekends. If you want to take him on an extended trip as I just did, I'm sure that could be arranged."

Since Kayla had only spoken with Sherry twice during the entire two weeks, she was fairly convinced that the "out of sight, out of mind" philosophy governed the Wagoners' approach to long absences. She doubted the couple would ever take Nathan on a vacation. Nevertheless, she said, "Nathan needs all of us in his life if he is ever to heal from losing his mother.

"There is one more thing," Kayla said.

"What now?" Paul snapped.

"I didn't tell you this before leaving for North Carolina, but one of my goals in making the trip was to connect with Nathan's biological father."

"His father?" Paul's face reddened. A vein worked in his temple.

"How did you know who he is?" Sherry asked.

"I got all the information from Susan. She has always kept track of this man in case she ever needed to contact him. And, as I learned from her before she died, she's always held a certain respect and fondness for the man."

Paul backed up to a chair and sat heavily. He shook his head. "I can't believe this. All those times I asked Susan about the man who did this to her. I wanted him to be responsible for what he'd done. And each time Susan refused to tell us anything about Nathan's father."

"There were reasons for her reluctance to divulge his identity."

"I'm sure there were," Paul said. "She was ashamed. He's a good-for-nothing bum, isn't he?"

Kayla held her breath for a moment until a pain in her chest subsided. It was as if Paul had made the accusation toward her, not Jace. "No, Paul, he is not, and Susan was not ashamed of herself or of him. He owns a business in western North Carolina."

"What sort of business?" Sherry asked. "Is he able to support Nathan?"

"That's not what is important now, Sherry," Paul ground out. "I want to know why he's never come forward to do his duty by our daughter and Nathan."

"Yes," Sherry agreed. "What sort of a man is he to have never recognized his own son?"

"The answer is simple," Kayla said. "Susan never told him about the pregnancy. He had no idea that Nathan even exists. He and Susan parted ways while they were both still seniors in college and never contacted each other again." She read the disbelief in Susan's parents' eyes. "Believe me, that's the way Susan wanted it."

"But she told you about him," Paul stated.

"Not at the time," Kayla explained. "I asked her, of course, but she wouldn't tell me, either. I only discovered his identity when Susan was facing her last days. She had his information in a safe-deposit box."

"This doesn't make any sense," Paul said. "If Susan didn't think enough of this...*boy* at the time, why did she suddenly change her mind and send you to find him?"

Kayla dreaded answering this question, but it had to be faced. "I'm ashamed to admit this to either of you, but when Susan told me that she had made me Nathan's guardian, I was overwhelmed, shocked. I'd always been fond of Nathan, but to agree to raising him full time… I wasn't willing to do that. I wasn't in a position to do that. That's when Susan informed me that there was one other option."

"And so rather than give the child to Sherry and me, which would have been the logical choice, she sent you off to find this so-called sperm donor."

Kayla stared at the ornate carpet on the floor of the great room. There was no way to soften the blow. What Paul had just said was basically the way it had happened.

Sherry sniffed loudly. "Why didn't Susan want us to raise Nathan? Did she tell you?"

Kayla did not want to provide details that would alter the Wagoners' opinion of their daughter or devastate them with its brutal honesty. She simply said, "She didn't exclude you from raising him, Sherry. She simply had other choices to consider. When I declined to accept the responsibility, and realizing that a young boy needs a parent to guide him, she thought finding his father might work out.

"At any rate," Kayla said, "the responsibility of Nathan's future is in my hands, and

I've decided to raise him myself." She focused the rest of her response on Sherry. "I love him, Sherry, truly, deeply, from the bottom of my heart. These last two weeks with him have convinced me that I can do this. And I want to. But I have no intention of cutting you and Paul from Nathan's life. You will always be his grandparents."

"And this Carolina man, what about him? Did you tell him what Susan had obviously kept from him for ten years? Does he know he's the father?"

"Yes, he knows."

"And let me guess...he's still not willing to step up and take responsibility." Contempt was evident in each of Paul's words.

"It was a shock to him, of course," Kayla said, remembering the night she'd told Jace the truth. She'd been so blunt. Maybe she could have said it differently, prepared him for the revelation. But all that was water under the bridge now. "But he handled the news well. In fact, he's become quite attached to Nathan."

Sherry's eyes widened. "You're not going to give the boy up, are you, Kayla? Why, the man is practically a stranger. I'll sleep more soundly knowing Nathan is with you than with a stranger we don't even know."

Paul coughed. "This whole thing is preposterous."

The Wagoners' reactions didn't surprise Kayla. The situation was out of the ordinary and difficult for anyone who hadn't just spent two weeks sorting it out to understand. But Kayla was certain of one outcome tonight. The Wagoners were at least minimally if not dramatically relieved that the burden of child rearing would not be on their shoulders. The Wagoners could go on with their lives, their social engagements, their extensive trips, without any guilt that they might be neglecting Nathan.

"The father's role at this point is uncertain," Kayla said. "I'm taking Nathan home with me and I will prepare him for school and begin looking for a bigger apartment. All you need to know right now is that Nathan will be loved in my care. If Nathan's father is involved in the future, I will of course let you know."

Kayla blinked hard. She would not fall apart now. But talking about Jace in such impersonal terms, as if he were just a piece of this puzzle they were all trying to figure out, was difficult. After recalling what he'd told her at the campground, after hearing what was in his heart, Kayla had believed every word he'd said. She'd been proud of him. She didn't question his determination to be Nathan's father in all ways. But still, she couldn't give Nathan up.

"Does Nathan know this man is his father?" Paul suddenly asked.

"No, not yet, but I'm going to tell him."

"That's it then." Paul stood, stared down at his wife. "We're out of it almost as if Susan had never been our daughter."

"But Susan was your daughter, and because of that, you will always be connected to Nathan," Kayla said.

"I suppose that's true. You take the boy now, Kayla. Tomorrow Sherry will have our housekeeper pack up his things and we'll have them sent to your place."

"Thank you, Paul." The words were difficult to speak because all Kayla could think about was that neither Paul nor Sherry had asked how Nathan had gotten on with his father, almost as if it didn't matter.

CHAPTER TWENTY-TWO

SATURDAY HAD BEEN a day for Jace to get his ducks in a row, and thereby arrange the facets of his life he could control. He'd spent the rest of Friday thinking about Kayla and Nathan, wondering how he could have stated his case any differently and finally coming up with the conclusion that he couldn't blame Kayla for questioning his resolve. Heck, he didn't think he'd believe himself, either. But everything had started to change for him when he had to say goodbye to them in the morning, and later, at the river rescue.

Something mind-boggling happened in that river. Something profound and lasting. And Jace had come away knowing that every child's life mattered; every child deserved someone in his life who would go to extremes for him in a crisis. Every child deserved unconditional love, the kind that made a man jump in an icy river to do what was right. On Saturday morning, Jace stood a bit taller knowing he was that man. And in the years ahead, he could be that man for Nathan. And even more profound, he wanted to be. The kid had gotten to him, and Jace finally understood the bond that comes with knowing a person is a part of you.

But now he had to make Kayla believe it. In preparation for the trip that he hoped would change his life even more than discovering he had a son, Jace went to Wilton Hollow on Saturday morning. After his first few days in school, Robert had shown significant and promising changes. He verbalized his enthusiasm at being with other children. He told Jace what he had learned to do. And he basked in Jace's praise of his accomplishments.

Jace had left that day knowing that it was time to integrate this half brother into the Cahill family. Once Jace had those ducks lined up the way he wanted them, he would bring Gladys and Robert to the Cahill home. Maybe Carter and Ava wouldn't support this decision, but it was going to happen. And knowing his siblings, Jace figured it might take all of five minutes for them to embrace this new member of the family.

On Sunday morning Jace gathered his family together. Usually Cora fixed a big Sunday dinner for anyone who could come, but today Jace volunteered to fix an old-time Carolina breakfast. He was standing in Cora's kitchen by 7:00 a.m., mixing flour for biscuits, choosing the right jam, peeling potatoes for his rarely made but never-equaled hash browns.

The family arrived by eight thirty: Ava, Carter, Miranda and Emily. Cora had been by his side since the early hour supervising and probably being a bit disappointed that there wasn't much to correct in Jace's cooking skills.

Along with the rest of the food, Jace served up over-easy eggs, bacon crisped in the oven for fifteen minutes and fresh fruit he'd picked up at the farm stand the day before. By the time breakfast was finished, there wasn't a morsel left.

"What's this all about, Jace?" Carter asked as he wiped his mouth and set his napkin on his plate. "I mean this was great, but pardon me if I say so, not really expected from you.

I mean you invited us, and frankly, that's weird."

"I know," Jace answered. "But I've got a couple of things to tell you all, and knowing how you can react on an empty stomach, I decided not to risk it."

Miranda smiled at him. Since she'd married Carter a few weeks ago, Miranda and Jace had buried all the hatchets of their past life. Jace had resented the Liggett Mountain girl for crushing his brother's heart all those years ago, but once she came back, and once she and Carter fell in crazy love all over again, well, bygones had to be bygones. Now Jace couldn't be happier for his brother.

"Tell us, Jace," she urged. "I hope this means what I think it means."

"I hope it means that Nathan is coming back," Emily said, having mentioned the loss of her good buddy several times in the last few days.

"First things first," Jace said. "I was at Wilton Hollow yesterday. Robert has shown remarkable improvement since attending school. In a few weeks I want to bring him to a family dinner."

He waited for a reaction. Since discovering that Cora had been paying money to support Gladys and Robert, Carter and Ava had resented the whole situation. Understandable since their father had cheated on their mother, but Jace had laid the groundwork for Robert's acceptance into the family.

"Are you sure about this?" Carter said, staring at their mother and waiting for a reaction.

Miranda quickly jumped to support Jace's decision. "I think it's time," she said. "Jace has been going to Wilton Hollow for a while now. None of the rest of us have, and that's not right. I trust his judgment that now we ought to introduce Robert to the family."

"And it's time to forgive and forget about the whole money thing," Cora said.

Carter leveled a questioning stare on Ava. She shrugged her shoulders, suggesting that if she wasn't 100 percent in favor, she was willing to meet Jace halfway. "Okay, then," Carter said. "But with Robert in school now, I'd like to discover that Gladys has gotten a job so she can quit taking from this family."

"And don't think I'm going to quit checking on the paper mill numbers," Ava said. "Since I've gotten involved in Mama's finances..."

She gave her mother a sheepish grin. "I've discovered things I question about the factory's books. I don't trust Uncle Rudy one bit."

"Fine. Next topic," Jace said. He turned to his mother. "Mama, I need to talk to you about the Christmas tree farm."

Her eyes narrowed in wariness. "What about it?"

"Do you still need a manager for it? A full-time guy?"

"You know I do."

"Then I know a couple of guys who'd like to apply for the job," Jace said.

"A couple of guys? We can't afford to pay two managers," Cora said.

"I know that, but we can afford profit sharing for two guys who have a personal stake in the business."

"What are you talking about?"

"Hear me out," Jace said. "We all know I've been avoiding any responsibility to the tree farm since…well, since forever."

"I certainly know it!" Cora said.

"That's because I didn't want to be tied down to five thousand living things every year. The rafting job gave me freedom to come and go as long as I had competent help. But putting me in charge of things that needed tending and shearing...well, I think we can all agree that it was a foolish idea."

"And now things are different?" Cora said.

"Yes. I've come to a conclusion that I'm not such a poor tender and shearer after all."

"So you're taking over the tree farm?"

Cora's voice was so hopeful, Jace smiled. "Not entirely on my own. It's a 24/7 job, and I'm still not ready to commit to those hours. But I've worked enough at the farm to know what's involved. I've talked to Billy Haverty, my best guy at High Mountain. He's graduating from college and needs a permanent position. He can't count on rafting trips to support him for the rest of his life." Jace chuckled, knowing rafting trips had done exactly that for him, but he never needed much. "And Billy doesn't even get the big bucks for playing a guitar."

"So what does this mean?" Carter asked.

"It means that Billy and I are going to be partners if Mama okays it. Partners in High Mountain, and two of three partners in Snowy Mountain Trees. Together we'll run the rafts, and with Mama remaining principal shareholder in Snowy, and getting her money first, Billy and I will split the remaining profits. We'll divide our time between the two and hopefully watch both businesses grow, and Mama take a few well-deserved vacations."

"And you would be happy with that?" Cora asked.

"I would." He laughed. "I have never had anything against Christmas trees, Ma. You've let me put the star on top of every one we've ever had." He leaned across the table and took his mother's hand. "I won't let you down, Ma. I'm ready to do this, and Billy is over the moon about it."

Cora pressed her hand to her chest and grinned. "This is what I've been waiting for you to say for years."

"Yeah, I know," he said. "It's been a long time coming."

"This will keep the farm in the family. And someone who really cares about its operation and success will be running it. Oh, Jace, what made you change your mind?"

"A number of factors, not the least of which is that I've grown up about ten years in the last two weeks, and I'm finding out that being an adult isn't so bad."

Carter threaded his hands on the table-top. "I'm with Mama, Jace. Why the sudden longing for stability in your life? These two operations will keep you tied to Holly River. Are you ready for this?"

"I'm ready. I love Holly River. It's my home."

Miranda smiled. "I bet Jace has one more thing to tell us. Go ahead, Jace."

He crossed his legs under the table, drummed his fingers on top. He never thought he'd make a statement like the one that was about to come from his mouth. "I'm trying my hardest to get custody of Nathan."

"Nathan's coming back?" Emily squealed.

Cora burst into tears. "Another grandchild. Jace, you've made me so happy."

"It's not a done deal, Mama," Jace said. "Kayla loves the kid, too. We have some issues to work out."

"You'll work them out," Cora said. "I know you will."

"Is that everything, Jace?" Miranda said with an all-knowing superiority evident in her tone.

"Not quite," Jace said. "I'm leaving here in a few minutes and driving to Virginia.

I'm hoping that tonight I can call you all and report that I've made a package deal. I want Kayla to marry me."

"Holy cow," Carter said. He looked at his wife. "Did you know about this?"

"Women always know such things," she said.

Jace stood. "Let's get the dishes picked up. I've still got to get gas before heading down the mountain."

"We'll do the dishes," Cora said. "You go before all the good sense you've acquired in the last two days suddenly vanishes."

Jace smiled. "One more thing. I need to talk to Carter and Miranda, just the three of us."

EIGHT HOURS LATER, Jace, driving his old pickup, entered the city limits of Washington, DC. He'd put Kayla's address into his phone's GPS and made good time—until he hit the beltway. Even though it was Sunday, traffic was still heavy and congested, making Holly River, North Carolina, seem like a world away, not just four-hundred-plus miles. He was creeping along to Banberry Street, where he would find Kayla's apartment.

She lived on a tree-lined avenue in what Jace figured was the heart of the city. He'd caught glimpses of the Capitol building, the Washington Monument and other national architectural treasures. He'd seen people walking the sidewalks, cramming into cafés and bistros that looked friendly and inviting. And though he missed the simplicity of Holly River, all the activity and pride in the city made him proud of his country.

Finally he reached 1228 Banberry Street. Parking was another nightmare. He squeezed his truck into a minimal space along the avenue, one that left him a three-block walk to get to Kayla's address. That part was okay. He needed to stretch his legs, and a five-minute stroll would help calm his nerves.

What would he do if she turned him down? What if she only agreed to be with him if they settled in Washington? Could he do it? Could a man who'd lived all of his life in the mountains give up the serenity and peace he'd come to love and commit himself to living in this ultra-city landscape? On the other hand, could Kayla give up the excitement and environment of packed city streets to live in a log cabin with a dog, a boy and a man who adored her? He darn well hoped she could.

He reached her address and made a mental note of the white brick facade, wrought iron stair railings and black shutters at the windows. He jogged up a short flight of cement stairs to the first level of apartments.

A narrow hallway led him to apartment C. He stood outside the door, took a deep breath and raised the brass door knocker. It resounded with a formal, sturdy thud that made him think of serious history through the years. Just enough early American charm that he figured Kayla loved it. He stood in front of the peephole in the door so the occupants could see him.

"It's Jace!" The voice echoed into the hallway and brought a smile to Jace's lips. His son was on the other side of the door. His *son*.

CHAPTER TWENTY-THREE

KAYLA RUSHED TO the door. She couldn't have heard Nathan correctly. She'd just left Jace two days ago. Why would he have driven all the way to Washington, DC? Had he come to take Nathan away from her? She didn't want to think about that.

Yet in the pit of her stomach, there was a quick spark of heat that soon spread to all her extremities. She shook her hands to relieve them of tingling. She blinked, bringing the door into clear focus. Jace was on the other side of that door. Maybe he had come for her. No. He'd come for Nathan, to break Kayla's heart.

"Stand back, sweetie," she said to Nathan.

"I want to open the door," he argued.

She peered through the peephole. Her heart raced. She wiped her hands on her shorts. "Okay. Open it."

He did and threw himself into Jace's arms.

"You came already. You said you would come and you did."

"I did," Jace said, ruffling Nathan's hair while his gaze remained fixed on Kayla.

She touched her hair, attempting to smooth the strands that had come loose from her messy ponytail. She'd been rearranging her bedroom to make room for Nathan's things. No makeup, a pair of cutoffs and a tank top. Her Sunday not-going-anywhere-today outfit.

And she could do no more than stare at Jace. His clothes, jeans and a T-shirt, were rumpled. His hair was messy; he needed a shave. Had he driven all those miles in that pair of scuffed sandals? Inside her chest, a deep sigh longed for escape. Jace looked wonderfully, staggeringly male, and her heart ached.

He smiled at her. "Can I come in?"

"Sure," Nathan said. "We were just going to order a pizza, right, Auntie Kay?"

The reminder of the dinner hour brought Kayla to her senses. She checked her watch. "Goodness, it's seven o'clock already." She stepped aside, letting Jace into her living room.

"I could eat some pizza," he said.

Nathan grabbed his hand and walked with him to the sofa. "It's so cool you're here," Nathan said. He lifted a couple of boxes and set them on the floor. "We can sit now. This is just some of my stuff."

Jace looked up at Kayla and mouthed the words, "His grandparents?"

She shook her head and pointed toward the bedroom. "We're learning to share our space," she said. "I think I'll order the pizza now. Who wants what?"

Jace and Nathan both contributed specific suggestions for their pizzas.

"I'll order two," she said, grateful to have something to do.

She stayed in the kitchen, fixing salad and setting out plates, glasses and sodas. She could hear the conversation from the living room. Nathan was talking nonstop. Jace contributed when he could get a word in. She was relieved to hear Nathan's enthusiasm when he told Jace that he would be staying with his Auntie Kay.

"You're a lucky guy," Jace said. "Your Auntie Kay is pretty cool."

"We're going to my new school tomorrow. Auntie Kay is going with me."

"You know you'll make friends in your new school, right?"

"I guess."

And then Jace said a strange thing—for him. In a perfectly serious voice he said, "How do you feel about making new friends? Do you think it's easy or hard?" He was learning to speak to a child, to draw him out.

There was a pause before Nathan said, "It's okay, I guess. I had friends when I lived with my mother. But they are not my friends anymore. Grandma said they live too far away. They've probably forgotten about me by now."

"Forget you?" Jace said as if that were the most preposterous thing he'd ever heard. "I don't think so. I couldn't even go two days without seeing you again."

In a low voice, so low Kayla had to step to the kitchen door to hear, Nathan said, "Did you come to see Auntie Kay, too?"

Jace's answer flooded her chest with warmth. "You bet I did."

Kayla pressed her hand over her heart. *And I'm so glad you did. Just please, Jace, don't take this boy away from me.*

After the pizza had been consumed, Kayla picked up the dishes while the guys watched television. When she was finished, Kayla came into the living room and reminded Nathan that it was time for bed.

"Jace is sitting on my bed," he said, pointing to the sofa sleeper.

"I know, but you can go to sleep in my room tonight. Get your jammies on and brush your teeth. We have to get up early to be at the school by eight."

Nathan looked up at Jace. "Will you come back tomorrow, Jace?"

"Maybe. Not sure yet."

"If you're not here, will you call us?"

"You know I will." Jace stood from the sofa and brought Nathan's head close to his chest. They looked so natural standing there, one small and eager to trust, the other tall and ready to protect, one so like the other in appearance.

Nathan took a step back. "I hope you come back, though."

"Me, too."

Nathan went into the other room. Kayla waited a few minutes before going in and checking on his progress. After she tucked him in bed, he stared up at her with some unidentified longing in his eyes. "Why do you think Jace came here tonight?" he asked.

"Sweetie, I don't know," Kayla said, sitting on the edge of the bed. "Maybe just to see us. Maybe he missed you."

"I think it's something else," he said. "Something bigger."

Yes, you're right, Kayla thought. And she was about to discover what his reason for coming to DC was. She wanted to know. Wondering all evening was making her crazy. Yet she dreaded knowing. Nathan was Jace's son. She was only the boy's guardian. If Jace wanted his son, she knew how the courts would rule.

She stood, smoothed the blanket over him. "You might be right," she said. "I've discovered you often are." She smiled. "Now go to sleep. You've had a fun night, and I'm sure whatever is in Jace's mind is nothing to worry about."

She wasn't sure at all, but it wouldn't do to let Nathan sense her anxiety. She turned off the bedside light, flicked on the small nightlight in her wall socket and left the room.

Jace was standing in the middle of the

room when she came out. He looked uncertain, almost shy, certainly not like the man she'd come to know the last two weeks. But then he smiled and all the reasons she'd discovered for loving him came flooding back. A sweet boyishness he didn't even know he possessed. A natural ease in every situation, his love for simple things evident in his clothes, his hair, his attitude.

He opened his arms, and she stepped into them. "I've waited all night for this," he said.

She lifted her face, and he kissed her. Long and hard and so filled with passion she almost allowed herself to believe that nothing bad could happen. At least not tonight. But that was foolish. He'd kissed her before, and it had been wonderful. But those times he hadn't driven eight hours to tell her something.

She spoke softly, not wanting to break the spell of contentment, of longing, that had filled her chest. "Nathan asked me why you came tonight. I didn't know what to tell him."

His arms still around her waist, Jace leaned back. "You could have said I missed you guys. It's true, you know."

"I did say that. But I know that's not the primary reason you came." She hoped her face didn't reflect the torrent of emotions in her heart. Would he leave DC tonight? Would he wait until tomorrow and take Nathan away?

"No, it's not," he said. "I came here on a mission from the town council of Holly River."

She'd imagined all sorts of explanations coming from his lips, but not this nonsensical phrase. "What do you mean?"

He took her hand. "Let's sit down."

They sat on the sofa, their thighs and shoulders touching. Kayla could feel the warmth of his skin through his shirt, tingling into her arm. She adjusted, turning slightly away from him so she could see into his eyes.

"Jace, tell me. The waiting is killing me. What's this about the town council?"

"Okay. I'm not sure how you'll react to my telling you this. I don't know how it's going to work out. Though Carter and Miranda agree it's a good idea."

"Carter and Miranda? What do they have to do with this?"

"They know all about Holly River stuff, what's going on, what needs to happen... Stuff I never paid much attention to."

"So tell me," she said. "What is this idea?"

He sighed. "Here goes. I don't think you know Alice Buchanan. She's a real nice lady, maybe in her sixties."

Kayla shook her head. "No, I don't."

"Well, she's served on the town council for something like ten years, done a good job, too. Has stood up to the mayor and many of our citizens at times. Even took on the hard-nosed chief of police last year over a public nuisance issue regarding a bear."

Kayla couldn't help smiling at the reference to Carter.

"Anyway, Alice is retiring at the end of this year, and the council needs to fill her spot. This may not seem like such a big deal to someone from Washington, DC, but it's a big deal to us. We don't have too many people who would take on the responsibility. I mean, the pay is lousy, the rewards practically nonexistent, unless you count the holiday buffet where council members can eat their fill without having to bring a dish."

"Sounds like a true reason for going into public office," Kayla said.

"Besides all that, council members have to listen to endless complaints before deciding which ones to take to the mayor. They have to read all kinds of ordinances and code enforcements. Boring, that's what it is. And the monthly meetings…that's the worst part, when folks have stored up their gripes for four weeks."

"Jace…" Kayla couldn't help smiling at him. "I think we established before that you've never actually been to a council meeting."

"Right."

"So what does all this have to do with you coming to DC tonight?"

"I'm getting to it. I talked to my brother about this upcoming vacancy. Also talked to Miranda about who she'd like to see fill the seat. We all agreed that we need someone who has a strong sense of community and responsibility, who wants to see change, and a knowledge of the workings of government." He grinned. "That last one will be a welcome change for Holly River."

"Makes sense…" Kayla was beginning to see where this was going.

"I started thinking—where have I been hearing this word *responsibility* lately, nearly every day to be exact? I seem to recall someone telling me to be responsible."

"Yes, someone did."

"So that must be a person who knows a lot about responsibility. And then it hit me. That person was you!"

Kayla laughed even though she knew she was being played. "Are you telling me, Jace Cahill, that you want me to run for town council in Holly River?"

"Not just me. Carter and Miranda, too. And Mama once she hears about it. And once we get a couple more people on board, that's practically the whole town."

"Interesting plan, Jace, but you are aware that we are in my apartment, where I live, in Washington, DC?"

"Oh sure, for now. But once you establish residency in Holly River, you'll be eligible to run for council."

Jace's eyes were bright, his voice enthusiastic. Kayla could almost picture herself listening to nuisance bear complaints. But she had to dig deep into her well of common sense and admit that this idea came with many risks. She couldn't leave Washington to take a chance in Holly River, even if this man was doing a darn good job of convincing her.

"First of all," she said. "I probably wouldn't win. I'm an outsider. A local person will be elected to fill the council seat."

He shook his head. "No one will run against you. Trust me, you'll be unopposed."

"You're saying no one else wants the job?"

"Pretty much."

"Anyway," she continued, "I have a job here in Washington. I work for a congressman, and I don't think he's going to fire me any time soon."

He took her hand. "Don't *work* for a congressman, Kayla. *Be* a congressman."

"What?"

"Holly River is only a beginning for you. After living in North Carolina for a year, you can run for state representative from our district. You might face a bit more competition in that race, but you'll win. And then it's off to Raleigh, where you can make the laws, not just advise someone else about how he should vote."

A state congressional seat? Could Kayla allow that dream to decide her future? What were the chances she could win on a state level?

"But you have to start with council-woman," Jace said. "And here's the really important part. We have a child to consider, you and me. And I want to be his father, but I don't want him growing up in a town that is short one council member. What kind of a future is that for a bright kid like Nathan?"

Kayla recognized the ridiculous exaggeration and thought about what Jace had said. "Wait a minute," she said. Suddenly all this eager persuasion made sense. "You're suggesting this just so I won't try to stop you from raising Nathan. You want me to give up everything I've worked for in Washington and move to Holly River so you can be a father to your son without feeling guilty over what that decision would do to me."

She stood, began to pace. "How convenient for you, Jace. Good old Auntie Kay is right there in case you have a problem slipping into your role as daddy. Any time fatherhood gets you down, and it will, you can call on me to smooth things over."

His eyes followed her as she walked around the room. "Sounds like a pretty sweet deal to me," he said.

She stopped in front of him and leveled a stern look at his placid face. "Well, sorry, Jace, but Auntie Kay is not going to be your backup plan. I'm not giving up everything I've worked for..."

His smile stopped her. "Auntie Kay? Oh, no. I forgot the most important part of this deal. You're no longer going to be his pretend aunt. I'm counting on you being his mother. Well, his stepmother to be exact."

He stood, took both her hands in his. "As soon as you marry me, anyway. I mean, take all the time you need—a week, maybe two if this all feels rushed."

"Marry you? I barely know you." Her head was swimming.

"Okay, a month. By then you'll be on the town council and planning your strategy for a congressional run. Our son will be at the top of his class at Holly River Elementary, and maybe we'll have another kid planned out for the future. I mean, once I decided I liked the idea of being a father, I figured why stop with that? Why not marry the woman I adore, have more babies and buy a bigger dining room table?"

All the tension of the last few minutes erupted in a burst of laughter. "Jace Cahill, the man who never wanted to be a father! What has gotten into you?"

He pulled her to him, kissed her forehead and then raised her face to accept a long, tender kiss. "*You've* gotten into me, Kayla. With your stubbornness and determination, you made me realize that the way I'd been living my life wasn't what I wanted. I've been lonely, and just too stubborn to realize it—until you and Nathan. We need you guys, honey. Copper and I need you. And the Snowy Mountain Tree Farm needs a manager.

"Come home with me, Kayla. I mean stay here as long as you have to in order to train a replacement, and then come to Holly River. We'll build on to my cabin and make every inch a home. And seriously, sweetheart, once I sell five thousand trees in a few months, I'm going to walk you down the aisle so we can celebrate the best Christmas ever as a family."

"This is crazy, Jace." She laughed through every word. "You know that, don't you?"

"It's love, and yeah, I guess love has driven many a man crazy." He kissed her again, deeply, warmly. "But if I'm going crazy, I'm taking you with me. What do you say?"

A small town that offered big dreams. A chance to have everything she could ever hope for. A way to help people by legislating better lives. A long, bright future with Nathan. A wonderful man who'd opened her eyes just as she'd opened his. And a way to fulfill a promise she'd made to a dying woman.

"What do I say?" She looked up into his eyes. "I say I hope there's room for both of us on that road to crazy."

EPILOGUE

JACE SLEPT ON the sofa in Kayla's living room after they stayed up late talking about families, the ones that existed now and the one they hoped for in the future. They admitted to the improbability of the connection they had found together and marveled that they had, indeed, found it. They recognized the differences between them as well as the wonderful sparkling qualities that now made them want to spend the rest of their lives together. They kissed and held each other close, and at the very last, discussed what they would say to Nathan in the morning.

Kayla and Nathan padded out of the bedroom shortly after the sun rose. "Jace is still here," Nathan had cried upon seeing the open sofa bed with Jace's body curled under the covers.

"Yes, he's still here," Jace said. He knew at once that the hand that came to rest on his shoulder was not Nathan's, and he was suddenly wide-awake and ready for whatever this day held in store. Together...*together*, the word that meant so much more now than just a man and his dog.

Kayla made coffee and explained to Nathan that the plans to take him to his new school today had changed. "We'll tell you all about it soon," she said.

After Nathan had consumed his cereal, they all sat in the living room, Jace in his jeans and T-shirt, Kayla in her robe and Nathan in his jammies. Jace started the conversation.

"We've come up with another idea for your school," he said. "But before I go into the details, I need to tell you something very important."

Nathan's eyes widened. His features reflected uncertainty, perhaps because he had learned to live with so much of it the last couple of months. "What do you know about your father?" Jace asked him.

"Only that he's not in our lives," Nathan said, as if he were repeating a fact he'd heard many times. "That's all Mom would tell me."

"Okay, I get that. And I'm sure your

mother had her reasons for telling you so. But I've got to say something that might surprise you. Your father didn't choose to be left out of your life. The truth is, he didn't know you had even been born. Had he known what a great kid you are, I'm sure he would have wanted to be part of every minute."

"How do you know that?" Nathan asked.

Jace cleared his throat. Never before in his life had he feared expressing what was in his heart more than he did today. "I know that because...well, because I am your father, Nathan."

Nathan blinked several times. His lips thinned as he processed the news. His little eyebrows came together in a scowl. "You're my father?"

"Yes."

"And you didn't know about me?"

"That's right. I didn't."

Nathan's fists bunched in his lap. His voice rose. "How can that be? When babies are born the fathers are there in the hospital. They hold the baby. They help name it. Didn't you do any of that?"

"I didn't have the chance," Jace said.

"Your mother never told me she was going to have a baby."

"You're lying! My mother would never have kept me from my daddy. She would have wanted me to have a father."

Kayla reached out a hand to comfort Nathan, but Jace held up his finger. He had this. He had to. "I didn't know because I lived in Holly River when your mother was pregnant. We weren't friends then, and she never told me you were born."

Nathan's face was stricken with trauma. "You didn't love her? People have to love each other to have a baby together."

Jace paused a moment and then smiled. "Oh, Nathan, I am quite sure that it was impossible for anyone not to love your mother."

"But you left her."

"We sort of left each other, but believe me, if I had known, I never would have left you." He looked up at Kayla. She was smiling her encouragement. "And I am thankful every day that your Auntie Kay came to Holly River to bring you and me together."

Nathan's bright eyes switched to Kayla. "You knew? And you didn't tell me I had a father?"

"I didn't know who he was until right before your mom died, sweetie. She wanted me to find Jace, tell him the truth and make you guys a family. And you know what? She was right to ask me to do that. You need a father, Nathan, and Jace is going to be a darn good one."

Nathan looked from one to the other. His features had calmed. He was in control, though it was doubtful he understood everything at this point. "So I'm going to live in Holly River?"

"That's the plan," Jace said.

Kayla pointed out the positive aspects she hoped would win Nathan over. "You'll be going to school with Emily. You can play at Cora's whenever you want…"

"And the best part is, you don't have to fish ever again," Jace said.

"But I want to fish," Nathan argued. "I like the fishing part. I just didn't like the going in the water with my clothes on part."

"Right. We won't do that again."

Nathan slowly nodded his head. "But where will I live?"

"You'll live with me," Jace answered.

"But…but…" Nathan's eyes filled with

tears, and Jace worried that his plan had hit a huge obstacle.

"What's wrong?" he asked.

"What about Auntie Kay? When I was gonna live with my grandparents, Auntie Kay said she'd visit me all the time. Now she'll be far away."

Kayla put her arm around Nathan. "No, I won't, honey."

Nathan stared up at her.

"We're saving the best for last, Nathan," Jace said, smiling at Kayla. "This lady right here won't be your Auntie Kay any longer. She's going to be your stepmother, and you can call her Mom, or Ma, like I call Cora, or just call her Beautiful, and I bet she answers."

Nathan's face lit up. "You like her like a girlfriend?" he asked Jace.

"I like her like the love of my live. You and Kayla are a package deal. We're going to be a family, Nathan. Just as soon as Kayla wraps up her job here in Washington, she's coming to Holly River to be with you and me."

"And Copper," Nathan said.

Jace laughed. "And Copper." He put both

hands on Nathan's shoulders. "So what do you say, sport? I promise to love you and be there for you and Kayla, whatever you guys need," Jace said. "And one more thing. I promise you the very best Christmas tree in Holly River come December."

Nathan sat very still for nearly a minute, the longest minute Jace had ever known. Then the boy catapulted himself into Jace's arms and hugged him for dear life. And that's what Jace knew they would have. A dear life.

* * * * *

Don't miss more romances from acclaimed author Cynthia Thomason:

THE CAHILLS OF NORTH CAROLINA
HIGH COUNTRY COP

THE DAUGHTERS OF DANCING FALLS
A BOY TO REMEMBER
THE BRIDESMAID WORE SNEAKERS
RESCUED BY MR. WRONG

Get 4 FREE REWARDS!

We'll send you 2 FREE Books plus 2 FREE Mystery Gifts.

Love Inspired® books feature contemporary inspirational romances with Christian characters facing the challenges of life and love.

Counting on the Cowboy
Shannon Taylor Vannatter

Reunited by a Secret Child
Leigh Bale

FREE
Value Over
$20

HOME on the RANCH

YES! Please send me the **Home on the Ranch Collection** in Larger Print. This collection begins with 3 FREE books and 2 FREE gifts in the first shipment. Along with my 3 free books, I'll also get the next 4 books from the Home on the Ranch Collection, in LARGER PRINT, which I may either return and owe nothing, or keep for the low price of $5.24 U.S./ $5.89 CDN each plus $2.99 for shipping and handling per shipment*. If I decide to continue, about once a month for 8 months I will get 6 or 7 more books, but will only need to pay for 4. That means 2 or 3 books in every shipment will be FREE! If I decide to keep the entire collection, I'll have paid for only 32 books because 19 books are FREE! I understand that accepting the 3 free books and gifts places me under no obligation to buy anything. I can always return a shipment and cancel at any time. My free books and gifts are mine to keep no matter what I decide.

268 HCN 3760 468 HCN 3760

Name   (PLEASE PRINT)

Address   Apt. #

City   State/Prov.   Zip/Postal Code

Signature (if under 18, a parent or guardian must sign)

Mail to the **Reader Service:**
IN U.S.A.: P.O. Box 1867, Buffalo, NY. 14240-1867
IN CANADA: P.O. Box 609, Fort Erie, Ontario L2A 5X3

* Terms and prices subject to change without notice. Prices do not include applicable taxes. Sales tax applicable in NY. Canadian residents will be charged applicable taxes. This offer is limited to one order per household. All orders subject to approval. Credit or debit balances in a customer's account(s) may be offset by any other outstanding balance owed by or to the customer. Please allow 3 to 4 weeks for delivery. Offer available while quantities last. Offer not available to Quebec residents.

Your Privacy—The Reader Service is committed to protecting your privacy. Our Privacy Policy is available online at www.ReaderService.com or upon request from the Reader Service.

We make a portion of our mailing list available to reputable third parties that offer products we believe may interest you. If you prefer that we not exchange your name with third parties, or if you wish to clarify or modify your communication preferences, please visit us at www.ReaderService.com/consumerschoice or write to us at Reader Service Preference Service, P.O. Box 9062, Buffalo, NY. 14240-9062. Include your complete name and address.

HRCBPA18

Get 4 FREE REWARDS!

We'll send you 2 FREE Books plus 2 FREE Mystery Gifts.

ROBYN CARR
Any Day Now

CARLA NEGGERS
the RIVER HOUSE

FREE
Value Over
$20

B.J. DANIELS
HERO'S RETURN

KAREN HARPER
SHALLOW GRAVE
A SOUTH SHORES NOVEL

Both the **Romance** and **Suspense** collections feature compelling novels written by many of today's best-selling authors.

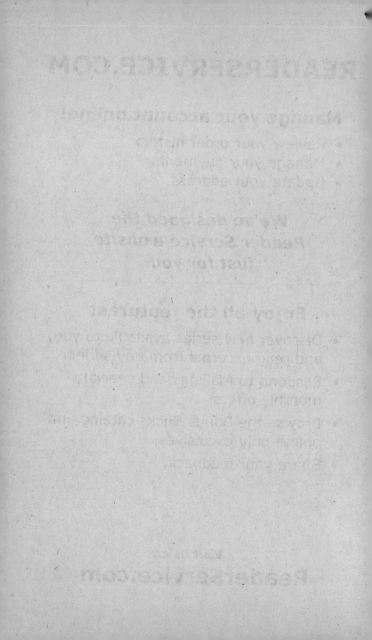